THE OTHEF

The Other Shore

Plays by Gao Xingjian

Translated by Gilbert C. F. Fong

The Chinese University Press

The Other Shore: Plays by Gao Xingjian
Translated by Gilbert C. F. Fong

ISBN 962–201–862–9 (Paperback)
ISBN 962–201–974–9 (Hardcover)

First edition 1999
Second printing 2000
Third printing 2000

THE CHINESE UNIVERSITY PRESS
The Chinese University of Hong Kong
Sha Tin, N. T., Hong Kong
Fax: +852 2603 6692
+852 2603 7355
E-mail: cup@cuhk.edu.hk
Web-site: www.cuhk.edu.hk/cupress

Printed in Hong Kong

Contents

Acknowledgements

The translator would like to thank the playwright Gao Xingjian for his patience, and Professor David Pollard and Professor Peter Crisp, who went over the translations and offered valuable comments. My thanks are also extended to Ms. Natalia Fong and Ms. Shing Sze-wai, whose assistance was invaluable in preparing the manuscript. I would also like to acknowledge Professor Jo Riley's translations of three of the plays in this collection. I have read her manuscripts, but all the translations are my own.

Introduction

You're a stranger, destined to be a stranger for ever, you have no hometown, no country, no attachments, no family, and no burdens except paying your taxes.

There is a government in every city, there are officers in every customs station to check passports, and man and wife in every home, but you only prowl from city to city, from country to country and from woman to woman.

You no longer need to take on any town as your hometown, nor any country as your country, nor any woman as your wife.

You have no enemies, and if people want to take you for an enemy to raise their spirits, it's purely their own business. Your only opponent — yourself — has been killed many times; there's no need to look for enemies, to commit suicide, or to do battle in a duel.

You have lost all memories, the past has been cut off once and for all.

You have no ideals, you've left them behind for other people to think about …

Gao Xingjian: Weekend Quartet

Gao Xingjian has been hailed as the first Chinese playwright to enter world theatre. His plays in fact have been performed more often outside China than inside it, in France, Germany, Belgium, Italy, the U.S., and in overseas Chinese communities such as Hong Kong, Taiwan and Singapore. While his plays have been condemned and subsequently banned in China, they have been heaped with kudos and honours in Europe. Individually, they have been applauded as "archetypal" and "extremely modern and poetic," as creating "a new and delicate language for the stage," and above all, as constituting a "*théâtre de l'asurde à la zen*." In 1992, he was awarded the *Chevalier de l'Ordre des Arts et des Lettres* in France, where he now resides. This can be seen as pointing to the fundamental differences in the idea of theatre and the arts in China and the West, the former rigidly subscribing to a set of utilitarian and political rules on what is legitimate and permissible — exactly the kind of constraints on artistic freedom that Gao Xingjian finds disconcerting. In fact, living in exile seems to have shaped and strengthened Gao Xingjian's convictions, and provided the impetus for the development of his ideas about the theatre. The questions may be asked: is there an essential "Chineseness" in his works? Does he, like many contemporary Chinese writers living overseas, still look to Chinese artistic and cultural traditions for inspiration? And in what manner has his exile and living as a marginalized member of society influenced his thinking and the creation of a "self-conscious" theatre?

Born in 1940 at the height of the Sino-Japanese War (1937–1945) in Ganzhou 贛州 in the Province of Jiangxi 江西, Gao Xingjian spent his youth growing up under the Communist regime that took over China in 1949. His mother, an amateur actress, introduced her young child to the art of traditional Chinese theatre. She also urged him to write, telling him to keep a diary of the happenings of his young life. At ten, he had already finished his first story and drawn some cartoons as illustrations. "I locked myself in my own little room, feeling happy about myself and my work."[1] (Gao Xingjian is proud of his accomplishment as a painter. Exhibitions of his paintings have been held regularly around Europe, in the United States, and in Taiwan and Hong Kong.)

Gao Xingjian went to the Beijing Foreign Languages Institute at seventeen as a French language and literature major. When in college, he became a member of the drama society and acquainted himself with the works of European dramatists such as Stanislavsky, Brecht and Meyerhold. He also developed into an avid reader of literature, saying that it was there that he could "discover the meaning of life." After his graduation in 1962, he worked as a French translator for the foreign language journal *China Reconstructs*. During the Cultural Revolution (1967–1977), he was at one time the leader of a Red Guard brigade, but was later banished to the countryside to work alongside the peasants and the masses.

For Gao Xingjian, the sufferings he witnessed during the Cultural Revolution were exactly like those he had read about in the great books of literature. Driven by a desire to "decipher the meaning of the cruel reality around him," he kept writing in secret and, to avoid detection, he wrapped his manuscripts in plastic sheets and buried them in the ground.[2] (It has also been reported that he had to burn a dozen or so of his playscripts and short stories to escape punishment.) Instead of serving the Party and the masses, for him writing was to be the means to self-knowledge and understanding of the value of human existence. This individualistic stance was of course anathema to the official dogma of socialist realism. With aspirations to become a published writer, he tried to avoid officially tabooed topics, even though he felt himself hemmed in by the restrictions imposed on him and his fellow writers. This dilemma apparently tormented the fledgling writer who, working under constant surveillance by officials and fear of censure, found himself in a constant state of siege mentality. He could only find comfort in the rationalization that perhaps his manuscripts would be allowed to be published posthumously. After the Cultural Revolution, he was sent to southwestern China as a schoolteacher for six years. It was in 1980 that he was able to publish his first piece of writing, a novella entitled *Hanye zhong de xingchen*《寒夜中的星辰》(Stars on a Cold Night). At that time he was already 38.

Of all the contemporary Chinese writers, Gao Xingjian was perhaps the most outward-looking. Through his knowledge of the French language, he could gain access, if only in a limited way, to contemporary developments in literature and literary criticism in the West. After a brief stint as a schoolteacher, he was for a short time a translator and he often gave lectures on French surrealist poetry and other avant-garde writings to his colleagues. In 1981, he published a booklet entitled *Xiandai xiaoshuo jiqiao chutan*《現代小說技巧初探》(Preliminary Explorations into the Techniques of Modern Fiction), which was based on ideas taken from the French structuralist school. The book was a rather crude attempt at theory, aimed at the self-enclosed circles of Chinese writers and critics who were still very much under the influence of the Maoist line of "revolutionary realism." The book proved to be too radical for the authorities and was condemned as a serious and blatant challenge to the party line. Soon the whole country was embroiled in a controversy over the pitfalls of modernism and the book's "bad influences" on young and old writers alike.[3]

In June 1981, Gao Xingjian was assigned to the Beijing People's Art Theatre, China's foremost theatre company. At the time, the company, like all the major theatre companies in China, was still deeply committed to realism and the Stanislavskian method of acting. The first play he wrote for the Beijing People's Art Theatre was *Chezhan*《車站》(Bus Stop), an absurdist play about a group of passengers waiting for a bus which never comes. The play was politely declined by the company because of its non-realistic tendencies. In 1982, Gao finished *Juedui xinhao*《絕對訊號》(Absolute Signal), which was given a test run in the rehearsal room of the Beijing People's Art Theatre. The play, featuring many flashbacks, disjointed temporal sequences and the interplay of subjective and objective perspectives, is a rather didactic prodigal son story — an attempted train robbery is thwarted by one of the villains who eventually realizes his mistaken ways. During the "previews," he and Lin Zhaohua 林兆華, China's best known director who also shared Gao Xingjian's views on experimental drama, decided against Stanislavskian realism and opted for a more modernist production with a minimum of props. The stage, an empty room with the audience on three sides, was equipped only with a few iron bars indicating the inside of a train coach, and the only lighting was a flashlight which the director used to shine on whichever actor was speaking at any given moment. The play had several full-house "previews" and was finally moved to the company's auditorium for a regular run. The production was considered a breakthrough and a trend-setter in Chinese experimental theatre, but it also aroused the authorities' suspicion and once again brought about a vehement war of words on modernism and realism.

Despite the threat of official sanctions, Gao Xingjian pressed on and continued with his efforts in experimental drama, supported by a host of famous dramatists such as Cao Yu 曹禺 and Wu Zuguang 吳祖光. In July 1983, he and Lin Zhaohua began reviving *Bus Stop* as a "rehearsal," which had a successful short run in the banquet hall of the Beijing People's Art Theatre. Cao Yu, then director of the theatre company, applauded the play and considered it a "wonderful" piece of work. But news of the "rehearsal" leaked out, and this time the political fallout was much more serious than with the artistic debate that followed *Absolute Signal*. It was the time of the "Anti-Spiritual Pollution Movement," and the new production was accused of being anti-socialist and of imparting a strong feeling of "doubt and negativity" against the existing way of life.[4] After thirteen performances the play was forced to stop, and Gao Xingjian was subsequently barred from publication for one year. Before further punishments were announced (reportedly he was to be sent to a labour camp in Qinghai to "receive training"), he went into self-exile in the mountains of southwestern China. The turn of events made him realize that exile was the only way to save himself and to preserve "one's values, integrity and independence of spirit."[5]

When he returned to Beijing, he was again allowed to publish his writings. A collection of his medium-length stories came out, followed by another collection of eight of his plays that included some short experimental pieces written to train actors. In November 1984, after settling down after his "exile" in the mountains, he finished *Yeren*《野人》(Wilderness Man) in ten days and nights, incorporating into the play his thoughts on ecology, the destruction of nature and the environment by civilization, and above all, a celebration of the primordial human spirit. According to Gao Xingjian, *Wilderness Man* was to be an experimental play, an "epic" describing events from "seven or eight thousand years ago to the present" and encompassing many issues such as those of "man and nature, and modern man and the history of mankind."[6] The play, aimed at creating a modern Eastern drama, has more than thirty atemporal scenes; it also features a plethora of nonrealistic masked ceremonies, wedding rituals, folk songs and a dance troupe of twenty members, whose abstract movements symbolize the masses, the earth, its floods and forests, as well as a wide range of emotions. *Wilderness Man* represented the pinnacle of the development of experimental drama in China at the time. It also gave notice that drama, or any work of art, did not have to be guided by the concerns for socialist education or political usefulness, and that interpretative lacunae in any piece of work, rather than determinateness, would enhance artistic effectiveness. Here Gao Xingjian's predilection for subjectivity gradually surfaced, and soon he would find himself increasingly uneasy, an individualist surrounded by a sea of collectivity which from time to time would threaten to overrun his personal peace and creative space in art. Regarded as politically innocuous, *Wilderness Man* was very favourably received, and the playwright and his work both managed to avoid political censure. But it was to be his last work to be publicly performed on his home soil.

In May 1985, Gao Xingjian was invited to give a series of lectures in Germany and France, where he apparently basked in the international recognition accorded to him in the foreign press. When he came back to Beijing in early 1986, he finished *Bi'an* 《彼岸》 (The Other Shore). Probably inspired by the freedom and individualism he had witnessed in Europe, the play, among its many different themes, expresses his reservations about the persecution of the individual by the collective rule of the masses, led by a deceiving and manipulating leader whose tactics and claims to power are highly questionable. The rehearsal of the play, done by the students of Beijing People's Art Theatre and under the direction of Lin Zhaohua, was ordered to stop after only one month, and subsequently the plan to establish a workshop on experimental drama was also dropped. This turn of events prompted Gao to go into exile in France in 1987, convinced that his plays would never be allowed to be performed in China again.

When he was living and writing in France, Gao Xingjian could give full rein to his imagination to explore and promote his ideas about a modern theatre, free from the interference of any overriding authority. In 1989 his *Taowang* 《逃亡》 (Exile), which tells the story of three characters running away from the pursuing soldiers during the Tiananmen incident (1989), again brought down the wrath of the Chinese government. As a result, his membership of the Communist Party was revoked. Ironically, the play also put Gao Xingjian at odds with the Chinese Overseas Democracy Movement, which considered the portrayal of intellectuals as susceptible to doubt and emotional vacillations an insult. However, he maintained that his play was concerned with the fate of the individual and his response to an adverse environment. One cannot be sure whether this development distressed our playwright, or if it was actually a predictable outcome of his individualism and personality as a loner. The fact remains that after *Exile*, he shied away from Chinese subject matter in his plays in the next few years.

Gao Xingjian is a highly private person. His unhappiness in China was due as much to his eremitic disposition as to the suffocating sociopolitical system he found himself born into, a totalizing regime bent on collectivization and a common ideology which pervaded every aspect of the life of the individual, including his creativity. To Gao Xingjian, such heavy-handedness strangles the freedom of expression, particularly in art. His response can be likened to that of a traditional Chinese Zen Buddhist, who chooses to detach himself from the "dusty" human world while being in it, casting a "cold eye" on everything, especially the absurdities and the shortsightedness of the unenlightened. But while the Zen Buddhist is keen on pursuing a supreme happiness, the understanding of the *tao*, Gao Xingjian does not consider himself so lucky, for as a modern man obligated to explore his own soul, he simply cannot afford the luxury of hiding his torment behind the *tao*. Instead, he forces his way into the self and compels it to reluctantly admit to its own inadequacies, its fragmentation, its impotence to act, and its inability to eradicate the evil in and around it. If we were to discern a progression in Gao Xingjian's dramatic career, it would have to be seen as a journey from the public subject matter of his early period to the later, more private concerns, a change from the culture and system specific to the more universal, and thus to the more neutral, his personal convictions having undergone, so to speak, a baptism of fire. This transition is clearly marked by *The Other Shore* in 1985, which features a mixture of private and public themes.

Gao Xingjian offers no solution to the problems of the self. Championing a new kind of modernism in contemporary Chinese literature, he claims in 1987 that it constitutes an affirmation of the self, not its negation, as in Western modernism, and a rediscovery of humanism, which has been lost among the insistence on the denial of rationality and the equation of absurdity with existence.[7] The self, as life itself, is always in a state of flux, encompassing past and present, good and evil, long-lasting guilt and brief happiness, and life and death. And like a mannequin, the self is made up of many separable parts which can be assembled and disassembled at will, and appear either in one piece or as dismembered fragments to the horrified owner who claims to have held them together. Such is the essence of existence, made meaningless by the horror, ignorance, and injustice surrounding it. But Gao Xingjian is not a complete pessimist; what matters most to him and to his characters is the materiality of living, of being able to live and, most importantly, to speak and write. Thus words, or discourse, are all and everything in life through which man gets to know his own consciousness, even though words may be mangled, rendered nonsensical, or even useless. As he says, the unknowable behind the words contains the real human nature, and the absurdity of language is the same as the absurdity of living.[8]

To Gao Xingjian, literature has no obligations — the moral and ethical controversies arising from literary writings are only figments of imagination trumped up by meddlesome critics and cultural officials. "Literature has no relation to politics. It is purely a personal undertaking, an observation, a look back at past experiences, a speculation, a cluster of sentiments, a certain expression of inner emotions, and a feeling of the satisfaction of contemplation." Therefore he advocates a "cold literature" (冷的文學 *lengde wenxue*), i.e., literature at its most fundamental, to distinguish it from didactic, political, social and even expressive writing.[9] However, a writer should not totally disassociate himself from society. While refraining from active intervention in social and political issues, he should "exile" himself but at the same time take a position on the margin of society, thus facilitating his undisturbed observations on life and the self. As such, "cold literature" is not art for art's sake, which he despises as being tantamount to "cowardice," [10] and which is only meaningful in so far as it is practised in a society which prohibits it. "Cold literature" survives by means of exile, and it strives to escape from the strangulation of society to conserve itself.[11]

Needless to say, Gao Xingjian is ambivalent on the question of the relationship between a writer and his society, betraying a love-hate attitude to man's involvement in society and detachment from it. Society is invariably made up of antipathetic masses, easily manipulated and prone to persecute the individual among them. But then what is a writer to write about apart from the society of which he is a member? This is Gao Xingjian's dilemma, one that he tries to solve by placing himself on the outside, a stranger to his own community, and by retreating into the innermost depths of the individual, his consciousness. Therein lies his Chinese heritage, not so much in the superficial display of traditional Chinese theatrical conventions which occasionally crops up in his plays, but in his reluctance to totally cut himself off from humanitarianism in an effort to save the human soul, if not collectively, as individual beings. He is characteristic of the modern Chinese intellectual who rebels against his own Chineseness and yet rejects a Western individualism which pays no heed to society. According to his way of thinking, the latter is injurious to human nature — the negation of the very essence of life itself.

Gao Xingjian does not purposely seek to construct a barrier between himself and his world. He is, so to speak, not much of a joiner; he only desires to seek his own personal peace and freedom. In one of his latest declarations, he proclaims the idea of "None-ism" (沒有主義 *Meiyou zhuyi*)[12], i.e., a refusal to believe in any of the "isms." "No matter whether it is in politics or literature, I do not believe in or belong to any party or school, and this includes nationalism and patriotism."[13] His "None-ism" advocates an unlimited and unbridled independence, so that the individual can empty his mind of all the shackles of convention to make the choices best suited to himself, to be sceptical of all blind acquiescence to authority, trendiness and ideological detainment, in other words, it is to be a liberation of the spirit. As a writer, Gao Xingjian steadfastly refuses to be categorized as belonging to any school, Chinese or Western. While he was still in China, he struggled to break free from realism and the Stanislavskian method which had dominated the Chinese theatre for more than three decades, considering them to be too logical, neat, and tyrannized by words. On the other hand, he is also particularly harsh about post-modernism. According to his opinion, the means of what is known as post-modernism has become an end in itself, and art vanishes as a consequence.[14] In other words, concepts have displaced art in the same way as dialectics and abstractions have taken over from genuine criticism, and anybody can become an artist because artistic skills are not required as prerequsites.[15]

Gao Xingjian's antipathy towards the canonized is derived from his constant search for a genuine renewal in art. Even though he pursues "the freedom not to peddle antiques," [16] he is nonetheless not iconoclastic. "When someone wants to go forward, there is no need to trample on one's ancestors."[17] He has not been able to sever himself totally from tradition: we can see him trying to seek inspiration from the theatricality of classical Chinese opera and from folk culture. The latter's emphasis on rituality and simplicity interests him as an artist, and its uncorrupted character is a kindred spirit to his understanding of the primeval self.

In rejecting the modernist label in 1987 (when he was still in China), he said that it was more appropriate to place himself at the meeting point between Eastern and Western cultures and between history and the present.[18] However, he also claimed that he has paid his debts to all things Chinese since the publication of *Lingshan* 靈山 (Spiritual Mountain) in 1990, a novel set in the mythical mountains and streams of southwestern China. In his latest plays, he has been striving for neutrality and universality, shying away from Chinese settings and characters.

We shall not dwell on the idea of interculturalism in Gao Xingjian. Suffice it to say that even our writer himself is conscious of the crosscurrents of the Chinese and the Western interacting in both his personal and artistic life. It is important to point out that he always values the self not in an egotistic manner, but in the knowledge of the imperative to comprehend the self, its relation to the world, and the value of existence. The key here is the Chinese concept of "*jingguan*" 靜觀,[19] or "peaceful observation," which encompasses the ideas of tranquillity, disinterestedness, and detachment. And it is through this concept that we can begin to understand Gao Xingjian's idea of the tripartition of the actor, i.e., just as a writer should observe himself and society with the indifference of an outsider, an actor should also be able to observe his performance and the character he is portraying with the same degree of "coldness" and detachment.

Acting and the Tripartition of the Actor

Gao Xingjian's idea of dramaturgy affirms the importance of what he calls theatricality (*juchangxing* 劇場性). When Aristotle talks about "action," Gao Xingjian claims, he is referring to action in its fundamental sense, i.e., the kind of action that the audience can see and hear,[20] unlike the "action" in contemporary drama which is limited to the conflict of ideas and concepts. This physical aspect of drama is what distinguishes it from poetry, which emphasizes lyricality, and fiction, which underlines narration. Drama is process, and while it may not necessarily be complete in itself, the changes, discoveries, and surprises in a play can be amplified and elaborated upon and made into elements of theatricality, thus generating dramatic action on the stage.[21]

According to Gao Xingjian, stage language can be used to indicate harmony or disharmony as in a musical structure. Like the notes in a symphony, the phonic qualities of words often highlight their materiality, effectively transforming the utterances into a non-narrational medium. In this manner, stage language acquires the charm and the almost magical power of chanting, and produces a deeply felt compulsion in both actors and audience. Such is the difference between the new language of drama, with its emphasis on materiality and physical impact, and the semantically inclined language commonly used in other literary genres.[22]

There is yet another aspect to the making of theatricality. Drama is nothing but performance, and the actions on the stage are meant for the enjoyment of the audience. In order to facilitate this communication and to enhance its directness, Gao Xingjian maintains that the actor has to be self-conscious of his craft, being aware not only of the character he is playing but also of the fact that he is putting on a performance as a performer. This awareness is in contrast to Stanislavsky's total immersion method, and to an extent it is also distinguished from Brecht's "alienation," which breaks the illusion of realism and underlines the distance between performance and audience. To Gao Xingjian, there is no denying that drama is ostentation — the many attempts at realism by the modern theatre are nothing short of spurious and futile efforts to achieve impossibility. Ostentation is helpful and also essential to communicating with the audience: in fact, an actor should highlight the act of pretending, as if he is saying to himself and to the audience, "Look how well I can pretend to be somebody else!" As in Beijing opera or the Japanese kabuki, even though the actor focuses his attention on how to perform his role, he still manages to retain his identity as an actor — his job is to give a good performance but not to live the life of the character.[23] The pretending still exists, and is even accentuated, but it coexists with a more direct and true-to-life actor-audience communication, in which the actor has become the centre and disseminator of artistic awareness. In other words, besides the character-centred and audience-centred theories of Stanislavsky and Brecht, Gao

Xingjian has ventured his own actor-centred theory in an argument for a more self-conscious art.

How does one achieve self-consciousness and yet still be "in" the performance and a good actor at the same time? The answer to this is Gao Xingjian's idea of the tripartition of acting. In traditional Chinese theatre, Gao Xingjian explains, when the actor gets ready for the role he is to play, he extracts himself from his everyday activities, relaxes his body and focuses his mind to enter into his performance. During this time, he "purifies" himself into a "state of neutrality"; in other words, he is in a state of transition between his everyday self and his role. This neutrality can be explained by looking at the convention of *liangxiang* 亮相[24] (literally "to reveal oneself") in Beijing opera. At the time of *liangxiang*, the actor freezes his movement for a few seconds to mark his entrance or the completion of a display of martial arts, dance sequence, etc., thus making himself "appear" before his audience, who applaud and voice their approval. The performance is briefly suspended, as the actor neutralizes his acting capacity and calls attention to the exhibition of his art.

Thus in any performance, there exists in the actor three identities — the self, the neutral actor, and the character. Neutrality is not tantamount to self-effacement; it demands a self-consciousness in the actor of his own make-believe. At the same time this also equips the actor with a "third eye" of inner vision which, because of the detachment from the character he is portraying, is capable of observing his performing self, the other actors on the stage and, more importantly, the audience. Neutrality then becomes a medium which enables the actor to control and adjust his performance, helping him to be in and out of his character not only before the performance but also many times during the performance. And because the actor is both experiencing (acting) and observing himself while performing, he is more able to project his feelings into the character for the audience's enjoyment. In any theatre, what needs to be communicated is not reality but the feeling of reality. By embodying the three identities on the stage, the actor can challenge the character he is playing, empathize with him, pity, admire and even criticize him. The dramatic tension resulting from this kind of acting is beyond that produced by mere yelling and shouting which disguise themselves as theatre. In this way, not only the plot but also acting itself can be interesting and become the focus of the audience's attention. And the actor, because his feeling for the character is not derived exclusively from his physical self, is awarded a high degree of satisfaction through an awareness of his own artistic creation.

Points of View in Drama

Gao Xingjian is concerned about acting, but being first and foremost a writer, he is also equally concerned about playwriting. He laments the demise of the playwright in the contemporary theatre. The playwright, according to Gao, has been forced to give up his former prominence to the director, who is now the absolute ruler of the stage. With the weakening position of the playwright, theatre increasingly relies on technology to support its predominantly visual presentation, and music, which is capable of generating tension through contrasts and variations (e.g. in a symphony), has also been abused, being given the task of covering up the inadequacies in performance. As the peripherals have taken over from real dramatic action, and abstraction, in the form of exegesis of ideas, emerges as the only objective, theatre tends to become non-drama or even anti-drama and comes closer and closer to the end of the road.[25]

As a playwright, Gao Xingjian is motivated by the desire to wrestle the centre stage from the hands of the director. He insists on the dramatic, the "drama" (戲 *xi*) happening on the stage. His plays may not feature a well-made plot, and they may even resort to abstractions from time to time, but there has to be structural integrity — expositions, contrasts, conflicts, and discoveries, the essentials with which drama is made, and which are seen as "action" by the audience. The dramatic is not confined to externalities; most of Gao Xingjian's recent works feature internal conflicts, the psychological drama within a character's consciousness.

Gao Xingjian admits that his idea of the tripartite actor is not universally applicable to all kinds of scripts, and he remains unsure whether this theory of his has been the driving force behind his style of playwriting or vice versa. The idea is part of Gao Xingjian's search for a new language for the contemporary stage; the drama of the modern man's frenzied schizophrenia demands such acting as a complement, or even prerequisite. His understanding of performance, namely, the coexistence of the self, the neutral actor, and the character in the actor, opens up new possibilities in playwriting. Just as consciousness is capable of being realized by the tripartite actor, so it can also be interpolated on the discourse level to project different modes of perception.

It is evident that Gao Xingjian's latest works, which are included in the present collection, all feature his newly developed ideas about narrative modes in drama and put into effect his demands on the actor. In these plays the characters not only speak in the first person, as is the case by dramatic convention, they also speak and refer to themselves in the second and third persons, being in and out of their own selves in the same play or even in the same scene. For instance, in *Dialogue and Rebuttal*, the hero and the heroine speak in the first person in the first half of the play, and then switch to the second and third persons respectively in the second half, when they are languishing in a state of apparent meaninglessness as spirits after their deaths.

Gao Xingjian's experiments in the narrative modes of drama may have been inspired by the special features of the Chinese language. Many times he has commented that the Chinese language, being an uninflected language, facilitates shifting the "angle" or perspective of narration. "As the subject in a Chinese sentence can be omitted and there are no verbal conjugations, it is quite natural to displace the 'I' as the subject by a zero subject. The subjective consciousness can be transformed, achieving a pan-subjective consciousness or even self-effacement. And it is just as easy to change the 'I' into the second person (you) or the third person (he/she). The 'I' as 'you' is a case of objectification, and the 'I' as 'he/she' one of detached observation, or contemplation. This really affords the writer tremendous freedom!" [26]

Commenting on the new possibilities of his dramatic strategy, Gao Xingjian says:

> The character, which usually appears on stage in the first person, can be divided into three different points of view and can speak in three different persons, and the same character will then have three psychological dimensions. The character as both agent and receptor is enriched by many perspectives, which enable a more complete mode of expression. And from his various observation platforms, the same character will be able to generate and express

> many different attitudes towards the outside world and towards his own experience of it.[27]

The shift in narrative mode is not a mere substitution of "I" by "you," "he" or "she"; it also has implications for the actor and the audience's point of view. With the "I" relating the story of "you," "he" or "she," the character is functionally divided into two separate roles of addresser and addressee, or narrator and narratee, even though they are both physically embodied in one person. The second or third person self functions as the observed, who operates in the external world made up of other characters. As the "I" is insulated from direct contact with the external world, he is equipped with a different perspective from that of his divided double, and in his capacity as a non-participating narrator, he can be more objective in assessing his own consciousness as that of someone other than himself.

The discourse situation in Gao Xingjian's plays mostly points to the exploration of the self, the centre around which all the happenings revolve and towards which all the meanings gravitate. In combining the narrating and experiencing selves, the narrative situation is capable of generating tension among the divided selves of the same character, with the "you" being closer to the implicit "I," but not less confrontational than the third person self ("he/she"), who is further removed. According to Lacanian psychoanalysis, "otherness" can never be firmly grasped. The other is basically a locus of the subject's fears and dears; they do not belong to an external category, but are internal and unchangeable conditions of man's existence. Viewed in this perspective, the dreams and speeches, when they are expressed on the stage, illuminate the split in the subject's imaginary register and its elements.

The process opens up new venues of communication for the theatre. For instance, the "you" in *Nocturnal Wanderer*, in its capacity as the observed self of the "I," is the main character in the play whose fate and emotions are on display. In this manner, the audience gets to see the play's actions with an awareness of the non-experiencing "I" and his implicit judgement on the "you." They are thus given a comprehensive picture of the drama, the complexity of the character and his inner conflicts which have been externalized, and his relationship with the world at large. In *Between Life and Death*, the heroine examines her own life in a series of narrated flashbacks. Here the implied "I" plays the role of narrator retelling the story of "she," who is the projected and experiencing self of "I." In this manner, a degree of objectivity is achieved because the narrating "I," detached from immediate experience, can be largely sheltered from self-pity. Thus on the level of expressiveness, shifting the narrative mode facilitates self-examination and makes it easier for the unconscious to reveal itself.

The modern stage has come a long way since the Stanislavskian method of realistic acting, i.e., total identification and immersion in the character being portrayed. Brecht's epic theatre introduces the third-person narrator, and highlights stage narratology by adding another dimension to communication in the theatre — the audience, made aware of the existence of a world outside the world of the play, are "alienated" from the performance and performers. For Gao Xingjian, his idea of the theatre goes beyond alienation and invoking the audience's rationality. It is inherent in and grows out of his conception of the world of the play, a world focusing on the consciousness of both actor and character, self-contained in its ostentation, yet made expansive so as to involve the audience both emotionally and intellectually. The key word is "self-consciousness." Gao Xingjian's self-conscious art reveals itself not merely in its self-reflexivity or in its relation to the world at large, i.e., how the world looks at the self; it can only be understood as self-observation in an alienated and detached manner. The relationship between the first-person self and his "other" hangs in a delicate balance, covering the whole spectrum of subjectivity and objectivity. The resultant potential for dramatic tension and conflict is part and parcel of his idea of the theatre, which encompasses both acting and playwriting.

Drama and the Modern Man

Gao Xingjian insists that his ideas should not be regarded as supporting technique for technique's sake, nor are they merely aimed at rhetorical purposes. His pursuit of a new theatre is intended to reveal the naked realities of modern man and his living conditions — privileging formalism would only bury the truth of these realities and conditions.[28] Gao Xingjian is not a fan of the modern theatre (so-called "spoken drama" in

Chinese) dominated by words and their meaning-generating functions. Far more concerned with the unstated emotions in language and in performance, he aspires to a "modern language," akin to the language games found in *Zhuangzi*《莊子》and in the *Diamond Sutra*《金剛經》, that will express a feeling of detachment and a kind of "free and easy" contemplation as embodied in Taoist and Buddhist texts.[29] In this he finds an ally in the Chinese language, which he tries to rejuvenate and develop into an appropriate medium of expression for the stage:

> … I am not at all a cultural chauvinist, and I don't have in me the incomprehensible arrogance typical of the Chinese race. The only thing I want to do is to rejuvenate this ancient language, so that it can be equally able to express the bewilderment of modern man, his pursuits, his frustrations in not being able to attain them, and in the final analysis, the sufferings and happiness of living, loneliness and the dire need for expression.[30]

Gao Xingjian's language is largely lyrical and at times even gossipy, yet it can be extremely powerful and moving in its indifference and apparent irrelevance, containing words of "unspoken wisdom." As with many Zen Buddhist texts, his words "speaks directly to the heart," striking at the innermost core of the human soul. When they are most effective, they are graced with an almost magical power derived from a spellbinding rhythm akin to chanting, evincing a materiality beyond mere utterance and primary referentiality. The idea is to allow the mind of the audience to "wander in contemplation" among the words so as to grasp their true spirit, which resides as a sublimated effect beyond the language being used.[31]

Gao Xingjian does not resort to yelling and screaming in his writings. He is not a revolutionary, and he refuses to fight other people's war other than the one that resides in his heart. In concentrating on the self, Gao Xingjian's writings can be regarded as subjective and individualistic. However, his is a distinctive kind of individualism, one that values the self but not at the expense of others. As he says of his novel *Spiritual Mountain*:

> My perception of the self has nothing to do with self-worship. I detest those people whose desire is to displace God with himself,

> the kind of heroism which aspires to defeat the world, and the kind of self-purgation which puts on the guise of a tragic hero. I am myself, nothing less, nothing more.[32]

In this way he rejects Nietzsche and the individualism of the West, which he considers destructive. His attitude is not unlike that of the traditional Taoist or Zen Buddhist who, bent on seclusion or exile from society to cultivating his inner virtues and strength, still casts an indifferent eye to observe the world of humans in his somewhat aloof and detached position. However, while Taoism and Buddhism aspire to understanding the *tao*, Gao Xingjian insists on knowing and studying the self and its inner secrets in all its complexities; while the former represents inner peace, Gao Xingjian finds only pain and suffering, and unfortunately, there appears to be no salvation. The individual is helpless in the face of this predicament, for he is impotent to change himself or his world. He can assert his existence only by way of thinking and of the production of discourse (he once proclaimed: "I discourse, therefore I am"[33]); ironically these tend to become as ineffectual and meaningless as the world he finds himself in — therein resides the frustration and insoluble dilemma of modern man.

The Plays

The Other Shore 彼岸 (Bi'an) *(1986)*

Written in early 1986, *The Other Shore* was originally scheduled to be performed by the Beijing People's Art Theatre under the direction of Lin Zhaohua, but the rehearsal was suspended because the play was considered politically sensitive. This marked a turning point in Gao Xingjian's thinking — he gradually came to the realization that the authorities would no longer allow his plays to be performed in China. (*The Other Shore* was subsequently performed in Taiwan by the Taiwan National College of Art in 1990 and by the Hong Kong Academy for Performing Arts in 1995. Both productions were directed by the playwright.)

The Other Shore is a short but complex play. The plot is made up of disjointed narrative units that do not apparently or necessarily connect with one another, at least in a structurally coherent manner. However, each unit can be seen as self-contained and is interesting and meaningful by itself. Gao Xingjian considers the play as his attempt at "pure" drama:

> *The Other Shore* is different from conventional drama. One of the differences is that the play does not attempt to put together a coherent plot. I only intend it to be a revelation, to portray some of life's experiences and feelings in a pure dramatic form, i.e., in the same way that music is pure.[34]

The title *Bi'an* (literally "the other shore" or "the opposite shore") refers to *paramita*, the land of enlightenment in Buddhism. According to Buddhist beliefs, one is able to cross the river of life — from the shore of delusion and suffering to the other shore of enlightenment — by cultivating and perfecting the *paramita* virtues of generosity, morality, patience, vigor, concentration (or meditation) and wisdom. The play reveals the fundamental tragedy of human life: even after crossing the river and reaching the other shore, the characters find that enlightenment is unobtainable, and that they are still trapped in the delusions and sufferings of everyday life from which there is no escape. As Gao Xingjian says, "It is destined that the individual will never be able to acquire the ultimate truth, which is known as God or the other shore."[35]

At least two issues stand out in the play: collectivism and personal salvation. In the opening scene, the game of ropes first illustrates the establishment of inter-personal relationships and the virtue and necessity of communal living. However, the ropes are soon subject to manipulation and control, and the relationships turn into unequal partnerships overrun by totalitarian rule. Then comes the river crossing by a group of actors, a difficult undertaking but hopeful of happiness upon its completion. After crossing the river to the other shore, the actors are accorded a temporary bliss through their loss of language. However, as soon as they are taught to speak again by Woman, a mother figure, they learn to distinguish between self and other and are anxious to seek out the outsider among them. Incited by their own words to irrational violence, they smother Woman to death and try to put the blame on one another. As the group tuns into an unruly mob, they need a leader to guide them. They try to pressure Man, who may be regarded as the *de facto* hero in the play, to take up the role.

When Man refuses, they let themselves fall into the hands of a manipulating card-playing Master, who tempts them with wine and coaxes them into making fools of themselves. In an attempt to please Master, they willingly confuse reality with illusion and compromise truth with falsehood. Together they ridicule and persecute Man, the individualist among them. The various episodes in the first part of the play, at first appearing fragmented, are now given a thematic unity underscoring the flaw of collectivism, that it can easily degenerate into blind obedience and violence and play into the hands of a manipulative leader.

The scenes that follow describe Man's search for personal salvation as he tries to assert his independence in the community of man. Besieged by adversities, he feels smothered by the unreasonable demands on his individuality. As a result, he is frustrated in every way, a total failure in human relations. With his non-conformist stance, he cannot get along with the masses, nor can he obtain any understanding from his father and his mother; even his yearning for love is denied him. An outcast turned cynic, he strives frantically to pick up the pieces of his life, doing so literally by rearranging the arms and legs of mannequins to make them whole again and, like God, he tries to create his own version of human society. But when the mannequins become too many, he finds himself helplessly drawn into their collective pattern of frenzied movements: this is mob behaviour once again. All the time his actions are haunted by the underlying presence of the Zen Master and his chanting, as if he is casting a "cold" eye of indifference on the futility of all of Man's undertakings. In the end, Man leaves the stage "a drooping, blind, and deaf heart," and the masses become actors again as the play reverts to the everyday life of the beginning, the world before the river crossing to "the other shore."

To an extent *The Other Shore* expresses the author's misgivings about collectivism and its darker consequences. The ending offers no salvation for the persecuting masses and their irrationality, and there exists no one, like the "silent man" in *Bus Stop* or the ecologist in *Wilderness Man*, who takes on the role of the harbinger of hope. Communication is impossible despite human interaction, or because of it, for language is highly suspect, a means of deception, violence, and the distortion of intentions. As a result the individual can only seek refuge in the "dark and shady forest" of his heart, reminiscing about his past life until life itself perishes. But all is not futile — for all its darkness and despair, the play also affords a glimpse of self-knowledge in the pursuit of an equilibrium between the self and the outside world.[36]

Of course we are treading on dangerous ground in attempting to interpret the unity and the meaning of the play. It is as if each interpretation leads to another that is its contradiction, and there is always the risk of oversimplification. Perhaps it is better to just regard the play, as Gao Xingjian suggests, as a training exercise for actors. To our writer, *The Other Shore* is an experiment in pursuit of a modern theatre, using Eastern drama as a starting point. As with Peking opera, it is actor-centred, and communication with the audience is mostly derived from the directness of the actors' performance.[37] The play is also the first piece of work by the playwright embodying his idea of the neutral actor:

> Crossing the river to the other shore is a key moment in the performance. After the rigorous movements of playing with the ropes and rapidly exchanging partners, the actors relax their bodies and lie on the floor to listen to the music. As they let the music evoke their feelings, their bodies are not motivated by ideas. This is a process of self-purgation.[38]

From this moment on the actors will be able to "forget" themselves and to effectively focus their attention on observing their own body movements and listening to their own voices. And Shadow, Man's super-ego, is the physical manifestation of the neutral actor on stage: he is there to observe, evaluate and even make fun of "Man" in the encounter of the self with his other.

Between Life and Death 生死界 **(Shengsijie)** ***(1991)***

In 1989, Gao Xingjian finished *Exile* (*Taowang* 逃亡), which is set against the background of the 1989 Tiananmen incident. The play describes the stories of three characters, a young man, a young girl student, and a middle-aged writer, who are in hiding and running from the pursuing PLA (People's Liberation Army) soldiers. It unmasks and examines the fundamental human weaknesses, such as fear and desire, and the naive idealism among the participants in the Democracy Movement, and casts doubts on the wisdom, and even the possibility, of the intelligentsia's intrusion into politics. In the end, the only way out for all the characters, as for the writer in real life, is to go into exile.

Between Life and Death, written two years after *The Other Shore*, can be seen as an attempt by Gao Xingjian to chastise the Chineseness in him (probably because of his displeasure with the adverse reactions to *Exile* in 1989) and pursue writing for a universal audience. The setting is unspecified and, except for the appearance of a Buddhist nun, there is no reference to anything specifically Chinese. The heroine, without any indication of her nationality, is just called Woman; she could be "everywoman." She serves as the play's narrator, describing her tortured life story, her fears and sensitivities, which are seen as typical of the female sex. In light of this, the play apparently champions feminism, especially women's sufferings at the hands of men. As the narrator-heroine says, "In her life, a woman is destined to suffer five hundred times more than a man." Even women help men to oppress other women, and they can be more vicious than men to their own kind. However, the play's concerns are actually more ambitious, as the collectivist themes in Gao Xingjian's previous works have been displaced by the more subjective question of the self and the existential.

The story is about a woman who faces the end of her life's journey in both mental and physical exhaustion. The various episodes in her monologue fall mainly into three categories. First there is her love-hate relationship with Man, who has no speaking parts but expresses his reactions to her monologue by performing pantomimes. She keeps nagging him, accuses him of infidelity and threatens to leave him. But when he disappears and eventually transforms into a pile of clothing, she is full of remorse, wishing that he could have stayed and made up with her. This is a sad comment on the fate of Woman, and of women in general — she attempts to assert her independence, but in the end she finds that she still has to depend on Man, at least for his companionship.

What follows are reminiscences of Woman's tainted past. She spent a harrowing childhood in a windowless house. She tried to get her mother's attention by cutting her finger with a pair of scissors. She was raped by her mother's lover. She had an affair with a woman doctor and her husband, in which she was used as a plaything to spice up their sex life. And then there was her irksome one-night stand with some unknown man. According to her own admission, she has abandoned herself to living a life of sin after being manipulated and exploited by both men and women. Feeling guilty and remorseful, she takes off her ring, her bracelet and her earrings, all tokens of her past experiences, to purge herself of her sins, but all is in vain. As her disappointment grows, she feels increasingly depressed about herself, thinking that she is unfit to be a mother and unworthy of a warm and comfortable home. She is alone in the world among its evil and squalor, with nothing to look forward to except the end of her life.

The latter part of the play features a series of hallucination scenes. Here Woman finds herself languishing in a state "between life and death" as she makes various frantic attempts to discover the meaning of her existence in her encounters with the supernatural. A masked man appears, chases her in his car and warns her of a bloody disaster. Then she slides down into the depths of icy water. A nun, whom Woman first mistakes as the Buddhist Bodhisattva, disembowels herself, cleanses her intestines, puts them on a plate and then throws them in Woman's face. A man dressed in black and perched on high stilts approaches, watching over her with a big black eye in his hand. A headless woman follows Woman, also with a big eye in her hand. The play ends with Woman musing aloud on the question of her identity while an old man tries to catch an imaginary snowflake with his hat.

As spectacle, the hallucination scenes in the last part of the play are the most dramatic and effective. The images are horrifying and dreamlike, and their accompanying earnestness and intensity make them disturbingly real. One recurring image in these scenes is the big eye, which appears twice and each time sends shudders down Woman's heart. The first one, painted on a man's hand, denotes the eye of other people and the opposite sex, and Woman feels that this eye has been following her all her life. The second is the eye carried by the headless woman, presumably embodying the soul of the heroine, and the eye is the inner eye. The fear of being spied upon lingers and terrorizes Woman as she feels that her judgement day is approaching.

In *The Other Shore*, Gao Xingjian resorts to externalization to realize his idea of self-examination by using different characters to portray the divided self, the observer and the observed. In *Between Life and Death*, he goes one step further towards subjectivizing and neutralizing the self: the two versions of the self are combined and contained in one character. The narrating "I" is the experiencing "she," even though the two are distinguished from each other in the use of deixis. The former, referring to her own story in the third person, distances herself not only from past experiences but also from the actions and emotions of the present. Ubiquitous in its presence, the "I" reveals itself only through narration, depending on discourse to prove her being (despite the fact that language is evasive and is itself in a state of chaos). The gap between the two selves remains unbridgeable from beginning to end. The narrating "I," like the big black eyes in the play, is always observing and implicitly evaluating, and so tends to transcend the immediacy of the moment. On the other hand, the "she," as the reification of "I" and the object of narration, can only aspire to the physicality of experience, the world of suffering and emotion. Thus the "I" plays the role of a "cold" and detached observer, but the irony is that it cannot be without the impassioned "she" and her worldliness.

The shift in narrative mode underlines the horror because of the need for objectification, but the play is more than the story of a fallen woman and her search for salvation. It is an examination of the dark secrets of a woman's inner world haunted by fears of rejection, ageing, death and the final judgement, and even of life itself, leading up to the impossibility of absolution despite her hysterical protestations. Narrated in the third person, these fears are given full expression, free from self-pity which tends to be inhibiting and selective. Apart from the psychological exigencies, the narrative situation eventuates in a split of the character, creating tension between the narrating "I" and the experiencing "she." In light of Gao Xingjian's idea of the neutral actor, the actress playing Woman, by positioning herself in an in-between space, can be in and out of her role in the course of performance. She addresses the character she is portraying as "she," and thus carries out a "disinterested observation" of her own performance in the same way that the two big black eyes observe Woman's actions. As the writer says in the postscript: "The narrator in the play, i.e., Woman, should not be regarded the same as a character. She is both in and out of the character, but still preserving her status as an actress." At times she appears to share the character's emotional torments, but mostly she is with the audience, on the outside looking in.

The playwright also requires that the props in the play, the coat-hanger, the building blocks, the jewellery box and the dismembered mannequin, etc. are to be "enlivened," regarded as living characters, in their encounters with Woman. As in traditional Chinese theatre, the props are the bases and extensions of the performance process. For example, Man turns into a coat-hanger after he has been strangled by Woman; the building blocks are a reminder of Woman's memories; and the jewellery box represents the grave in which Woman buries herself and her past. Together with the other on-stage but non-speaking actors — the actress who performs the various psychological manifestations of Woman and the actor who plays Man, the ghost, the clown and the Old Man — the props as "living" characters combine to create a "psychological arena" where the drama of Woman's consciousness is revealed and played out, not only within the heroine herself but also among the various performing roles.

Dialogue and Rebuttal 對話與反詰 **(Duihua yu fanjie)** *(1992)*

Gao Xingjian appears to have a love-hate relationship with language. He has said that he wants to enhance the expressiveness of the Chinese language, yet he also condemns the ascendancy of language in modern drama, which he says has deprived the stage of its theatricality. With *Dialogue and Rebuttal* he claims to have made a determined effort to destroy language[39] and to cast doubts on its meaning-generating functions.[40] The play is made up of a series of dialogues between a man and a woman, generically known as Man and Woman, two strangers who have just had a brief sexual encounter. In the aftermath of their physical contact, they shut themselves out from each other in the ensuing conversation, refusing to engage in any meaningful communication. Woman flaunts her sexuality and laments her plight as a woman, but her fear of ageing and dying fails to arouse any sympathetic response in Man. Man is only interested in gratifying his prurient curiosity, as when he listens with relish to Woman's stories of her sexual caper in India and her alleged rape by her physical education teacher when she was a young schoolgirl. In the absence of love and understanding, only desire is left as the embodiment of physicality, and their conversation merely serves to uncover the loneliness, boredom and futility of their lives.

The dialogues between Man and Woman, invariably short, non-expressive and generally indicative of an indifference towards each other, are interrupted by the characters' monologues narrated in the second (Man) or the third person (Woman). These digressions evince a move away from the drama between the two characters, who then become the objects of observation, evaluation and commentary by their own alienated selves. At times the monologues, as in the moment of "sudden enlightenment" in Zen Buddhism, serve to expose the truth of the predicaments in which the characters are trapped, but they also further neutralize their relationship. Even though the plot is dependent on the presence of Man and Woman, it is even more dependent on the absence of interaction between them. Communication is only one-way, from the narrating self to the experiencing self, not between the characters, as each is preoccupied in their own cocooned world.

At the end of the first half, the non-communication eventually leads to boredom and a bizarre game of sexual perversion, in which Man and Woman stab each other to death. As in *The Other Shore*, language inevitably alienates and ushers in violence. In the second half, communication remains impossible between the kindred spirits, for in most cases, the ghosts of Man and Woman are not talking to each other but to their own dead bodies or to the other's head lying on the stage floor. At this time, even sexual desire, which was the only channel of interaction in the first half, has lost its attractiveness. Man keeps looking for a door to escape from his predicament even though he knows that there is nothing behind that door, and Woman is preoccupied with reminiscences of the violence and suffering in her life, striving fruitlessly to ascertain her existence by the production of discourse. They are like dancing partners who nonetheless insist on being distanced from each other and shy away from any direct emotional contact. In the end, words have lost their referential function and the game of free association, with its occasional and accidental overlaps of meaning, is the only hint of their participation in a dialogue and of their existence. The irony is that both Man and Woman are already dead, their physical being already taken away from them by their nonsensical game of desire, which was meant to verify their being alive in the first place.

Their deaths have prevented them from talking to each other — only their souls are talking to their bodies.[41] All that remains in language is a "crack," the ever-increasing communication gap between humans. At the end of the play Man and Woman have become crawling worms; the reification of their human selves signifies a regression, or a recognition of their true identities and the true nature of human existence.

Witnessing and punctuating this drama of futility is the Monk and his acrobatic tricks. Like Man and Woman, he is also enwrapped in his own world and he makes no effort to communicate, or as Gao Xingjian puts it, there seems to be an invisible wall between the Monk and the other two characters. In one sense he is a foil, for while the acting of Man and Woman is naturalistic, his is highly ritualistic, and when they are hysterical and metamorphosed in the realm of the dead, he is composed, indifferent and above all, wordless, in sharp contrast to their rambling, meaningless verbosity. Even though he remains unfazed from beginning to end, he is not beyond laughing at himself. His attempts at a one-finger headstand, standing an egg on a stick and other antics are illustrations of the futility and frustrations of human endeavours.[42] He is transcendental but not totally otherworldly, his antics being the follies of his own humanity. He listens carefully (this is symbolized by cleaning his ears, a gesture imbued with Buddhist meanings), and he observes with indifference that he has seen through the emptiness of human desires and sufferings. Perhaps the personification of Gao Xingjian's idea of "indifferent observation," he is content in the wordless wisdom accorded to him by his attainment of the state of Zen. If the drama between Man and Woman is "dialogue," the Monk's pantomime tricks are a "rebuttal," an unspoken challenge to and ultimate denial of any possibility of meaning in language and in life's activities.

Monk's on-stage presence invokes a meaning beyond words. His role is meaningful in its meaninglessness, evincing a negative capability discernible in the hopeless world of Man and Woman. There remains in this paradox a capacity, a virtue that comes with the loss of referentiality, an attitude towards life derived from the understanding of the illogicality and the unstated meaning of language in Zen.[43] Gao Xingjian claims that he has no intention to promote Zen Buddhism or to expound its teachings: he is only interested in nudging the audience into contemplation, so that they can come close to the state of wordless and unspoken wisdom.[44] At the end, the Monk reveals a greyish blue sky, which is eternal and peaceful, a symbol of the quiet acceptance of the way of the universe.

Nocturnal Wanderer 夜遊神 (Yeyoushen) *(1993)*

The subject matter of *Nocturnal Wanderer* is a dream, and through the dream the inner world of the protagonist, Traveller, is revealed in all its horror and insidiousness. The world of reality, with which the play begins, inspires the dream and provides the dramatis personae for the dream world. Traveller enters the dream world and becomes Sleepwalker, who embarks on a journey of self-discovery in his encounters with Tramp, Prostitute, Thug and Master, the various characters corresponding to the passengers Traveller meets on the train. The metamorphoses of people in the real world into dream world characters are accomplished in and through Traveller's psyche and its workings: they are imaginings and representations indicative of his secret fears and desires. In this way the dream is set up as an exploration of Traveller's consciousness.

Gao Xingjian has said that the play is about good and evil, about man, Satan, and God, and about man's self-consciousness.[45] In the dream, goodness, seen as Sleepwalker's conscience and innate sense of rectitude, is invariably suppressed and displaced by evil, either voluntarily or as an expedient. And Sleepwalker, an everyman figure whose only wish is to take a stroll in the night, just cannot escape being encroached upon by evil — Thug who threatens his life, Master who wants to control his thoughts, and Prostitute who tempts his soul (she later turns into his friend and critic exposing the lies in his life). Man is not born evil; in the case of Sleepwalker, evil is thrust upon him by a world infested with crime and violence. Consequently he is transformed into a murderer more flagitious than Thug or Master, someone who readily abandons his sensibility, his conscience and his sense of morality. He kills Tramp, who with the sagacity of a Buddhist monk represents salvation for his soul, thus depriving himself of any chance of redemption. He even rejects his head, which symbolizes thinking and reason, as he tramples upon it and breaks it into pieces.

At the end of the play Sleepwalker becomes fascinated by evil; in fact, he is obsessed with it. But just when he manages to bury his guilt by rationalization, feeling happy for himself in his newfound pleasure in violence, he encounters his double, perhaps the narrating "I" in the nightmare. The two grapple with each other in a fight: Sleepwalker still has to run the gauntlet of his own self. Traveller has embarked on a journey of being and existence, but he discovers only violence and horror. Evil is ubiquitous in the outside world, but the real horror is that it also lurks inside the self, jumping at any chance to rear its ugly head. Traveller as everyman, or "archetypal man"[46] thus finds himself threatened by what surrounds him and what resides within him. In dream as in reality evil is invincible and irresistible, for as Sleepwalker finds out, it is the only means with which to fend for oneself; however, even this recourse to evil represents nothing more than a meaningless resistance against a world of meaninglessness. In the final scene Traveller and all the other passengers are gone; what remains is nothing but an open book which has inspired the nightmare.

There are three levels of consciousness in *Nocturnal Wanderer*, each one penetrating deeper into the psyche of the protagonist. The first level is located in the real and objective world of the train coach; here Traveller speaks in the first person. On the second level, Traveller becomes Sleepwalker in the dream. And as he speaks in the second person, he creates a third level of reality made up of self-reflections, where he takes on the role of observer, insulated from the experiencing self of evil, violence, and gratuitous sexuality, a world he finds inexplicable. What happens in the dream world also reflects on the world of reality, for the characters in the dream, Tramp, Prostitute, Thug, and Master have been transmuted into being through and by Traveller's feelings towards the world he is living in. The products of his mental processes, these "images of the heart" 心像 have ironically become the masters controlling his consciousness. Gao Xingjian has commented that:

> *Between Life and Death*, *Dialogue and Rebuttal*, and *Nocturnal Wanderer* are concerned with the state of liminality between life and death or between reality and imagination. They also reveal the nightmare in the inner world of man. In these plays, the relationship with reality only serves as a starting point. What I strive to capture is the reality of the feelings in the psyche, a naked reality which needs no embellishment, and which is larger and more

> important than all the exegeses on religion, ethics, or philosophy, so that human beings can be seen as more human, and their true nature can be more fully revealed.[47]

In *Nocturnal Wanderer*, the key concepts are subjectivization and detachment: subjectivization transforms objective reality so as to delve into the meanings hidden behind the facade of the perceptible, and detachment objectifies such transformations as the other, so that a truthful picture of the subject becomes obtainable. Just as he demands that his actors be neutral observers of the performing self, Gao Xingjian also insists that his characters should observe themselves as the other through shifts in narrative mode. In this way the actor and the character he is playing are divided yet unified, and life as a multifaceted reflection of the self is incorporated into art.

Weekend Quartet 周末四重奏 (Zhoumo sichongzou) *(1995)*

Gao Xingjian believes in the constant renewal of his craft. With *Weekend Quartet*, his latest play, he appears to have made a determined effort to try his hand at something different — a realistic play devoid of the rituals and magical spectacles of his recent works. Whereas the previous plays are not keen on characterization, *Weekend Quartet* is peopled by characters with names and individualizing traits. With their varied backgrounds and personalities, they react differently to the dramatic situations in the plot, functioning like the different musical instruments in a quartet ensemble.

There is very little action in the four scenes ("quartets"), and there are no crises pushing the characters to the brink of their sanity as in *Between Life and Death* and *Nocturnal Wanderer*. The story is made up of the kind of everyday happenings one finds in real life — an elderly couple, owners of an old farm in the country, is visited by a young couple whose relationship is as unstable as their older counterparts, and the uneventful plot revolves around their romantic entanglements which, like all of their lives, lead nowhere. Bernard is an old and famous painter. Increasingly weary of living, he is nonetheless afraid of loneliness and of growing old, and he tries to prove what remains of his virility by chasing after the young girls he employs as models. His companion Anne, a more sober and worldly type, has been an aspiring writer all her life, and she is equally obsessed with ageing and dying. To compensate for the lack of attention from Bernard, she flirts with their guest Daniel, a middle-aged writer. Daniel is at the end of his writing career — he has run out of things to write. A lost soul without any commitments, whether it is in ideology or love, he has nothing left in his life except his cynicism. Among this insipid bunch, Cecily, Daniel's girlfriend, is like a breath of fresh air, even though her liveliness could easily have been contrived. An ordinary girl except for her attractiveness, she does not hesitate to use her charms to her advantage. She has no lofty goals but wishes to find a mate to provide her with food and a roof over her head. Towards the end of the play even she grows tired of her role as the *femme fatale*. Her outward liveliness can hardly contain the same death in spirit as that of the other characters.

As with most of Gao Xingjian's plays, *Weekend Quartet* is not made up of external actions but of the interior landscapes of the soul. It is a play about characters and also about their self-examinations: they are likened to musical instruments playing life's sorrowful tunes. Unlike the other plays in this collection, its concerns are not so much existential in a philosophical sense as the fears and worries of ordinary living, the realities of how to accommodate oneself to the banalities of day-to-day living. There are no real crises but trivial conflicts and verbal squabbles which, as in a musical quartet, make up the changes in the mood of the play. Quartets 1 and 2 are expositions and complications, while Quartet 3 is made more sombre with the expose of the characters' dark inner secrets, and the final Quartet is spirited and gay, ending with a game of disjointed words and phrases in an acceptance of life's impossibility of meaning. It is as if the play has finally come to terms with life in exploring into the truth of man's existence.

While the characters are built up in the traditional manner, the audience, in a typical Gao Xingjian manner, also gets to know the truth of their private selves through their monologues, comprising dream sequences, hallucinations, and memory flashes. These lapses into the subconscious punctuate the realistic setting and situations and resonate with a disharmony that characterizes the world of the play. The characters' self-examinations are unprovoked and are mostly unrelated to the action — as if the play willingly and deliberately suspends itself, forfeiting its illusion of reality and forcing the actors to neutralize their roles under the watchful eyes of the audience. During these monologues, the actors speak in the second or third person to carry out an "indifferent observation" of the characters they are portraying. Despite its realistic subject matter and characters, *Weekend Quartet* purposely flaunts its mechanical nature and achieves an artificiality which, coupled with the seemingly contradictory demand for real-life emotions, approximates the playwright's concept of a modern dramatic performance.

Notes

1. Gao Xingjian 高行健, "Lun wenxue xiezuo"〈論文學寫作〉(On Writing Literature), in his *Meiyou zhuyi*《沒有主義》(None-ism) (Hong Kong: Cosmos Books Ltd., 1996), p. 57.
2. *Ibid.*, p. 59.
3. Gao Xingjian, "Geri huanghua"〈隔日黃花〉(Day-old Yellow Blossoms), in his *Bi'an*《彼岸》(The Other Shore) (Taipei: Dijiao Chubanshe 帝教出版社, 1995), pp. 86–87.
4. Zhao Yiheng 趙毅衡, "Gao Xingjian chuangzuolun"〈高行健創作論〉(On Gao Xingjian's Creative Writing), unpublished manuscript, p. 34.
5. Gao Xingjian, "Bali suibi"〈巴黎隨筆〉(Random Thoughts in Paris), *Guangchang*《廣場》, Feb. 1991, p. 14.
6. Zhao, p. 43.
7. Gao Xingjian, "Chidaole de xiandaizhuyi yu dangjin Zhongguo wenxue"〈遲到了的現代主義與當今中國文學〉(The Late Arrival of Modernism and Contemporary Chinese Literature), in *Meiyou zhuyi*, p. 102. First appeared in *Wenxue pinglun*《文學評論》, No. 3, 1988.
8. Gao Xingjian, "Ling yizhong xiju"〈另一種戲劇〉(Another Kind of Drama), in *Meiyou zhuyi*, p. 191.
9. Gao Xingjian, "Wo zhuzhang yizhong lengde wenxue"〈我主張一種冷的文學〉(I Advocate "Cold Literature"), in *Meiyou zhuyi*, pp. 18–20. Also in *Zhongshi wanbao*《中時晚報》, 12 Aug. 1990.
10. Gao Xingjian, "Lun wenxue xiezuo"〈論文學寫作〉, p. 54.
11. Gao Xingjian, "Wo zhuzhang yizhong lengde wenxue"〈我主張一種冷的文學〉, p. 20.
12. Gao Xingjian, "Meiyou zhuyi"〈沒有主義〉, in *Meiyou zhuyi*, pp. 8–17.
13. *Ibid.*, p. 9.
14. Gao Xingjian, "Lun wenxue xiezuo"〈論文學寫作〉, pp. 34–35.
15. Gao Xingjian, "Ping Faguo guanyu dangdai yishu de lunzhan"〈評法國關於當代藝術的論戰〉(The Controversy on Contemporary Art in France), in *Meiyou zhuyi*, p. 281.

16. Zhao, p. 72.
17. Gao Xingjian, "Chidaole de xiandaizhuyi yu dangjin Zhongguo wenxue"〈遲到了的現代主義與當今中國文學〉, p. 104.
18. *Ibid.*, p. 105.
19. Gao Xingjian, "Wo zhuzhang yizhong lengde wenxue"〈我主張一種冷的文學〉, p. 20.
20. Gao Xingjian, "Juzuofa yu zhongxing yanyuan"〈劇作法與中性演員〉(Dramaturgy and the Neutral Actor), in *Meiyou zhuyi*, p. 254.
21. Gao Xingjian, "Yao shenmoyang de xiju"〈要甚麼樣的戲劇〉(The Kind of Drama I Prefer), *Lianhe wenxue*《聯合文學》, No. 41, 1988, p. 133.
22. *Ibid.*, pp. 136–37.
23. Gao Xingjian, "Wode xiju he wode yaoshi"〈我的戲劇和我的鑰匙〉(My Plays and the Key to My Writing), in *Meiyou zhuyi*, p. 238.
24. *Ibid.*
25. Gao Xingjian, "Meiyou zhuyi"〈沒有主義〉, p. 14.
26. Gao Xingjian, "Wenxue yu lingxue: Guanyu 'Lingshan'"〈文學與靈學・關於《靈山》〉(Literature and Spiritualism, About *Spiritual Mountain*), in *Meiyou zhuyi*, pp. 174–75.
27. Gao Xingjian, "Juzuofa yu zhongxing yanyuan"〈劇作法與中性演員〉, pp. 262–63.
28. Gao Xingjian, "Ling yizhong xiju"〈另一種戲劇〉, p. 191.
29. Gao Xingjian, "Wenxue yu lingxue: Guanyu 'Lingshan'"〈文學與靈學・關於《靈山》〉, p. 175.
30. Gao Xingjian, "Guanyu *Bi'an*"〈關於《彼岸》〉(On *The Other Shore*), in *Bi'an*《彼岸》, pp. 68–69.
31. Gao Xingjian, "Wenxue yu lingxue: Guanyu 'Lingshan'"〈文學與靈學・關於《靈山》〉, p. 175.
32. *Ibid.*, p. 174.
33. Gao Xingjian, "Liuwang shi women huode shenme?"〈流亡使我們獲得什麼〉(What Have We Gained from Being in Exile?), in *Meiyou zhuyi*, p. 128.
34. Gao Xingjian, "Guanyu *Bi'an*"〈關於《彼岸》〉, p. 69.
35. Gao Xingjian, "Guojia shenhua yu geren diankuang"〈國家神話與個人癲狂〉(National Mythology and Personal Lunacy), *Ming Pao Monthly*《明報月刊》, Aug. 1993, p. 117.
36. Zhao, p. 88.
37. Gao Xingjian, "Guanyu *Bi'an*"〈關於《彼岸》〉, p. 69.
38. Gao Xingjian, "*Bi'an* daoyan houji"〈《彼岸》導演後記〉(Written After Directing *The Other Shore*), in *Meiyou zhuyi*, p. 225.
39. Gao Xingjian, "Meiyou zhuyi"〈沒有主義〉, p. 13.
40. Kong Jiesheng 孔捷生, "Xiao wutai he da shijie: Yu lu Fa dalu zuojia Gao Xingjian duitan"〈小舞台和大世界：與旅法大陸作家高行健對談〉(Small Stage and Big World:

Dialogue with the Dramatist Gao Xingjiang, a Chinese Expatriate in France), *Minzhu Zhongguo*《民主中國》, No. 16, July 1993, p. 86.

41. Gao Xingjian, "*Duihua yu fanjie* daobiaoyan tan"〈《對話與反詰》導表演談〉(On Directing and Acting in *Dialogue and Rebuttal*), in *Meiyou zhuyi*, p. 208.
42. *Ibid.*, p. 194.
43. Gao Xingjian, "Meiyou zhuyi"〈沒有主義〉, p. 13.
44. Gao Xingjian, "*Duihua yu fanjie* daobiaoyan tan"〈《對話與反詰》導表演談〉, p. 196.
45. Kong Jiesheng, "Xiao wutai he da shijie: Yu lu Fa dalu zuojia Gao Xingjian duitan"〈小舞台和大世界：與旅法大陸作家高行健對談〉, p. 86.
46. Gao Xingjian, "Ling yizhong xiju"〈另一種戲劇〉, p. 191.
47. *Ibid.*

The Other Shore

Time: The time cannot be defined or stated precisely.

Location: From the real world to the nonexistent other shore.

Characters:

An actor playing with ropes	Shadow
Card Player	Heart
"Dogskin" Plaster Seller	Mother
Woman	Father
Young Girl	Zen Master
Mad Woman	Old Lady
Model	Stable Keeper
Man	Actors
Young Man	Crowd

(The play can be performed in a theatre, a living room, a rehearsal room, an empty warehouse, a gymnasium, the hall of a temple, a circus tent, or any empty space as long as the necessary lighting and sound equipment can be properly installed. Lighting can be dispensed with if the play is performed during the day. The actors may be among the audience, or the audience among the actors. The two situations are the same and will not make any difference to the play.)

The Other Shore. The Hong Kong Academy for Performing Arts, Hong Kong. Directed by Gao Xingjian. 1995.

The Other Shore. The Hong Kong Academy for Performing Arts, Hong Kong. Directed by Gao Xingjian. 1995.

Actor playing with ropes Here's a rope. Let's play a game, but we've got to be serious, as if we're children playing their game. Our play starts with a game.

Okay, I want you to take hold of this end of the rope. You see, this way a relationship is established between us. Before that you were you and I was I, but with this rope between us we're tied to each other and it becomes you and I.

Let's try running in opposite directions. See, now you're pulling me, but then again I'm also holding you back, like two locusts tied to the same string, neither of us can get away from each other. Of course, we're also like husband and wife. *(Pauses.)* But that's not a good metaphor. If I were to pull the rope real hard towards me, then we'd have to see who's stronger. The stronger one pulls and the weaker is being pulled. It becomes a tug-of-war, a competition of strength, and there'll be a winner and a loser, victory and defeat.

Now if I carry this rope on my back like this and pull even harder, you'll be like a dead dog; likewise if you manage to gain control of this rope, I'll be like a horse or a cow, and you'll be able to drive me around like cattle. In other words, you'll be running the show. So you see, our relationship is not at all constant, it's not at all unchanging.

Or we can establish an even more complex relationship. For instance if you revolve around me, I'll be the centre of your orbit, and you'll become my satellite. But if you don't wish to revolve around me, I can rotate on my own, thinking that all of you are revolving around me. Are you revolving or am I the one who's revolving? I could be revolving around you or you could be revolving around me. Who knows? Perhaps we're both turning at the same time, or maybe we're both revolving around other people, or maybe those other people are revolving around us both or maybe all of us are revolving around

God — maybe there isn't a God after all, maybe there's only a universe rotating by itself like a millstone — now we're touching on philosophy. Never mind, we'll leave philosophy to the philosophers, let's just continue to play our game.
Everyone of you can pick up a rope and play different kinds of games, the possibilities are endless. Playing with ropes is such a game, that it can be a manifestation of all kinds of interpersonal relationships.

(The actors each choose a partner to play the game, using a piece of rope. They can switch partners or briefly make contact with other pairs of players, but the contacts are soon broken. The game becomes increasingly lively, tense, and exciting, accompanied by all kinds of salutations and screams.)

Actor playing with ropes Okay everybody, let's knock it off for a moment. Let's make this game bigger and more complex. Now I want all of you to hold on to one end of your rope and give me the other end. This way you'll be able to establish all kinds of relationships with me, some tense, some lax, some distant, and some close, and soon your individual attitudes will have a strong impact on me. Society is complex and ever-changing, we're constantly pulling and being pulled. *(Pauses.)* Just like a fly that's fallen into a spider's web. *(Pauses.)* Or just like a spider. *(Pauses.)* The rope is like our hands. *(He lets go one rope and his partner also lets go. The rope falls on the ground.)* Or like an extended antenna. *(He lets go another and his partner follows.)* Or like the language we use, for instance when we say "Good Morning" or "How are you!" *(Another rope falls to the ground.)* Or perhaps it's like looking at each other, *(Replaces another rope.)* or like the thoughts in our minds. *(His back is against his current partner, but the two sides are still communicating.)* Either you're thinking of her, or she's thinking of someone else. *(He brushes*

past her shoulders. She and someone else are gazing into each other's eyes.) In this way the rope is pulling all of us, binding us together.
We look —

(The actors are communicating with one another through pieces of imaginary ropes.)

We observe —
We stare —
Then there's temptation and attraction —
Orders and obedience —

(In the following, the performance is accompanied by all kinds of sighs and screams but without resorting to the use of language.)

Conflicts —
Intimacy —
Exclusion —
Entanglement —
Abandonment —
Emulation —
Evasion —
Repulsion —
Pursuit —
Encirclement —
Congregation —
Fragmentation —
Dismiss!
At ease!
Now there is a river in front of us, not a piece of rope. Let's cross the river and try to reach the other shore.

Actors *(One after another.)* Yes, to the other shore! To the other shore!

The other shore! To the other shore! To the other shore!
The other shore!
Oh — Oh — Oh
The water in the river is so clear!
So cool!
Watch out, the stones are killing my feet!
How nice!
(Gradually there comes the sound of running water.)
My skirt's soaking wet!
Is the river deep?
Let's swim across to the other shore!
Don't go by yourself!
Look at the water spray, how it sparkles in the sunshine!
What fun, just like a waterfall.
A dam, a river flowing gently down the dam.
Form a line in the middle of the river.
Further down the water's dark blue, it's got to be really deep there.
I've got some fish wriggling between my legs …
So exciting!
I'm going to fall.
Don't worry, hold on to me.
There's an eddy over there —
Look after one another, hold hands.
To the rapid waters.
To the other shore!
No one can see the other shore.
Cut the poetry crap! I'm falling.
Hold tight, one after another now.
Over there the water is deep blue …
Aahh! The water's over my waist all of a sudden!
I'm getting dizzy.
Close your eyes for a while.
Look in front of you, look ahead, keep your eyes open!
All looking at the other shore.

How come I can't see it?
We'll drown, all of us.
We'll all be fish food.
If we're going to die, let's die together.
Girls, stop blabbing, try to concentrate.
The current is very strong, tread in the shallows, try going up stream!
I can't make it across, I'm sure I can't make it.
Where's the other shore?
Sometimes it's dark, sometimes it's bright.
Are there lights on the other shore?
There are flowers, lots of flowers on the other shore, it's a world of flowers.
I'm afraid I can't make it, please don't leave me behind. *(Sobs.)*
Can you feel it? We're drifting in the river.
Like corks on a string.
And like water weed.
Why are we going to the other shore? I really don't understand.
Right, why do we want to go to the other shore?
The other shore is the other shore, you'll never reach it.
But you still want to go, to see what it's like over there.
I can't see anything.
No oasis, and no light.
In total darkness.
It's like this …
No, I can't make it.
We haven't been there before.
We must get there.
But why?
To make a long-time wish come true, the other shore, the other shore.
No, I can't make it, I want to go home!
None of us can.

Can't go back at all.
O — !
Who is it?
Don't know.
(Silence, only the sound of water gurgling.)
Was somebody screaming? Did you hear it?
You must have heard it, but nobody answered.
(Silence. Sound of sobbing.)
This is a ditch of dead water.
There's only oblivion.

(Bewildered, the Crowd slowly walk out of the dead water. Music is faintly heard. The Crowd gradually reach the shore and lie down totally exhausted on the ground. Woman appears in darkness. Like a strand of light mist, she walks around to inspect the people who have lost their memories. She drifts among them, touching and waking them up one by one. They lazily open their eyes and look up, turning their bodies and staring at her. They try to speak but in vain.)

Woman *(Raises her hand.)* Look here, this is a hand.

(The Crowd utter muddled sounds from their throat.)

Woman This is a hand.
Crowd *(Still mumbling.)* Th … The … This … ee … ha … han … hand.
Woman Hand —
Crowd Hand — band — sand — hand —
Woman This is a foot.
Crowd Th … Th … This … ee … fo … foo … foot.
Woman *(Pointing to her eye.)* Eye.
Crowd Ee … ee … eye … eye …
Woman *(Gesturing.)* Your eyes are looking at your foot!
Crowd *(Totally confused.)* Eyes … cook … cook your … own … coot …

(Woman laughs, and the Crowd join in the laughter with her, giggling.)

Woman (*Stops laughing, somewhat sad.*) This is a hand —
Crowd This is a hand, this is a band, this is a sand, this is a hand …
Woman This is a foot —
Crowd This is a boot, this is a hoot, this is a root, this is a foot …
Woman This is a body — your body —
Crowd This is a body, this is a body, this is a body your body, this is your body is a body is a body is your body your …
Woman *(Shakes her head, gesturing more slowly and still being patient.)* My hand — my body — my foot — this is me.
Crowd My band, my hand, my body, my coot, my hand's body's foot's my coot's hand's foot's body this is my hand's foot's body is meat!
Woman Say, me —
Crowd Say me say me say me say me say me!
Woman *(Shakes her head and points to herself, from her eyes to her mouth, and from her body to her feet.)* Me.
Crowd *(Together at last.)* Me.
Woman Good!
Crowd Food! Hood! Good! Wood!
Woman *(At once she waves her hand in disagreement. After thinking for a moment, she points at one person among the crowd.)* You.
Crowd *(All pointing at the person.)* You!
The person *(He looks around him and then points at himself.)* You!
Woman *(Shakes her head and helps him to point his finger at someone else.)* You.
Crowd You.
Woman *(Gesturing.)* Me and you.
Crowd Me and you.
Woman *(Laughs.)* Good!
Crowd *(Also laugh.)* Good!

(Music. Gradually the tempo of the music becomes faster.)

Woman Me and him!

Crowd Me and him!

Woman Them and me.

Crowd Them and me.

Woman Me and you.

Crowd Me and you.

Woman You and us.

Crowd You and us.

Woman Now follow me when you're seeing with your eyes —

Crowd See —

Woman Tell me, who do you see?

Crowd *(One after another.)* See him, see you, see me, see them, they see you, you see us, we see them …

Woman Now say touch, give, like, and love, and you won't feel lonely any more.

Crowd *(Becoming active.)* I touch you, you give me, I like him, he loves you, you touch me, I give him, he likes you, you love me …

(Man comes out from among the Crowd.)

Man Who are you?

Woman I'm one of you.

Man Where are we now?

Woman The other shore, which we wanted to reach but couldn't.

Man Are you the same person who drowned while we were crossing the river? *(Woman shakes her head.)* Are you her soul? *(Woman still shakes her head.)* Have you been hiding in our thoughts, do you appear only when we think of you? Or are you something like a kind of consciousness? Did you guide us to the other shore so that we wouldn't get lost?

Crowd *(At the same time.)* I detest you.

You touched me!

I'll beat you up!
You hate me?
I'll torture her.
He cheats on me.
You're swearing at him!
I'll tell on you.
You punish him!
He plots against me!
I hate you!
You curse him!
I'll kill you …

Man *(To Woman.)* You're so kind.

Crowd *(Turn to face Woman one after another, playing with words.)*
You're so generous.
You're so lovely.
You're so despicable.
He's a bastard.
You don't say what you mean, you're a crook.
You're a double-dealing no-good tramp!
She butters you up, but she's actually jealous of you.
You're snaky, you teach us words so that you can talk to our men and seduce them!
You may look so kind and gentle, but who knows if you're a whore or not?
She's trying to seduce our husbands!
Stirring up trouble among our brothers.
A buttered bun, look, just look at her —
Keep the girls away from her, she'll turn them into whores.
She may look prim and proper, but she's really more corrupt than a common whore.
She's the one, she makes people panic, there'll be no more peace in this world.

(Woman draws back as the Crowd surrounds her from all sides. They are excited by their own increasingly venomous language.

She cannot escape from the stares of the Crowd, so she turns to Man for help and hangs on to him.)

Crowd *(Getting more angry.)*
Whore!
Venomous snake!
Witch!
Shameless slut!

(Woman holds on to Man and pleads for his protection. The Crowd go wild.)

Crowd Look, go and take a look!
Pooh!
Dump her!
Drag her away!
Get a hold of her!
Strip her!
Wring her neck! The shameless whore!

(The Crowd drag her away from Man and jump on her. In the confusion they strangle her to death. When Man pushes his way into the Crowd and shakes her body, there is no response.)
(Witnessing this, the Crowd is stunned.)

Crowd Dead.
Dead?
Dead?
She's dead!

(The Crowd disperse in a hurry.)

Was she strangled to death?
It's you —
No, he started it.
You shouted first!

I was only following you, you were all shouting.
Who shouted first? Who?
Who shouted first to grab her, strip her and strangle her? Who?
We all shouted.
I shouted because you did.
I shouted because all of you were shouting.
But she's dead! Strangled alive!
I didn't kill her.
I didn't kill her.
I didn't kill her.
I didn't kill her.
I didn't kill her.
I didn't.
I didn't.
Didn't.
Didn't.
Didn't.
But she's dead for sure, so lovely even when she's dead.
So beautiful, nobody could help loving her.
Her skin is like jade, it's got no blemishes, it's so pure.
Look at her pretty little hands, they've got her endless tenderness in them.
My, she's like a statue of the Bodhisattva!
So pure, so prim and proper.
She gave us language, she brought us wisdom, but she was murdered!
This is the greatest sin of all, you despicable lot!
Who are you talking about?
Murderers! You, all of you!
How dare you smear me? You bastard!
You're a thug!
You're a rascal!

(The Crowd fight among themselves.)

Man Are you finished? We killed her, there's no question about it. It's you, it's him, it's me, and it's all of us. We're all in it together! On this desolate other shore, she gave us language, but we didn't know how to cherish it; she gave us wisdom, but we didn't know how to use it! We ought to be shocked by what we did, but we're cowards, we're too spineless to feel any shame.

Crowd What do you think we should do?

We need a leader, a flock of sheep also needs a leader. We'll follow you.

Man I detest you, I detest myself. It's better for us to go our separate ways.

Crowd No, don't abandon us.

We've made up our mind to follow you, and you want to leave us?

Man Follow me where? Where can I lead you? *(He leaves by himself. The Crowd follow behind.)* Don't follow me! *(Troubled.)* I don't even know where I want to go myself. (*Stops and tries to figure out where to go. The Crowd still follow him at a distance.*)

(Mother appears in front of him.)

Mother Do you still remember me?

Man Yes, mother.

Mother You've almost forgotten me, haven't you?

Man *(On his knees.)* Yes, mother.

Mother *(Stroking his head.)* Find yourself a girl, you really should start a family.

Man But I want to make something of myself.

Mother You're too ambitious.

Man *(Looks down.)* I'm still your son.

Mother Are they all following you? Where are you going to take them?

Man I don't know. I only know we should go forward, is that right, mother?

Mother My good son. *(Embraces his head.)*

Man Your hands are cold! *(Shocked by his discovery.)* Mother, is this the world of the dead? Am I in another dimension?

Mother There's nothing to be scared of, son. It's just a bit dark, a bit cold and damp, that's all.

Man *(Leaves her.)* How do I get out of here? Mother, I haven't lived long enough!

(Mother turns and disappears. He hesitates for a moment and then follows in a hurry. A young girl blocks his way.)

Man Who are you? I've seen you somewhere, but I can't recall your name. It seems like we used to live on the same street or something, many years ago. Every day on my way to school I always hoped that I could catch a glimpse of you, even if it's only your back. My heart would keep on pounding whenever I saw your long ponytail and your crimson red dress, you seemed to be wearing that crimson dress all that time.... I used to follow you, follow you right to your doorsteps, hoping that when you turned around to close the door, you'd at least say one word to me before you went inside, or smile at me just once. But every time you'd only look at me, saying nothing. Oh, I can see those eyes of yours again ... *(He rubs his eyes and looks more closely, but she has disappeared into the dark shadows of the Crowd.)*
(To the Crowd.) We've got to get out of this ghastly place. Once we're away from this darkness we'll find light ahead of us. With the light there'll be houses, and we'll be able to dry our clothes around the stove and drink some hot tea. *(Incitingly.)* We'd be able to return to our homes, see our families, our wives and husbands, our children and parents, and all our loved ones and those who love us!
(Young Girl appears again from behind the Crowd.) Who are you?

(Blocking her way.) Wait, your name is on the tip of my tongue! It seems like I used to write poetry for you, that we used to go to the movies together and I held your hand in the dark, those tiny frail hands of yours ... *(She turns and gets away from his grasp. She is now behind him, becoming more illusory. He turns around but cannot see her, no matter how hard he tries.)*

She always appeared in my dreams to torment me whenever I was worried and couldn't set my mind free. I couldn't recall her name, I couldn't see her face clearly, I couldn't even get hold of her presence in any way, but she still kept on tormenting me.

(Speaking to the shadowy Crowd.) Why do you keep following me? I need some peace and quiet, I need to be alone! I don't need to be stared at by a crowd, I don't need you, just as you don't need me. What you need is someone who can guide you, to show you the way, even though once you've found a way out, or think you have, you'd put on a spurt, darting away faster than rabbits. And you'd abandon your guide without even taking a second look, just like throwing away a worn-out shoe. I understand, I understand it only too well. You've all experienced loving and being loved, possessing and being possessed. I, too, have a right to be in love, to love a woman and to possess a woman, and to be loved and possessed by her. I'm human just like you are, so full of desires and ambitions, I'm what you may call a career-minded man, a man who is competitive yet extremely weak sometimes, and a man who is righteous, compassionate, willing to sacrifice himself and ... *(He rolls on the ground and wails loudly like a fretting and self-indulgent child.)*

(The Crowd is stunned. When Man has had enough wailing and is totally exhausted, he settles down and gets up from the floor. He continues his way forward and the Crowd follow

silently behind him. A faint light in the dark becomes brighter. A man is seen drinking and playing cards alone under an oil lamp. Man mimes knocking on the door. The Crowd clap their hands three times.)

Man Sorry to bother you.
Card Player *(Without lifting his head.)* Come in. Take a seat.
Man May I ask —
Card Player *(Tosses a card from his hand. Looks up.)* You play cards?
Man I've played before.

(The Crowd try to squeeze in through the door.)

Card Player Come in, come in. Do you all want to play cards? Close the door for me. I hate draughts, they make the light flicker, which is bad for a card player's eyes. Alright, let's form a circle, I'll be the banker here. All of you will each take a card, and I'll take one myself, only one, just like you. That's only fair. The card in my hand will be the trump, there's got to be a trump, right? And it's better if I choose the trump card instead of you, it's more convenient that way. *(Turns over his card.)* My card is the two of spades. I'm not trying to fly low, luck is all you need when you're playing cards. Now if you pick a spade, any spade, you'd have a higher number than mine and I'd be the loser and you'd be the winner. But if you didn't pick a spade, you'd lose no matter what, it doesn't matter which card you've picked. You got me?
Man What happens if one wins or loses?
Card Player The winner gets to drink the wine in this pot.
Man And the loser?
Card Player There'll be a penalty.
Man I have no money, no land, no property, and no wife.
Card Player But you do have a face, haven't you?
Man I don't get it.
Card Player You'll find out soon enough. All of you, anyone who loses will stick a piece of paper on his face for me.

Crowd That's easy enough.
How big is the paper?
Any paper?
The thing is, have you really got wine in your pot?

Card Player Have a taste first.

Crowd It's good.
What aroma!
Of course, it's the real thing.
Let me have a sip.
It's worth playing for.

Card Player In a moment you'll pick your cards. I've shown you my card, all of you have seen it, right? Now you can only look at your own card, no ganging up, that's a no-no.

Crowd *(Eager to pick their cards.)*
That's nothing, it's fine with me.
We should play our own games.
Don't worry, I won't look even if you let me.
Me, I'm honesty personified.
Integrity comes first, winning and losing second.
Hear! Hear!

(Those who have picked their cards are silent.)

Card Player *(To the person who picks first.)* Show me your card. You lose.

This Person *(Nods.)* What's the penalty?

(Card Player takes a piece of paper and spits on it. He sticks the paper onto the cheek of This Person, who mutters something. The Crowd watch and laugh. This Person is relieved and laughs with them.)

Card Player *(Turns to another person.)* My friend, how about you? *(That Person shows his card.)* You lose too.

That Person Well, give it to me.

Card Player Stick it under your chin.

(That Person takes a piece of paper, spits on it, and sticks it under his chin. He is somewhat embarrassed, but when he sees the Crowd laughing, he is himself again.)

Third Person (Female) It's fun.

Card Player *(Turns towards her.)* And you? *(She shows her card and hurriedly takes it back.)*

Crowd Did you win?
You won!
Did you really win?
(She frets demurely and shakes her head.)
Why aren't you sticking the paper on your face?
Stick the paper on, stick it on!
Come on, it's the rule, no exceptions allowed.
If you don't stick it on, we won't either.

Third Person (Female) It's too embarrassing.

Crowd You think we're not?
That won't do. Stick it on the ear.
Right, on the ear.
Stick it on the nose!
It must be different with everybody, okay? No repetitions.
Everybody gets one.

(When the Card Player looks at someone, the person will show his card and then obediently stick a piece of paper on his face.)

Crowd *(Sticking paper to their own faces.)*
Fair and square.
No doubt about that.
Nobody tells you to lose, but when you do, you've got to take what comes.

Everyone gets a penalty, everyone sticks a paper on their face.
If you haven't got a paper on your face, you'll look odd and out of place, and people will be afraid of you.

(The strange-looking, papered faces all turn towards Man.)

Card Player My friend, it's your turn now.
Man I don't play.
Card Player Everybody plays, why don't you?
Man I find the whole thing very silly. What's more, I've got to go.
Crowd Yes, that's right. We should all be going.
Don't go by yourself.
Where are we going?
Right, where exactly are we going?
Man In any case I've got to go.
Card Player I've got the whole place lit up and I've prepared wine. I went through all these troubles just to play cards with you people. I've never heard of anyone who comes here and leaves without playing. You shouldn't have come in the first place!
Crowd *(Stopping Man.)* Play!
Come on, be a good sport. Don't be such a party popper.
Just play one game. Just one.
Play once and then we'll go.
Man Don't you understand? You're not really playing cards, he's playing a trick on you. You can't win. Your card, yours, and yours are all no trumps, including all the cards still in the deck. The only spade in the deck is in his hand! *(Card Player giggles.)* Let's go! Why waste our time on this guy.
Card Player There is no such thing as time here. *(He blows on the oil lamp and the light flickers, and it gradually turns brighter again.)* There is only eternal light. *(He takes the lamp and shines on everyone from below the chin. The papered faces*

look like gargoyles.) I'm a sucker for big crowds. You're scared, aren't you?

Man You're a devil.

Card Player Why don't you try feeling their arses? They've all got a bristly tail down there! *(He points to the Crowd's bottoms and laughs out loud. Then he pushes a deck of cards in front of Man.)* Take a card! Let everyone see if it's a spade or no trumps? *(Turns over a no trump card and flashes it in front of the Crowd.)* What is it, is it a spade or not?

Person A I can't really tell.

Card Player What'd you say?

Person B It looked like —

Card Player You must have seen it clearly.

Person C I think I saw a — spade.

Card Player That's right! Young lady, what do you think?

Obedient Girl Spades.

Card Player That a girl. You've made my day. Old Sir, how about you?

Person D Spades, how can it not be spades?

Card Player Bless you. *(Suddenly explodes.)* How can we let him bullshit us like this and tell us that they're all no trumps? Huh?

Crowd It's spades.

Of course it's spades. It can't be anything else.

No mistake about it.

We all saw it.

We're all witnesses!

Card Player You heard what they said, didn't you? Why did you lie, why did you insist that a spade is no trump? You're scared, aren't you? Have you ever tried eating rat meat? A bouncing baby rat, its hair not fully grown and its eyes unopened, the little creature still squeaking when you dip it in the sauce and put it in your mouth, ready for a bite? If you had, then you'd be brave enough to tell the truth. My friend, I'm gonna give you one more chance to tell the truth. Tell me, was it spades or a no trump?

Man I think … that's still a no trump.

Card Player You're no fun, you make people miserable. Tell me, people, is this guy bad or what?

Crowd *(Passing the wine pot and taking sips one after another.)* Bad, bad, bad, bad, bad, bad, bad, bad …

Card Player *(Takes the wine from them.)* What shall we do with this bad guy?

Crowd *(Surround Man.)* Throw him out!
Tell him to get out of here!
Trouble-maker.
A real pest.
When he's here, we've got no wine to drink.
Teach him a lesson!
Spank him!
Strip him!
Take off his pants!

(The Crowd try to take off Man's pants.)

Card Player I'm gonna give you a second chance. Think clearly. Think again!

Man *(Holding up his pants.)* But I remember … it looked like a … no trump.

(Card Player tucks the wine pot under his arm and turns away. The Crowd pull at Man as if they were teasing a bird.)

Crowd Tell him to fly!
What? What did you say?
Fly like a bird!
Men are not birds, why should they learn to fly like birds?
Wow, it's so fun!
Fly!
Lower your head, let your arms fly!

Card Player My friend, I refuse to believe that you're a stubborn man.

Obedient Girl *(Takes pity on Man.)* You can't turn a spade into a no trump. What's with you? Please, try to take hold of yourself.

Man Maybe it was really a spade …

Obedient Girl Then why did you say it was a no trump?

Man I think it should be …

Obedient Girl But what should be is not necessarily the truth.

Card Player You're a loser because you're a pighead. What do you mean by "should be"? It either is or isn't. To hell with "should be."

Man But why can't we have "should be"?

Card Player *(Irritated.)* Should be my foot! What do you say, should be or not should be?

Crowd *(Immediately tear at Man.)* We don't want any "should be"!
We want "yes" or "no"!
We want spades, not no trumps!
Down with no trumps!
Spades are the best!

Man It … seemed … like a … sp …

Crowd *(Beating their chests and stamping their feet.)* Speak up!
Louder!
Can't hear you!
You've got to clear this up!

Man Sp … Spa … It's spades … *(On his knees and collapses.)*

(The Crowd surround Card Player and perform a strange and awkward dance. They exit.
A woman dressed in a white cotton skirt appears. She covers Man with her skirt, bends down and wraps herself in it as well. The two form a white object which disappears with the gradually approaching drumbeat. The drumbeat builds up into a heart-thumping bang. A scrawny monk comes out jumping and beating a gigantic drum with his fingers, palms, elbows, and knees as if he were bewitched. Zen Master enters, dressed in a Buddhist robe of kasaya, his hands clasped together and his right shoulder bare. Other monks and nuns, all cloaked in

grey kasaya, follow Zen Master onto the stage. The Crowd enter in a single file, chanting "Amitabha" as they come. Their chanting is not in any particular order, each singing their own tune and at their own pitch. The chanting comes and goes, combining with the drumbeat into a cacophony of intersecting sounds. Man is following the Crowd; he also chants and looks around him at times. The Crowd all put down a futon, on which they sit with their legs crossed. Man does the same. The drum stops, followed by the sound of a wooden fish and an inverted bell.)*

Zen Master *(Recites the Vajraccedika prajna paramita sutra, his palms clasped together and his right knee on the ground.)* "... How much the Bodhisattvas, the great beings, have been helped with the greatest help by the Tathagata, the Fully Enlightened One. It is wonderful, O Lord, how much the Bodhisattvas, the great beings, have been favoured with the highest favour by the Tathagata, the Fully Enlightened One. How then, O Lord, should good men and women stand, who seek the supreme wisdom, how progress, how control their thoughts?"
After these words the Lord said to the Venerable Subhuti: "Well said, well said, Subhuti! So it is, Subhuti, so it is as you say! The Tathagata has helped the Bodhisattvas, the great beings with the greatest help, and he has favoured them with the highest favour. Therefore, Subhuti, listen well, and attentively!..."

(Incense smoke permeates the whole place during the chanting. The Crowd close their eyes in meditation, and Man gradually does so as well. Young Girl appears, her eyes slightly closed. She is squatting in a corner and doing her mental exercise, like a baby who is sleeping not too tightly in

---

* A percussion instrument made of a hollow wooden block, used by Buddhist priests to make rhythm while chanting scriptures.

a transparent egg shell, its hands and feet pressed against the four walls of the shell. Young Man, who has been hiding behind her, gets up slowly and walks towards Young Girl in gingerly steps. The chanting gradually fades. The Crowd disappear.)

Zen Master *(The sound of chanting can still be heard faintly.)* "Monks of the Buddha, nuns of the Buddha, I will teach you how they should stand, who seek the supreme wisdom, how progress, how control their thoughts."
"So be it, O Lord. With a joyful heart we long to hear," the Venerable Subhuti replied to the Lord.
The Lord said: "Here, Subhuti, someone who seeks supreme wisdom should produce a thought in this manner …"

(Young Man stretches his hand to touch Young Girl's fingers. Surprised, she wakes and withdraws her hand immediately.)

Young Girl Stop it!
Young Man Are you doing your mental exercise?
Young Girl Yes.
Young Man May I ask what kind of exercise are you doing?
Young Girl They say it's called Small Circular Heaven.
Young Man Is there a Big Circular Heaven as well?
Young Girl I don't know.
Young Man You're doing something you don't know anything about?
Young Girl *(Nervously.)* Stop interrogating me! Just stop it!
Young Man *(Mischievously.)* Then perhaps you don't know what's the use of this exercise? *(Grabs her hand.)*
Young Girl No, don't, you can't do that —
Young Man Why not?
Young Girl I'm scared …
Young Man What's there to be scared of?
Young Girl Don't touch me!
Young Man What if I do?

Young Girl Then I'd feel the pain.
Young Man So you don't feel any pain right now?
Young Girl *(Painfully.)* I can't say for sure …
Young Man *(Grabs her hand by force.)* Then for once I'll let you feel the pain!
Young Girl *(Begging him and trying to struggle free.)* Oh no, don't …

(Father enters carrying an umbrella. The chanting Zen Master and the meditating Crowd have all disappeared. Only Man is left sitting on the futon with his eyes closed.)

Young Man Father!
Father Don't get into trouble. Come home with me, now!

(Father drags Young Man along.)

(Young Girl disappears.)

Young Man *(Turns back to look. Nonchalantly.)* Why? It's not raining.
Father I tell you it will.
Young Man But it's not raining now.
Father It'll be too late if it does.
Young Man What if it doesn't.
Father It's going to rain sooner or later! Look, what do you think I've brought my umbrella for?
Young Man You've brought it because you have nothing else to do.
Father I've been carrying an umbrella all my life!
Young Man You've brought it upon yourself.
Father How dare you talk to your father like that?
Young Man Fine, I won't say anything then.
Father Get away from me! Go as far as you possibly can! Don't even bother coming back to see me. I don't have a son like you! *(Exits angrily.)*

(Young Man is bewildered. Man is still sitting on the futon meditating. The sound of chanting approaches, but there is no sign of Zen Master.)

Chanting Sound The Buddha said: Here, subhuti, someone who seeks supreme wisdom should produce a thought in this manner: "As many beings as there are in the universe of beings, comprehended under the term 'beings' — egg-born, born from a womb, moisture-born, or miraculously born; with or without form; with perception, without perception, — as far as any conceivable form of beings is conceived: all these I must lead to Nirvana, into that Realm of Nirvana which leaves nothing behind...."

(Young Man turns and finds a wall of people behind him. He tries unsuccessfully to find a way to get over it. Old Lady comes out from a crack in the "wall.")

Old Lady Young man, do you want to go over there?
Young Man I just want to take a look.
Old Lady Look, look. Everybody wants to take a look. Do you have any money?
Young Man *(He searches all his pockets and finally takes out a coin.)* Here.
Old Lady *(Laughs out loud.)* You want to take care of me with this? Don't you have anything valuable on you at all? Something your mother gave you, for example?
Young Man *(Suddenly understands.)* I've got this fountain pen, it has a gold nib, my mother gave it to me for my birthday. *(Takes the pen out and hands it over to her.)*
Old Lady *(Takes the pen and inspects it carefully.)* Hmm, this is quite nice. *(Stuffs the pen into her waist bag and steps aside to reveal a crack in the "wall.")* Now you can go ahead.
Young Man *(Hesitating.)* I'm afraid my mother might find out ...
Old Lady Will she beat you?
Young Man I ... I can't say ...
Old Lady You'll just have to lie to her, tell her that you've lost it. Don't you know how to lie?
Young Man Mother wouldn't allow it.
Old Lady That's why you're still such a kid. I'm telling you, there's no adult who doesn't lie, and you know, without lying

there'd be no more happy days. All right, just go right through.

(Crawling, Young Man goes through the crack of the wall of people. When he looks up he sees Young Girl sobbing quietly on the other side, her hands covering her face. He tries to get up, but two thugs approach and take turns beating him up. Young Girl and the sound of chanting disappear at the same time. Only Man is left sitting on the futon and meditating with his eyes closed.)

Plaster Seller Dogskin Plasters! Dogskin Plasters! Thirteen generations in the family. Give me internal wounds, external wounds, fractures, strains and contusions, give me rabies, heart-attacks, infant convulsions, geriatric strokes, lovesick young men and women, unspeakable depravity and the possessed, stick one on and you'll be as good as new. The first don't work, the second will.... Dogskin Plasters! Dogskin Plasters! Taken junky home remedy? Swallowed the wrong drug? No problem! Infertile women, impotent men, sinners and delinquents? Sure thing! Oh yes, and the stutterers, the crooked mouthed, jealous women, avenging men, fathers who love not the mothers, sons who listen not to their old men, pock-marked faces, tinea feet, one plaster cures all. The first don't work, the second will. Satisfaction guaranteed or your money gladly refunded.... Dogskin Plasters! Come and get the miracle Dogskin Plasters! Don't miss this golden opportunity! Your chance in a life time!

(Young man, on the outside of the Crowd's circle, finally manages to get up from his feet. Mad Woman enters.)

Mad Woman *(Approaching Young Man.)* They say I'm a whore, but they didn't say anything when they sneaked into my bed to sleep with me. They say I'm bad as if they haven't been bad before, as if they haven't had fun with a woman's body before!

(Young Man retreats and hides himself from her. The Crowd turn to face them.)

Crowd Here comes the mad woman.
The mad woman's here!
The mad woman's here!

Mad Woman You're mad!

Crowd Look, look at her.
She's talking crazy again.

Mad Woman You're talking crazy.

(The Crowd happily break out in laughter.)

Plaster Seller *(At the same time.)* If you've got money, give me money, if you don't, stay and watch the show! Dogskin Plasters for sale! *(Throws a bundle of plasters on the ground.)* Big sacrifice! Everything must go! Pay what you will. Cheap! Cheap! Cheap! … Pooh! You stinking whore! *(Puts away plasters and exits.)*

Mad Woman You're cheap! *(The Crowd laugh at her again.)* What are you laughing at? Go laugh at yourselves! What things you wouldn't do to get into a woman's pants! You all look like you're human, but actually you're all dogs, dogs, dirty dogs.

Men in Crowd *(To women in the Crowd.)* Stop her wagging tongue.
Take her away.

Mad Woman Why? You're scared because I'll tell on you, right? You're hiding something, aren't you? Right, keep away from me, as far away as you can. I know exactly what's going on in those shitty little heads of yours. *(Snickers.)*

Men in Crowd Take her away! Take her away!

(Women in the Crowd come forward to drag Mad Woman away.)

Mad Woman You're afraid too, aren't you? You're afraid I'll say that all of your husbands, every single one of them, have slept with me? Afraid because you'll become like me, dumped by your men after they've gotten their rocks off? Afraid your husbands will know you've screwed other men? Afraid people will find out you'd lost your cherry before you got married?

Crowd Gag her!
With horse shit!
With bull shit!
Shut her big mouth!

Mad Woman *(Grappling with Women in the Crowd.)* Haven't you got off with a man before? You're like me, you can't take your hands off your men after they've screwed you ...

(The Crowd move forward to tie up Mad Woman with ropes and gag her mouth. Crying and wailing, she becomes hysterical, but is finally dragged away by the Crowd. Young Man watches in astonishment and leaves with the Crowd. Man, who has been sitting and meditating on the futon, also disappears at the same time. Immediately afterwards, he returns from the other side with his Shadow. Shadow is dressed in black and has on black headgear which covers his face. Man and Shadow do not look at each other. They talk only to themselves, but their steps and movements are synchronized.)

Man A seed falls on to the soil —

Shadow A child is born onto the world —

Man A gust of wind blows through the forest —

Shadow A horse gallops on the plateau —

Man A grain of sand falls into the eye —

Shadow An eye is crying tears —

Man The tears fall on the parched desert —

Shadow Like entering a bustling marketplace —

Man People squashing people, but their eyes can't be seen —

Shadow Seeing dead fish one by one —

Man That's a lonely city —

Shadow Pop singers are yelling and screaming to exhaustion —

Man Only the stars can hear the wind chimes ringing —

Shadow It is not our hearts that are ringing —

Man It's the electric guitars picking your nerves —

Shadow You jump three times, nine times, eight times, seven times and you're out of breath —

Man Just because you're no hero —

Shadow More like a popular and low-minded farce —

Man An out-of-tune trumpet blows, blows, blows, blows and blows —

Shadow The conductor has to be right —

Man Everyone says he's 180% painful —

Shadow Only one minute's happiness —

Man It's not the time for drinking beer —

Shadow Chicago Nuremberg —

Man Once there was a war —

Shadow Only sparrows were killed —

Man Soldiers didn't fight, they only stood on guard —

Shadow And those standing on guard got to wear medals —

Man Who is the person speaking to me?

Shadow It is your shadow, your thoughts spoken out loud —

Man You're always following me —

Shadow When you have lost your self —

Man You'll come and remind me and double my trouble?

Shadow What are you looking for so desperately?

Man Now that you've reminded me! I've definitely lost something, can you tell me where to look for it?

Shadow *(Sarcastically.)* You probably do not know what you are looking for?

Man It appears to be … isn't everyone looking for it?

(The Crowd enter. They form a circle and bend down to look for something in the circle, like children at play.)

Shadow It would not hurt to ask them what you are looking for. *(Takes the chance to leave and disappear.)*

Man Excuse me, are you looking for —

Person A A needle, they say you can lead a camel through the eye of this needle.

Man *(To another person.)* Excuse me, can you tell me what you're looking for?

Person B Looking for a place where I can sit comfortably and securely. Once I'm there, I won't leave the seat ever again. *(Whispering.)* I have haemorrhoids, I can't sit on any wooden bench.

Man And, what are you looking for?

Person C *(Stuttering.)* I … I … I am … looking for a … a … mouth … which can … s … s … peak … for me. I … I … have to s … s … speak a lot … of … of … words ev … every … every day.

Man And you, young man?

Person D I'm looking for a rice bowl! You have everything, but I don't even have a rice bowl!

Man Of course, I know, I know it's very important to have a rice bowl. Go for it. Keep looking. *(To another person.)* Excuse me, I didn't do it on purpose. *(Removes his foot.)* What are you looking for?

Person E I'm looking for a pair of shoes that fits. I don't know why my shoes pinch. I want to know —

Man I'm also looking for —

Person E Do your shoes pinch too?

Man My shoes don't pinch, but I don't know where my feet should be going.

Person E You just have to follow other people's footsteps.

Man Are you also looking for other people's footsteps?

Person F *(Laughing playfully.)* I'm looking for a hole I can sneak through without anyone noticing me. And then I'll come out on the other side swaggering.

Man How about you, my friend? You don't look like the sneaky type.

Person G You're right.

Man Can you tell me what are you looking for?

Person G Looking for my childhood dream.

Man It must be a very beautiful dream. *(To another)* And you? Are you looking for a dream too?

Person H No, I'm looking for a sentence.

Man Are you writing a poem?

Person H Everybody can write poetry, just like everybody knows how to make love.

Man Then you're —

Person H Thinking! Everyone's got a mind, but not everyone can think.

Man You're right. What you're looking for must be an epigram.

Person H I'm not sure if it's an epigram. The problem is, if I didn't find this sentence my thoughts would be cut off, and thoughts which have been cut off are like a cut-off kite, you'll never be able to retrieve it again. Without a sentence you just can't think, because thinking is like a chain, each ring is linked to the next one. You understand?

Man Young lady, how about you? What are you looking for?

Young Lady Take a guess.

Man It must be something to do with love.

Young Lady You're so right! I'm waiting for a pair of eyes, tender, profound, and burning with passion —

(He avoids the young lady, but he bumps into another person.)

Person I Don't step on my toes!

Man Oh, I beg your pardon.

Person I Never seen anyone who walks like you.

Man	Neither have I. I'm going that way.
Person I	Everyone's looking here, what are you going to do over there?
Man	There is nothing I want here.
Person I	What are you looking for?
Man	*(Troubled.)* I don't know what I'm looking for.
Person I	Everybody, look! The man is a weirdo, he doesn't know what he's looking for!
Person J	He must have found it already.
	(The Crowd surround Man.)
Man	No, I haven't. Really I haven't. *(Walks away.)*
Stable Keeper	*(Coming out from the Crowd.)* Where are you going?
Man	Over there.
Stable Keeper	You haven't found anything yet, right? How come you're going over there?
Man	I'm not going to look for anything any more. I just want to go over there.
Stable Keeper	We're all looking here, but you insist on going there.
Everybody	Shall we let him?
Crowd	No!
	Absolutely not!
	He can't go.
	Just wait until we've all found it, then you can go.
Man	Let me explain.
Crowd	There's no need, we already know.
	We've been looking, you've been looking, everybody's been looking, but no one's found anything. Why do you want to go there now?
	It won't do.
	When we say no, we mean no.
	If you quit looking and we quit looking, then you can go there. But everybody's still looking right now and you insist on going, of course we won't let you.
	How can you?

If we're going to quit, we should all quit. So if we're going to look, we should all be looking, right?

Man I don't have anything to do with you.

Stable Keeper My friend, we're treating you like a friend, don't you see? *(To the Crowd.)* Try again to make him understand. Okay, let's start from the beginning.

Crowd *(One after the other.)* That's to say, yes, no, everybody looks or nobody looks, even if nobody looks or everybody looks, not looking is not the same as not wanting to look, the question is whether we can look and find it —

Man What if I don't want to look?

Crowd You don't want to look, sure, okay, we can't force you to if you don't want to, if you don't want to look, it doesn't mean nobody should look, and if everybody looks then you can't be not looking, nobody looks you don't look no more, everybody wants to look and you don't look, everybody looks for everybody, you don't look for everybody, you don't look and everybody looks, you look or not you don't look everybody looks you look or not nobody looks you look everybody looks —

Man *(Can't control himself.)* I'm going my way! I'm not bothering anybody, and nobody's going to bother me, okay?

Stable Keeper I'll give it to you straight: No way! You've found it but we haven't, it just won't wash!

Man But I haven't found anything!

Stable Keeper Then keep looking.

Man I'm not looking here any more. I — want — to — go — there.

Stable Keeper Don't you know the rules here? We've told you over and over again, why can't you admit that you're wrong and change your ways?

Crowd What's happening?
What's happening?
Son of a bitch, he's looking for trouble!

Stable Keeper Wait, this is no good, it's so uncivilized. If he doesn't want to repent, let him. We won't make it difficult for him. Just tell him to crawl through here. *(Pointing to his crotch.)* What do you say?

Crowd *(Bursting into laughter.)* Wonderful!

(Silence. Surprisingly, Man crawls through Stable Keeper's crotch. The Crowd is shocked and disappears. Man picks up a key while he is crawling. Shadow enters immediately.)

Shadow A key? That is correct. You must have been looking for a key like this one. Yes, yes, the key is what you have been looking for!

(Man is on his knees, inspecting the key in his hand. He then stands up and walks to centre stage and uses the key to open an imaginary door. He pulls hard on the big and heavy door and manages to open it. He walks inside. Shadow exits. Silence everywhere.)

Man *(Inquiring.)* Hello — *(Echo: Hello — hello — hello — hello … hello …)* Ah — *(Ah — Ah — Ah — Ah … Ah … Ah … The echoes seem to make the room more hollow and deserted.)* Anybody home? *(Echo: Anybody home? Anybody home? Anybody home? Anybody home? Anybody home? Anybody home? …)* Nobody has ever set foot in here before for sure … *(Echo-like murmuring: so lonely, so lonely, so lonely, so lonely.)* *(Man looks around and finds that some objects are hidden under the cover of a piece of black cloth. He carefully pulls out a bare woman's arm from under the black cloth.)*

Man *(Shocked.)* O —

(Simulated female voice sighs, echoing: O … O … O … O … O…. The voice seems to make him more enthusiastic. He begins to clear out what lies beneath the black cloth more diligently, and he pulls out a woman's leg.)

Man *(Excited.)* Ah!

(There is another series of simulated female voice calling urgently: Ah! Ah! Ah! Ah! Ah! Ah! ... Finally Man discovers a female mannequin hidden under the black cloth. He lifts the mannequin out and lays it down carefully. He admires it and then starts to move its hands and feet. And with increasing passion and energy, he fiddles with its shoulders, arms and the whole body, bringing it to a rather awkward forward leaning position. He turns the head around, and groping and touching, he manages to create various facial expressions. Every change he makes on the mannequin is accompanied by a simulated female voice akin to mechanical sound. The different expressions on the mannequin's face, including joy, pain, bewilderment, and peaceful staring, are also accompanied by music expressing the same sentiments in a simulated female voice. He puts the head straight so that it is staring at a not-so-distant place in front.... Then he stops and tries to figure out what to do next.

He becomes more excited now. One by one he pulls out more male and female mannequins and arranges them into a kind of pattern. After thinking for a while, he decides to put a piece of headgear on the first model. He keeps rearranging the pattern, his feet dancing to the beat of the increasingly loud music. The pattern changes according to one or more rules of his own making and at a speed which can only be observed in an instant. Gradually he finds himself hemmed in by the pattern and becomes one of its composite parts, and he crawls busily back and forth in between the mannequins. The process is a sustained and intense consumption of will power and strength.

Now the mannequins form a gigantic collective pattern using the first mannequin as its centre. As they move about, the pattern keeps changing slowly yet unstoppably. Man runs around in a hurry, jumping, moving, and rolling among his own creations. Highly excited, he calls out and responds to the mannequins in all kinds of non-language shouts and screams. This is a process of constant discovery, renewal,

rediscovery, and further renewal. But gradually the objects no longer obey his commands and the sounds they make begin to overwhelm his shouts. As he is totally drawn in among them, he gradually becomes weaker, and it becomes difficult for him to get out. After a long while he finally manages to crawl out like a worm, utterly exhausted. His creations roaringly gyrate past him and slowly disappear.)
(Shadow appears again, keeping a certain distance from him.)

Shadow *(Narrates in a serene voice.)* Then winter came along. It was snowing hard that day, and you walked barefoot on the ice to experience the bone-chilling cold. You seemed to feel that you were Jesus Christ, that you were the loneliest person, the only person who was suffering in this world. You felt that you were pervaded by the spirit of self-sacrifice, even though you were not sure for whom you would be sacrificing yourself. Yes, you did leave your footprints in the snow, and in the distance was a hazy, misty forest.

(Totally worn out, Man walks into a simulated forest made of human bodies.)

Shadow *(Following him.)* You walked into the dark and shady forest. The trees, every one of them, had already shed their leaves, stretching out their shaven branches like naked women. Somberly they stood in the snow, lonely and speechless. You could not help wanting to tell them about your sorrows and torments. You recalled the time of your youth, when you waited for her on the roadside for a long long time. That day it was also snowing, and you were determined to tell her that you loved her. You want to say that at the time you were still young and innocent, but now you have sinned deeply, and you will never be able to go back to those early days any more.

You have long lost your faith in people, your heart has grown old and it will not love again. Your only wish is to go walking among the trees in the forest until you are totally exhausted. Then you will collapse somewhere, hoping never to be found.

(Finally Man leans against a tree to take a breath. Shadow comes closer and closer, observing him.)

Shadow In fact it is nothing more than a kind of self-pity. You are unwilling to end like this, you are so vain. *(Exits.)*

(The tree Man has been leaning against bends down its trunk and speaks in a human-like voice: "Oh, here you are." Then all the trees in the forest move slowly towards him like monsters. They reveal their human forms and become the Crowd, all dressed in mourning clothes.)

Crowd *(They speak and move, but they are unfeeling and expressionless.)*
We've been looking all over for you.
Come on, take us to the pub to have a drink.
You're our host, how come you're here in the snow?
You're a giant, and we have to look up to see you.
You're famous, so famous that we're scared of you.
We admire you, but we don't want to idolize you.
You're no more than a crook, only we don't have your tricks.
Get up and come with us.
You should donate money to our charities for children, you must know that children need money the most.
You went through the forest alone, a forest even the devil fears to tread, you're number one.
You're a pathfinder, you've walked out a road nobody wants to walk on, you've led people astray.
You're lucky, not everyone is as lucky as you are.

It's not that you're more talented than the others, it's only that they don't get the chance to show what they've got.
You're the tops, let's us give him a pat on the behind!

(The Crowd laugh coldly and sinisterly. Some start to pull at him and grapple with him.)

Crowd *(Suddenly.)* Here he comes!
Talk of the devil.
Make way.

(Shadow backs in as the Crowd step aside to make way for him.)

Man (*Weakly.*) Who are you?
Shadow Your heart.

(As the Crowd watch the drooping, blind, and deaf heart slouching past them, Shadow quietly drags Man away. The Crowd slowly follow behind the heart which is extremely old and actually invisible. All exit.)

(One by one the Actors enter from the other side.)

Actors We set off before dawn. The morning dew was thick, and in the dark we heard the cows breathing while they were chewing grass on a small hill nearby. In the distance, the river bend was enveloped in a shade of deep blue light brighter than the sky.
He told us a fable.
I dreamed that there's a piece of ivory in my stomach, it scared me to death!
Have you thought of becoming a bird?
Why a bird? I'm happy with the way I am, and he says he loves me.

Faulkner.
I like "Roses for Emily."
I called you up many times.
Do you know how to read palms?
No need for any explanations, you don't have to explain any more!
This kitten is so cute.
I think I've seen you somewhere.
I have a sweet tooth, and I'm also a sucker for sour milk.
Your hair looks so nice, is it real?

(The sound of a baby crying.)

Sweetie, oh, sorry, I forgot to change your diapers!

(The sound of a car engine starting.)

How are you going to get back?
It's so bad, what kind of stupid play is this anyway?
Are you doing anything tomorrow? Shall we have dinner together?

(Sounds of a baby crying, a car engine starting and running, bicycle bells and the trickle of running water from a tap, and in the distance, the siren of an ambulance.)

The End

Some Suggestions on Producing *The Other Shore*

1. The so-called "spoken drama" (*huaju*) tends to emphasize and highlight the art of language; in order to free drama from its constraints and to revive drama in all its functions as a performing art, we have to provide training for a new breed of modern actors. As with the actors in traditional operas, these new actors must be versatile, and their skills should include singing, the martial arts, stylized movements and delivering dialogues. They should also be able to perform Shakespeare, Ibsen, Chekov, Aristophanes, Racine, Lao She, Cao Yu, Guo Moruo, Goethe, Brecht, Pirandello, Beckett, and even mimes and musicals. The present play is written with the intention of providing an all-around training for the actors.
2. An ideal performance should be a unity of somatics, language, and psychology. Our play is an attempt to pursue this unified artistic expression and to assist the actors to achieve this goal. In other words, we should allow the actors the chance for linguistic expression in their search for suitable somatic movements, so that language and somatics are able to evoke psychological process at the same time. For this reason, during rehearsals and actual performances, it is not advisable to separate dialogue from movement, i.e., to memorize only the dialogue, to do reading as in common practice, or to strip the language and transform the play into a mime. Certain scenes in the play do not feature dialogue, but there are still other aural expressions, which could be regarded as a kind of sound language.
3. Even though our play is abstract, the performance should not aim at sheer conceptualization in the stark fashion of the play of ideas. Our aspiration is to achieve a kind of emotive abstraction through performance, i.e., a non-philosophical abstraction. The play seeks to set up the performance on the premise of non-reality, and to fully mobilize the imagination of the actors before evoking abstraction through emotion. Therefore the performance requires not only the unity of language and somatics but also the unity of thought and psychology.
4. Except for a few simple props, the performance does not require any scenery. The characters' relationships with their surroundings and other objects are contingent upon life-like dialogue and communicative

exchanges in the play. In the case of monologues or in the absence of dialogue, music, sound effects, movement, the look of the eyes and changes in posture could also take on performing roles, so that the props and surroundings will not be relegated to being inanimate objects or mere adornments.

5. The play highlights the performance's ability to ascertain in the mind of the audience the existence of non-existing objects, for instance a decrepit heart, a concrete or abstract river. We may say that this is the inherent difference between a film and a theatrical performance. Even though the play itself relies heavily upon imaginary surroundings, relationships and acting partners, real and life-like objects can be deployed as stage props at the beginning of the performance. For instance, an interpersonal relationship could be established through a piece of rope. Once an actor is equipped with the capability to relate with others, he can easily communicate with his non-existent partners anytime, anywhere. He can also materialize his non-existent partners through his power of imagination, making them come to life and communicate with them, even though they have been created through his own imagination and are actually non-existent.
6. Grotowski's training method aims at helping the actor to discover his own self and to release its potential through big-movement exercises which also relax both body and mind. Thus he calls this type of performance a form of sacrifice. Our play's performance helps the actor to ascertain his own self through the process of discovering his partners. If the actor, without being obsessed with his own self, is consistently able to find a partner to communicate with him, his performance will always be positive and lively, and he will be able to gain a real sense of his own self, which has been awakened by action, and which is alert and capable of self-observation.
7. The play demands that the actors abandon completely the kind of performance dependent upon logic and semantic thinking. The liveliest performances are exactly those which are intuitive, improvisational, and on the spur of the moment. On the stage as in real life, the actor sees with his eyes, hears with his ears, and captures his partners' reactions with his free-moving body. In other words, a performance can only be lively without the use of intellect. Therefore it is best not to

resort to literary analysis outside of theatrical performance or to uncover hidden meanings in the text in performing the play.

8. Our play aims at training actors who can be as versatile as the actors in Chinese traditional operas, but it is not our intention to create a new set of conventions for modern drama, because the latter aspires to the kind of acting which is non-formulaic, unregulated, and flexible. Before the actual performance, the actor should enter into a state of competitiveness similar to that of an athlete before a game, or of a cock preparing to slug it out in a cock-fight, ready to provoke as well as to receive his partners' reactions. Thus the performance must be fresh, regenerating, and improvisational, which is essentially different from gymnastic or musical performances.
9. The play's performance strives to expand and not to reduce the expressiveness of language in drama. The language in a play is voiced language, but it is not limited to beautifully written dialogue. In this play, all the sounds uttered by the actor in the prescribed circumstances are also voiced language. If an actor has learned to communicate using fragmented language which features unfinished sentences, disjointed phonetic elements, and ungrammatical constructions, he will be better able to make the unspoken words in the script come to life as voiced language.

The above suggestions are for reference only.

Between Life and Death

Characters:

An actress playing Woman
A clown playing Man, Ghost, and Old Man
A female dancer playing Woman's imagination

Objects:

A clothes rack on which is hung a man's suit
A woman's jewellery box
A mannequin's arm and leg
A small house made of toy blocks
A withered tree and its shadow
A piece of rock

Between Life and Death. Théâtre Renaud-Barrault Le Rond-Point, Paris, France. Directed by Alain Timárd. 1993.

(above) *Between Life and Death*. Centre for Performance, University of Sydney, Australia. Directed by Gao Xingjian. 1993.

(left) *Between Life and Death*. Dionysia Festival mondial de Théâtre contemporain, Veroli, Italie. Directed by Gao Xingjian. 1994.

(An empty and dimly lit stage. Woman has on a long skirt and a large black shawl. She has a pale complexion. Man is behind her to one side. He is wearing a black tuxedo; his complexion is even more pallid. The two remain motionless for a long time.)

Woman *(She wants to say something but stops. Eventually she cannot hold back and speaks in an indifferent voice.)* She says she's had enough, she can't take it any more!

(Man raises his hand slightly.)

Woman *(Cannot control her outburst.)* She says she can't understand how she's managed to endure it, to put up with it for so long until now. Him and her, she says she's talking about him and her, their relationship just can't go on like this, it's not living or dying, and it's been so difficult, so enervating, so uncommunicative, so muddled, and so entangled. It's so sickly and so tense that her nerves are going to snap at any time. She's talking about her spiritual being, the spirit and the nerves are all but the same thing, there's no need to be so picky about words!

(Man shrugs his shoulders.)

Woman *(Keeps on talking garrulously in the same manner as before.)* She says she can't understand, really can't understand how it could've come to be like this. She can't explain it clearly, it's just like a ball of unruly hemp, all tangled up. She's not talking about him, she knows perfectly well what he's thinking in his head; she's talking about him, who's been disturbing her to no end, driving her to be so jumpy and so harried. She doesn't know what she's talking about, she doesn't know whether she's made herself clear enough.

(Man makes a face.)

Woman *(Somewhat irritated.)* She says this is exactly what she can't put up with, the cynicism, the quizzical attitude! But she's dead serious, she wants to talk it over with him calmly and in control of herself. Don't you think he understands? But once their talk touches on the subject, he'll put on the same old expression, and she just can't help getting herself all stirred up! She can't stand it any more, she can't keep on like this any longer, she means the relationship between him and her.

(Man puts on a bitter expression.)

Woman *(Somewhat weary.)* She says she knows exactly how he'll react once she mentions it. She's seen it countless times, she has long had a taste of his hypocrisy. He's a coward, he has no manliness left in him whatsoever, yet he still wants to pull a fast one and pretend to be somebody. She doesn't understand how she could live with him, eat dinner with him at the same table, stay with him in the same room, and sleep with him on the same bed, go places together like a man and his shadow, and still have nothing to say to each other.

(Man is silent.)

Woman She says she knows he's got nothing to say, what more can he say? He's said all he wanted to say and could say, the beautiful lies and all that sweet talk, with so much gallantry and so much flattery. He could've readily repeated them to anybody, any woman. Only when he's with her, he'll pretend and conceal himself behind his silence —

(Man opens his mouth and attempts to speak.)

Woman No, it's better for him not to say anything. She says she knows he'll just repeat the same old tune again. She's grown sick and tired of it, she can't take it any more. She doesn't want to hear that hypocritical voice coming from the bottom of his throat, the reluctant laughter, a laughter which is cold and obsequious and harbours an insidiousness which cannot contain itself. His sophistication and his manners, they're a sham, a total sham! He was only playing to the occasion, but now the play is over. He had planned everything, he knew how the whole thing would end even before it got started.

(Man presses his lips together, quite at a loss.)

Woman She says she knows him only too well, she can read him like a book, now there's only indifference in her eyes. The astuteness, intelligence, and passion that she saw in his smiling eyes, they all came from his glasses. Now that the glasses are taken off, there is no more glitter, only weariness, iciness, and cruelty, just like his selfish heart, where there is only egotism and unconcern. He only wanted to take without giving, to possess her, and to enjoy himself, he got what he wanted, he has used her and played with her, now there's only boredom and apprehension. But he's still holding back, waiting for her to explode first. She's no fool, who doesn't know about his bag of tricks? *(Snickers.)*

(Man pouts his lips and keeps shaking his head.)

Woman She says there's no use shaking his head. No shaking can shake her determination, no shaking can change her mind, and no shaking can ever refute or erase the harm he has done her. Any more shaking will be meaningless, it won't cover up the hypocrisy in his heart. He's never been faithful to her, never —

(Man raises his right hand, attempting to explain.)

Woman *(Shouts.)* She doesn't want to hear it! She doesn't want to hear the lies! Save them for the bobby-soxers! His sugary talk has been a fraud from beginning to end. She'll never again believe that there's true love in the world, don't talk to her about loving or not loving!

(Man opens his left hand, so that his right hand faces up and his left hand faces down, striking a strange pose.)

Woman She says if she wanted to possess she'd possess everything, if she wanted to love she'd love with all her heart, she wouldn't allow even the tiniest bit of untruth, otherwise, she'd rather have nothing at all. She wanted to possess him, to possess all their feelings together, even if they should be darkness personified, all the sounds and movements of darkness. But she'd already known that there was no way she could possess this man completely. The darkness, the whispers, suffocation, tolerance, agony and happiness they shared together, he also shared them with other women in the same way. She's not the only one, she might as well sever their relationship and leave him once and for all.

(Man changes his pose. Now his right hand faces down and his left hand faces up, striking an equally strange pose. He then raises his hands up high and does a flip in the air, landing with his back facing the audience.)

Woman *(Starts muttering.)* She says she doesn't understand how there could be so much disloyalty and betrayal, so much indifference among people and between men and women, it's so frustrating, so disheartening, and so unbearable. The dating games, trendy clothing, genuine and fake jewellery, woman's vanity and man's attention are all deceptions. Movies, pop stars, dancing parties, theatre-going, and even taking a trip together are nothing but excuses to flirt and make out, what follows is either contraception or litigation. The disapproval on a man's face and a woman's tantrums, they don't mean anything to her any more, all she wants to do is to cry her heart out, just like a small child —

(Man slowly turns his head. Somewhat moved, he takes out a dark blue silk kerchief from his suit pocket and squeezes out a teardrop.)

Woman *(At a loss.)* But she says she's run out of tears, there is only hopeless solitude now. She just wants to lock herself up and refuse to see anybody. She's afraid when the telephone rings, the sudden ringing makes her heart jump, she has unplugged the phone. She can't stand the noise of cars coming and going, when they brake or when someone starts the engine outside her window, she's agitated to no end. She is also afraid of lights, the colour of the lampshade, the crimson carpet, the pillow cases with violets embroidered on them, and the leather slippers on the shaggy carpet. What she detests most is this picture of him in the gilded picture frame beside the tulip-shaped wall lamp, so shamelessly full of himself!

(Man lowers his head.)

Woman *(Somewhat tired, she takes off her shawl and casually throws it on the floor.)* She says she doesn't know why she has said all this. What was said has been said already. She feels relieved once it's said, once it's said it's over and done with, isn't it? (*Turns her head to take a look at him, and then turns back.*) You can speak too, that is, if you've got anything to say. She only fears that you've got nothing to say, then all you could do is to play dumb and act the part of some well-behaved fool. Why don't you try saying something? It wouldn't hurt, you know. Good or bad she has been living with you for some time, don't you have anything else to say besides "let's go to bed"?

(Man moves slightly, then slowly disappears.)

Woman You know, you can explain if you think there's been a misunderstanding, but she can't stand people not responding like that! You know why she's broken out for no reason? It's because she can't stand the loneliness any longer. If you can't even understand that, then you might as well go your separate ways and you'll both have some peace and quiet. *(Turns around to look for him.)*

(Silhouette of Man's back appears dimly on the other side of the stage.)

Woman *(Facing silhouette of Man's back.)* She says she's only saying it, actually she doesn't want to leave him. And she's not really kicking him out either, she just hopes that he'll offer her some explanation and tell her that his feeling for her hasn't changed, then she'd be relieved and comforted, and she'd be able to prove that all her doubts and worries are groundless. How come he can't even understand that? He doesn't understand women, he doesn't understand a woman's feelings, does she really need to spell it all out for him? If he has to go, then just let him go, she can't force him, she's only saying please, please ask him to explain himself clearly. It's not that she can't go on with her life without loving him. What more does he want her to say? She's already said all that she can — *(Approaches him.)* She begs him not to go like this, she begs him to turn around, to take one more look at her, just like when they first fell in love. She just wants to see his eyes again, those engaging, penetrating eyes he had when he was courting her, or the gentle look in his eyes when he stared at her later, even if they were uncertain, pensive, or engaged in thought, they all managed to send shivers to her heart. If only she could bring back the same look in his eyes, if only he could turn around and look at her once more, all their problems would be over, they'd be as loving as before, and she'd snuggle up to him in his arms to enjoy his fond caress once more.

(Leaning against him.) Then she'd never nag him, she'd never say anything to hurt him ever again. She says she knows all about men, their pride, their temper and their idiosyncrasies. When they don't get along with their boss in the office, they'll take it out on their family when they come home. She says that sometimes she's a nervous wreck herself and that she does break out every once in a while. She also knows that this isn't good, but she never thought that men also had their problems. She might not solve his problems for him, but at least she can offer him some understanding and comfort.

In fact all the tantrums she's thrown at him have been his fault, because she loves him and cares for him so much, that's why she's so demanding towards him.

She also says that there are actually no problems between them, only that she's suspicious, only this funny feeling of hers. If she were wrong, then he should help her to get rid of her worries, he shouldn't just turn and walk away like that.

She also says that she doesn't mean to stop him from going out with other women, she's only afraid that such things might happen. She says too that she's actually not that stuck up. Even if he had something going with another woman, it'd just be one of those one-time flings and he'd be in it only for the pleasure, and besides, he'd probably forget about the whole thing in no time. When it's over, it's over, isn't it? Not that she

doesn't understand, she just thinks that he should at least lay it all out for her and give her an explanation.
She says she doesn't want to possess him, she only wants him to truly love her, that'd be good enough for her. She has said so much already, shouldn't he at least have the courtesy to say one word in response?
(Grabs his shoulders and turns him around.) God! *(She suddenly withdraws her hands as Man turns into a piece of clothing on the rack.)*

(A bald-headed clown appears at the side of front stage. On his nose hangs a pair of glasses made for extreme shortsightedness. He has on a collarless black shirt, his legs crossed. He looks up and stares at a non-existent raindrop in the air, which after a long while lands in front of him. Then the rain falls down with a pitter-patter. The clown gradually disappears in the dark.)

Woman *(She kneels on the ground before a pile of folded clothing. In front of the clothing lies a pair of men's shoes; on top of the shoes is a man's hat. Next to her is a leather jewellery box.)* She says she's never, ever in her life thought that it would end like this, that she would actually kill her man, her darling, her treasure, her little zebra, her sika deer, her sweetheart, her life and destiny.
(While speaking, she takes down her ring, bracelet, and earrings and puts them into the jewellery box one by one.) What a real nightmare! She's just woken up from it, she feels a bit cold.
(Wraps the shawl tightly around herself.) The cold rain and autumn wind raging outside the window, when will they ever end?
(Listens.) There'll be no more telephone rings in the middle of the night, its endless ringing scares her and makes her heart jump, she wants to answer it but she wouldn't dare, but then if she didn't she'd feel guilty.

(Sighs.) There'll be no more sweet-nothing whispers, the whispers with so many pauses in between. Neither of them was willing to hang up the phone, even when they were too drowsy to talk any more.

Right now she's cut off all her ties with the outside world, she's cut off her ties with her lovers, friends, and enemies, and with those she once loved but no longer loves, those who admired her but whom she didn't admire. She doesn't even have the courage to step out of this room to go to a pub, any pub, to pick up a man, any man. She knows exactly what's going to happen if she does: when the hangover goes away in the morning, she'll find herself sleeping beside a naked man with hair all over his chest and whose name she's already forgotten, and all that's left is the feeling of emptiness and disgust. At this time, she doesn't even have the courage to pick up her clothes from the floor and run away in a hurry. She's totally down on herself, she doesn't have a desire for sex any more, she even finds her own body repulsive.

She doesn't need to put on make-up and beautify herself any longer, even that necklace, the one her mother gave her before she died, has now become a burden.

(Takes off the necklace and throws it into the jewellery box.)

All this jewellery is superfluous, is there any reason left for making herself beautiful? And for whom? She detests herself, detests being a woman, her tantrums, her possessiveness, her irrational jealousy and her groundless anxieties, and then there's her never-ending nagging that nobody ever wants to listen to, she can't even find the energy, she only feels totally exhausted. She knows her face looks tired and her skin is coarse, she doesn't have to look in the mirror. She knows her breasts have become saggy and insensitive, they can no longer arouse a man's passion. She, a woman, her prime has ended, become depleted and consumed, what else has she got to hope for? Even this body of hers, nobody wants it. *(She wraps the shawl tightly around her. Her eyes droop and she looks down.)*

(Half a wooden leg, whose paint has peeled off, slowly stretches out from under her skirt.)

Woman *(Startled, she puts a hand on the floor to support herself and draws back.)* This is impossible! This is not real! *(Stooping down to inspect.)* How could this possibly be her? Is this her leg? She must find out if this is real or if it's just a nightmare.

(The leg stretches out further until it finally comes off her skirt.)

Woman *(She retreats further, holding her breath. She wraps the shawl tightly around herself.)* She wonders if at this moment she is still alive, if she is still breathing. She must have some proof, proof that her heart is still beating, that it is still feeling. Is all of this just her imagination? Is it just an illusion? Or is her existence, this living body of hers, also a mirage? She must find some definite proof. *(She pinches herself on the arm.)*

(An arm appears from inside the shawl. Its palm is pale and white, and the fingernails are covered with a coat of shell-like paint.)

Woman *(Panting.)* No … *(Beginning to feel terrified.)* She wants to know if her fear is real. Maybe she only thinks she's afraid but actually she's not? She must experience death once to find out what death is and to feel its pain, in other words, a living experience of death, then, and only then can she prove that she is still alive, and then she'll know if life is worth living, if it's really necessary. She's too hurt to free herself from suffering now, but she still keeps on analysing herself in desperate pursuit of her true self, to find out for sure if she's real or just a body without a soul.

(The arm falls off from the shawl. From the palm up, the paint has peeled off as with the detached wooden leg.)

Woman No!
(Runs away.) This is too horrible, she can't continue to be cut up like this, she can't keep on butchering herself to death! She must run now, run away from this room!
(Simulates action of opening a door.) Strange, she can't open the door, how could she be so stupid? How could she possibly lock herself in?
(Crawls all over the room in a circle around the pile of man's clothing, the jewellery box and the detached arm and leg.) She can't find the key! How can this be possible? She remembers clearly that when she opened the door she was holding the key in her hand, but now she's forgotten where she put it. Where could it be?
(Stops, staring blankly at the detached arm and leg.) She just can't understand, can't understand what's happening here. Her home, this warm and comfortable little nest of hers, has turned into a horrifying abyss overnight, how could this be? … She's got to get out.
(Shouting.) She wants to get — out —, but nobody hears her, nobody cares, she's in her own room, she's locked herself in, she's got in and now she can't get out….
(She kneels on the floor and looks around, at a loss what to do.)

(Clown comes out from one side and backs up the stage until he reaches the centre, his head hanging down and looking at the floor. A rat appears from where he came from. The rat, under his guidance and enticement, crawls gingerly and

timorously to his feet. The audience then discovers that he is actually pulling a very fine thread in his hands. He puts the rat into his pocket and exits.)

(The tick-tock of an electric clock is heard, gradually increasing in volume.)

Woman *(Murmuring.)* She doesn't know what time it is, she doesn't dare look at the clock, she doesn't want to know whether it's midnight or dawn, she can't pull up the blinds, she has no strength, she has no courage to …

(At the back of the stage, the shadow of a woman appears, her back facing the audience. She is carrying an umbrella and marking time.)

Woman *(Staring at the woman's shadow.)* She says it appears that she sees a woman waiting in the rain, she's all alone, she doesn't know how long she's been waiting, she doesn't know when she's going to stop waiting, but she's still waiting, waiting for that someone she hasn't got a date with, she knows he won't come, yet she still insists on waiting in vain. She wants to warn her, she wants to tell her that to live is to be destined, destined to be alone all your life, so why keep on dreaming an impossible dream? But she refuses to come to her senses.

(The woman slowly turns around. She is still marking time, her face hidden by the umbrella as before.)

Woman *(Quietly approaches.)* Who is this woman? She can't help wanting to know, but she keeps on turning this way … then that way … she can't see anything, she can't see her face clearly. *(Disappointed, she covers her face with her hands.)*

(The woman suddenly disappears.)

Woman *(Lifts her head, dejected.)* She's just realized that she's the one who's lonely in the whole wide world, not the other people, whose loneliness she has been observing. Other people may be waiting, downcast, forlorn, and all by themselves, but after all they're still waiting, and they know in their hearts where they want to go, but she doesn't, she doesn't know if there's anything left for her to do, or if there's anywhere else she can go.
(Very troubled.) So she tries to search her memory. Where did she come from? Why is it that she hasn't been able to control herself, why does she have to be down and out like this? Has it been a dream all along? And merely a dream?
(Closes her eyes.) Ah, what a strange dream!
(Opens her eyes.) Just now, at that fleeting moment ... she saw it, she saw a wall, its plaster was crumbling away piece by piece, ... exposing the cold and damp concrete, a coffin was lodged there, ... it was placed there neatly, sideways, buried in poured concrete ...

(A large wall appears back stage. The wall is dark grey and is illuminated from the side. There is no coffin in the wall.)

Woman *(She wobbles and feels her way along the wall, her head leaning against it.)* She doesn't know what this dream means ... No, she knows, she knows that right now her mind is not clear, she needs to sort things out, how did it all begin? There's got to be an end to all of this somewhere, nothing'll go wrong as long as she finds a clue.
(Turns, leaning against the wall.) But she can't even remember a single incident from her childhood! Does this mean that she has never been alive, or is she just a shadow, the shadow of some nonexistent person? Is her existence just an illusion? No! She definitely had a childhood, she remembers! *(Determinedly gets away from the wall.)*

(The wall gradually disappears.)

Woman She says she's got to pour it all out. It was a long time ago, at that time, her family still owned this small house ... It was an old building, and everywhere there were rats scurrying around ... The family had an old cat, so old that it was too lazy to run after the rats, and it was always dozing off on top of the stove in the dingy kitchen ... She wants to say that it was an old building, when a gust of wind blew you could hear it creaking and squeaking, and the lumber would give out a musty smell. The old cat's always crouching on top of the stove, and when the fire went out completely, one could see nothing but a pair of green eyes glowing in the dark and spying on her every move. She seems to remember the first time she discovered her own nakedness in the mirror, and the old cat was right there behind her ...

(A small house made of toy blocks appears centre stage.)

Woman That's right, her room was behind that window on the second floor.

(Smiles and starts to narrate, facing the house.) Downstairs just past the front porch was the living room. There was a rocking chair, her grandpa always sat on it. He had a head of white hair, when he died nobody knew how old he was. The house had no doors, only windows, and more strangely, her family always locked themselves inside, it was so dark and so damp. The first one to escape from the house was her father, then it was her mother, and they'd never come back since.

(Becoming more interested.) He, she's talking about her father, escaped during the night. Later they only found a string of footsteps in the rain-soaked muddy ground under the window. The next one to go was her mother, they said that there was a man, whenever he passed by

the window, he'd always be humming a popular tune, it'd been like this for some time, and her mother must have heard him, then she disappeared. And then it was her brother, he always screamed and yelled and generally made a big racket. Once he knocked down a really old vase in the house, her grandpa said it was an antique and a family heirloom. The last one to escape was herself. She thinks the building is still there, in her memory it's wobbling, as if it's going to collapse any second.

(Somewhat delighted.) She says this is a children's story, maybe it's a fable, she's always wanted to talk to people about something, to talk about something that happened in the past, or to talk about her memory, or better yet, to tell a story, a fable.

(Totally immersing herself.) She says when she was small she was always curious, she yearned to get out of the house to take a look at the outside world. She grew up in a town, and the house was located at the edge of the town, a building all by itself, on top of a small hill. She also says that she'd never seen the places beyond the wall in the yard.

Of course she knew every thing within the wall inside out, she knew where there was a peach tree, where there was a doghouse, even where there was a vegetable plot with tomatoes growing in it, but when the tomatoes had grown ripe and fell to the ground to rot, she refused to go there any more. She says she can't remember how her grandpa died, they all said he'd swallowed opium, his whole body was in unbearable pain, there was something wrong with all his joints, according to the present day doctors, it was probably cancer spread to the bone marrow, he'd scream out loud at night, it was very scary, he screamed that he'd burn the whole house down. She knew that actually her grandpa couldn't get out of bed, he needed someone to hold him even when he tried to turn his body a little ...

She doesn't believe her grandpa killed himself, especially by swallowing opium, it seems like a made-up story. She doesn't know why she's telling all this, perhaps she's beginning to make up stories, making up a childhood she never had, but she still wants to make up some more things, something beautiful, make up some ... some ... She says that her arrival in this world was entirely a misunderstanding, but isn't life a series of misunderstandings?

But she does recall a young boy, ... he used to stand under her window in the snow waiting for her to appear, at the time she'd hide behind the curtains, she thought that it was fun, a bit laughable perhaps, and she also felt a bit sorry for him, but in the end she still held back, because her best friend in her class told her that she'd also received a love letter from the same boy. Afterwards she stopped going out with both of them.

She wants to tell a romantic story. Besides physical contact there should be some poetry in the relationship between a man and a woman, but everything has been so hypocritical, hypocritical, so hypocritical that it's made her utterly sick and tired of the whole thing.

She remembers that her mother had two lovers, whenever her father was out on business, her mother'd make herself especially beautiful. She spent all her money on herself, she never cared about what her children were wearing, and she'd lose her temper about almost anything and everything. Once a girl student came to ask her father something, they were together for a long time, until dinner it was, and her father asked her to stay and eat with them. Suddenly there came the sound of banging dishes from the kitchen, and her heart cringed, because she was sure that once the girl student left, her mother would blow up. Afterwards, she heard her mother and father quarrelling in their room as expected, her mother said her father had something going with the girl student, he repeated many times that there was nothing, but her mother insisted that she saw the whole thing through a crack in the door! She couldn't stand her mother the most, as soon as she got upset she'd whoop up a storm.

Oh yes, and they also had a neighbour, a single woman, she was also unbearably neurotic. She was keeping this dog she called Sicko. Here, Sicko! There Sicko, run! She'd keep horsing around all the time with the dog until it yapped and yelped and never stopped, and then she'd caress it with all her tender loving care as if it was her lover.

Her mother was the same, she only quieted down when she was on her deathbed. She had broken her spine in a car crash, when she died she was still quite young, the skin on her arm was smoother and fresher than hers is now, but her head was all wrapped in bandages, her lips swollen, all pale and ashen. It was the first time she'd been so close to death. When she died she didn't cry, she only felt a bit surprised, a bit regretful, she cried only after she'd left the hospital and stayed up alone at night, suddenly she felt she'd lost something ... *(Covers her face with her hands.)*

(A woman appears behind her. She is completely dressed in white, and her head is wrapped in bandages except for her mouth and her nose. She is wearing a necklace with a small watch attached to it.)

Woman She choked and burst out crying, was she crying for herself or was it because she'd lost her mother? She couldn't say for sure. She and her mother were never close, there was always a barrier between them which could never be removed. The necklace she has on now belonged to her mother, she knows that one of her lovers gave it to her..., she had her eyes on her mother's small silver

watch inlaid with sapphire even when she was a little girl, once she wore it without telling her, when she found out, she jumped down real hard on her and she cried her eyes out for a long time. She gave the watch to her before she died, as something to remember her by, and she also whispered in her ears, begging her not to hold anything against her.
When she was alive she always said that it was difficult being a woman, she says her mother said women suffer five hundred times more than men. She didn't understand why women had to suffer from so many more deadly sins. She also knows that it wasn't her mother but an old woman who had said these words first, perhaps women like to talk about these things when they're together, and her mother just repeated them to her. Yes, sins, she'd brought sins upon herself. Whenever the lover, the one who gave her the watch, came calling, she'd have to make a real fuss of it, she'd bath and dress herself up from head to toe for him and then she'd look for some excuse to send her away, all this got her really peeved and that was why the relationship between mother and daughter became so tense. Today, well, of course she's forgiven everything. *(Turns around.)*

(The woman turns around, still behind her.)

Woman But at the time *(Pauses.)* she only wanted her attention, so that she'd notice her, notice her anger, that was why she stabbed a scissors blade into her middle finger. They say that the ten fingers are linked to the heart, and she wanted her heart to suffer the pain too.
(Looking at her hand.) She watched the blood oozing out, it streamed down the centre of the palm along the middle finger, and then it seeped through the fingers to the back of the hand, she could have stopped the bleeding, but she didn't, rather she hoped the blood

would bleed much faster. She watched her wrist turn purple red, *(Raising her arm.)* but she still let the blood flow, she just wanted to drown her whole body in a pool of blood. She didn't know how much longer she could hang on like that, she just felt faint and dizzy. At last she heard her mother calling out after her, the water's all gone, the kettle's going to be burnt into ashes, go take a look! Her mother found her in her room and asked her why she had pretended to be deaf and dumb. Only then did she see that her hand was covered in blood, she immediately snatched the trembling scissors from her and gave her a big smack across the face. *(Raises her head.)*

(The woman walks away quietly.)

Woman *(Watching the back of the woman.)* She doesn't know if it's a dream or reality.

(Only the shadowy image of the woman's back is visible.)

Woman *(Takes one step forward to follow her.)* Is it a real dream? Or does she only think she's dreaming?

(The woman disappears.)

Woman *(Shakes her head.)* To tell the truth, she once had a very weird dream, in the dream her mother was holding down her legs, she was actually helping a man to rape her, and the man appeared to be her mother's lover. At the time she knew that she might be dreaming, she wanted to scream but she couldn't, she only managed to sob quietly, though there were a lot of tears. Strangely enough, at this moment she also wants to cry, but she just can't. If only she could cry, if she cried she'd be able to find some relief, she knows that, but unfortunately at her age she's already grown out of crying. She used to be a cry baby. At that time there was a peach tree outside her window, whenever she saw the peach blossoms being ravaged by driving rain and there were nothing but a few raindrops left on the bare branches, she'd break down in tears. Of course she wasn't crying for the peach flowers, she cried because she didn't understand why she was crying, no, not now, she's not talking about now, she's talking about those early days, talking about a young girl who had no knowledge of the world and who had to live a life of misery. In fact, it's all her own fault, she asked for it, and at the same time she also gave other people a lot of troubles. She says that she wasn't the only one, most girls were like that, they liked to bore her with their tattered stories about men.

She says she's talking about a bad girl, and the bad girl is herself. When they first taught her to walk, they told her not to let her soles touch the ground, instead she should tread on the sides of her feet, *(Looks down at her feet.)* and she should raise her arms a little, they said men found this more attractive, all this made her uneasy for a long period of time ...

(A girl's laughter is heard.)

Woman *(Listens.)* When a woman wants to do it to another woman ...

(The laughter disappears.)

Woman She can be even more vicious than a man. She says at one time she knew this woman, a woman doctor, she had a husband and a lover, but she still said that she loved her, telling her that when she saw her she was seeing herself when she was young and in her prime. She said she was her big sister, and that she was willing to be her mother if she wanted it, she hoped that some day she'd have a daughter like her. She also said that when she grew tired of men she'd live with her and nobody else. She said you only lived once, so you must try to live happily, she also wondered why she was still living by herself at her age, without a man by her side. The woman was just like a witch, when her eyes were staring at her, it was like they were going through her body from one side to the other. She loved to flash her breasts and her body in front of her, she'd change her clothes in her presence, and then suddenly she'd laugh out loud for no reason, at the time she was just like a she-devil. She never held back anything from her, she told her that she couldn't live without men. But she didn't understand why she always brought her along even when her lover took her out to dinner. She wanted her to spend the weekend at her place all the time, saying that she was afraid of being alone. Whether it was a set-up or not, she sometimes left her alone with her husband, and the two would sit face to face in silence. She had nothing to say to him, this very decent man, he was never without a tie even when he was at home, and his clothes were always pressed, neat as a pin he was. One time, perhaps just this one time, the phone rang before dinner. The woman answered the phone and said that it was an emergency and she had to go out at once to see a patient, and she told her to wait for her to come back no matter what happened. First she heard the car driving away, then she heard the man telling her that she had really beautiful hands. She said he was not the first one to tell her that, but he replied that when he said her hands were beautiful he meant the hands were a reflection of all of a woman's beauty. And she said what was the use even if her hands were more beautiful? He said it depended on whether one knew how to make use of them. *(Lowers her eyelids.)*

She can't remember clearly how the whole thing began or how it ended, it was all so hurried and panicky, then she heard the sound of the car again.

(A female voice laughing coquettishly.)

Woman *(Raises her eyelids.)* She felt that she was compelled to join in with their foolish laughter, this woman and her husband, her husband and her, all of them couldn't stop laughing, as if there was really something laughable or something worth laughing about —

(Laughs nervously, then stops suddenly.) The woman played with her, and she also played with herself. Since she'd used her to spice up their marriage, why shouldn't she return her favour, why not give her a dose of her own medicine? So she phoned up her lover for a date and she made sure that she also knew about it. She knew that she was playing with fire, but she was keen to make the woman jealous. Yet she couldn't prevent herself from falling into her trap, just like sinking into a muddy swamp, the more she struggled to be free the more she'd dirty herself.

She saw this woman coming towards her, she was all dressed in black, her thin lips were closed tightly and emitted a layer of disdain, she ignored her, as if she did not see her. She knew that she was looking her over to check out if she was as low down as she was. She reciprocated with a similarly disdainful look.

(Drops her shawl.) And the woman just walked away.

(Dragging her shawl and walking giddily.) She says the first time she made love to a man and saw the semen flowing down her leg, she felt so disgusted that she almost threw up, now she doesn't have the same reaction any more, the world is in fact a very filthy place, including herself. At first she really wanted to lead a clean life and to love just one person with all her heart, but now she has also learned how to have some fun for herself.

She says all men are dogs, every one of them, but they're not as loyal as the real dogs, and women are worse than

cats, not only do they covet comfort, warmth and a full stomach, they're also vain, jealous, and insatiable.
(Stops and covers her head with her hands.) She says she has sinned deeply, she hasn't gotten anything out of it, and she also hasn't been able to obtain forgiveness.
(Dejected, she drops her hands and clasps them.) She says when she reached puberty, she once thought of becoming a nun in a temple, for a long time she couldn't eat meat, it made her throw up. She says she thought that good or bad she must have faith, that she should be a follower of the Buddha or she should believe in God. Whenever she passed by a church, she'd always be deeply moved by the singing at mass.
She also says she also wanted to have a dog. *(A quiet laugh.)*
Or simply have a baby, it wouldn't make any difference with whom, and she wouldn't even think of having an abortion, she'd keep the baby.
(Restrainedly.) And she'd look after it, she'd give it her undivided attention.
But she also says, *(Shaking her head.)* she's not equipped to be a good mother, and she couldn't find a man to make such a sacrifice worthwhile! She says she's not a good woman either, and she doesn't deserve a good family. It's in her destiny, who knows, when …
(Unattentively.) She's afraid of driving alone at night, always worrying that something might go wrong …

(A masked man in a long black robe appears in the dark.)

Woman She says she sees someone standing in the middle of the highway, and she flashes the headlights again and again —

(Light flashes twice. A masked man appears waving a red semaphore flag with his right hand. Sound of car braking hard.)

Woman Fog is everywhere, she can't see anything in front of her …

(In the dark, the masked man turns around and blocks her way. He raises his left arm and a wide red sleeve falls down.)

Woman She says she understands, he's warning her of the calamity of blood! *(Dodges.)*

(Masked man turns around again, still with his back towards her. He raises his left sleeve in front of her. She dodges one more time, but she still cannot get away from him.)

Woman *(Closes her eyes.)* She says she's not afraid of death, she's only scared that nobody'll know when she's dead. She's even more afraid of a prolonged death, afraid of being crippled, being half dead and half living, nothing is more horrifying than that, it's better to end it once and for all, to wrap it up totally and completely.

(Masked man disappears.)

Woman She feels like she's gliding on a glacier and she can't stop, she sees only a big mass of blackness, any time now she's going to slip into the cracked icy layers and plunge into the deep dark water of death, after she dies all will vanish in an instant like snowflakes in water, the world is such a large place, she's not the only person living in it, she's not important, just let her vanish, let her be forgotten, ignored, and let her end it once and for all … But she still can't free herself from the old grudges, the jealousy, the greed, the worries, and the anxieties. It's not that she doesn't know what the Buddha has said, that the four elements of life are mere emptiness, it's just that she can't free herself from the vanities of human

life. So she prays in a whisper, pleading the merciful Bodhisattva to look after her, to help her to sever her ties with the mortal world.
She says she sees her filthy body rolling in a puddle of muddy water, in broad daylight, on the side of the road, and in public view, everyone's trampling on her. She's covered with scabies, her voice hoarse, she's crawling and begging, but everyone's swearing at her and turns their back on her. *(Slowly opens her eyes.)*

(A nun with an iron-like grey complexion appears. She is enwrapped in a grey kasaya, a Buddhist robe, her eyes lowered and her hair worn in a bun. She is sitting up straight on a futon in a high place with her legs crossed and her palms clasped.)

Woman She says she sees a Bodhisattva, her palms clasped together, sitting on top of a lotus flower platform.
(She approaches slowly and cautiously.) She looks more closely and it's not a lotus flower … she looks again and it's not a Bodhisattva … and she looks even more carefully and it's a nun meditating with her eyes closed and her hands clasped together —
(Inspects closely.) Her brows are slightly knit, and her clasped hands are holding —
(Comes nearer.) a pair of scissors!

(The nun slowly lifts the scissors. Suddenly she stabs them into her own stomach.)

Woman *(Screams.)* God! *(Drops to the ground with her face down.)*

(The nun bends forward and backward, her lips tightly closed.)

Woman *(Creeps forward.)* Why is this happening?
(Looks back.) For no reason at all, she replies flatly.

(The nun bends over and places the scissors in front of her.)

Woman *(Creeps backward.)* What is she doing? There's got to be a purpose.
(Lowers her head.) She's intent on dissecting herself.

(The nun holds her stomach, then offers her intestines on a plate.)

Woman *(Holds her breath, then inhales.)* Is it worth it? Why suffer such pain?

(The nun lowers her head and rubs the intestines.)

Woman *(Gets up on her knees.)* She says she must cleanse the intestines, this big mess of filth and blood.
(Leans forward and watches attentively.) How can they be cleansed? After all, they are so bloody and filthy!
(Takes one step forward and listens.) She says she must cleanse them whether they can or can't be cleansed.
(Pressing.) She knows there's no way she can make them clean, but why does she still insist on cleansing them?

(The nun picks up the intestines and cards them one by one, using her dainty fingers.)

Woman *(Staring for a long time.)* She keeps on cleansing and carding, will it ever end?

(The nun lifts the plate. She disappears instantly just as she is going to hurl the plate at Woman.)

Woman *(Covering her face with both hands.)* She sees countless heads swimming in the sea of bitterness, this boundless sea which has no end. Perhaps the merciful Bodhisattva is to release her from purgatory, but unfortunately she just can't be exalted to paradise and *sukhavat*, the land of the pure. All the while she is wandering between the misty clouds and among the big Chaos, she's looking for her way, hurriedly, yet aimlessly, she feels that she has degenerated to the lower depths. Then she sees the door of a dark and secret valley, behind which a mammoth eye keeps watching her every move, nothing can escape its attention. *(Lays down her arms and stares attentively.)*

(Behind her appears an immeasurably tall and thin man on stilts. He is cloaked in a long black robe which touches the ground, and the tall headgear he has on extends to cover his face. He holds out his long arm and reveals a palm painted with a big, staring eye the size of a copper bell.)

Woman He makes her sweat, he makes her heart jump, he makes her scared, she is always agitated, she can never have peace, she suffers from all kinds of torments, they all stem from the man's eye in the dark. Ever since she was a young girl she had been shy and bashful, mischievous, self-indulgent and even masochistic, she realizes it now, it was all because of him. His staring has been the cause of all her sufferings. Has he become her only *raison d'être*? Is it possible? No! *(Turns and tries to escape.)*

(The eye in the palm of the man in black robe is high above her. It stares at her steadily and never lets go.)

Woman *(Screams.)* No — ! *(Runs.)*

(The man in black does not chase after her. He just raises the painted eye on his hand up high to observe her, as if it is a light shining on her every move. When she stops, he places it behind her head again.)

Woman *(Screams.)* No — *(She kneels on the ground with her face down, her hands holding her head.)*

(The man in black still covers her head with the painted eye on his hand.)

Woman *(Murmuring in rapid succession.)* She says no, she says don't, she says don't say a word, she says it's very good, she says ah, she says she does not want what she says she wants, she says when she says no she doesn't mean no, she says when she says no she doesn't mean yes, she says she is not saying no! She's not saying yes either, she only says, she no longer wants, wants it no longer, no longer wants, no longer can, no longer willing to see this stranger's eye again, it keeps staring at her and never lets go …

(The man in black takes off his headgear and reveals a hideous-looking face. His bloody red tongue is drooling, giving out a screeching laughter resembling the wind tearing open a paper window pane.)

Woman *(Falls on her back and murmurs slowly.)* She says she doesn't know what she was saying, she doesn't know what she really wants to say, maybe she didn't say anything, if what she said is useless, then she might as well not say it, she says she doesn't know what she ought to say, and what else she has not said. But what more can she say?

(The man in black disappears. At the same time a grey white shirt slowly comes up in front of Woman. It faintly reveals itself as the body of a headless woman.)

Woman *(Lifts her head.)* She says she's had enough, she feels drowsy, … *(Lies down.)*

(The headless woman drifts in front of her and extends an arm to stroke Woman's forehead.)

Woman *(Startled, she sits up and covers her eyes with her hand.)* She see it again, this time it's a woman's eye! It's floating and appearing in front of her eyes ... *(Pushes away the hand.)*

(The headless woman draws back her hand.)

Woman *(She stands up and thinks deeply, searching her brain.)* She doesn't know ... if ... she's witnessing ... her own soul leaving her body?

(The headless woman again holds out her hand and waves it menacingly in front of her eyes.)

Woman *(Staring.)* She can even see her own eyes! In these eyes she sees her own naked body again. *(Shakes her head.)*

(The headless woman immediately withdraws her hand and recoils.)

Woman *(Lowers her head to look at herself, startled.)* She saw herself just now, very clearly, naked, lying down and floating in the nether world: she gradually moved up, and then she slowly went down ... when she was going to sink to the bottom, she floated to the surface again ... she was pushed up ... by surge after surge of black waves she couldn't touch or feel ... from an unfathomable depth ... her body moved up again ... and then plunged into a deeper valley of darkness ...

(The headless woman holds out her arm again and waves her palm again in front of Woman's eyes.)

Woman *(Shudders.)* This icy and unfeeling eye's making her shiver with cold, she can't take this prying any more! *(Looks around.)* Who are you? Are you a nightmare? Or are you a ghost? *(Tries to extricate herself from the indistinct headless woman's body.)*

(The headless woman reveals a hand and a leg, teasing and keeping Woman occupied at the same time.)

Woman *(Screams.)* Go away!
(Angered, she tries to grab hold of the hand.) She wants to get rid of this thing!
(Spreads the fingers.) Trample it to pieces!
(Grips the centre of the palm.) Wipe it all out!

(The headless woman flees.)

Woman *(Laughs hysterically, then stops at once.)* Finished … who finished whom?

(The headless woman slowly turns into a floating shirt and disappears at the back of the stage.)

Woman *(Puzzled.)* She has no thoughts, those searching thoughts which once troubled and tormented her, which remained incomprehensible even after long hours of thinking, the various causes and effects, the interminable analyses, the possibilities and conclusions built upon voluminous hypothetical premises and deduced through thousands of inferences and conclusions which are not necessarily reliable. She has no more words, the meaninglessness of meaning which is full of sound and colour, unending eloquence, definition, relatedness, and content. She also has no more feelings, they have all faded away, no matter whether they are hot or cold, light or heavy, visible or invisible, coloured or colourless, sentimental or unsentimental. Everything is enshrouded in the big Chaos, only a glimmer of secret light still exists in her heart, sometimes it's bright and sometimes it's dark, and if she can't even prevent it from disappearing, then all will return to Nothingness …

(The quiet and empty sound of someone beating on a monk's alms bowl, in succession.)

Woman *(On her knees.)* She gradually hears a sound, from far to near, from near to far, like water gurgling, quite intangible, but it flows through her heart …

(The light at the back of the stage becomes brighter, revealing a huge wall on which a bare sapling is indistinctly projected. Only a crooked branch is seen; it becomes increasingly visible.)

Woman *(Kneels down and speaks as if she is singing.)* The world is too small … the world is too large …

(The projected tree branch on the wall extends longer and longer.)

Woman The world is finite … the world is boundless …

(The projection on the wall presently becomes more indistinct.)

Woman The world has a form … the world is elusive … the world is like the wind … the world is like a dream … the world is crude … the world is clamorous … the world is lonely … the world is monotonous …

(An old man holding a walking stick wobbles along and comes close to the wall. He is wearing a greyish white stormcoat, a grey hat and a scarf.)

Woman Is this a story? A romance? A farce? A fable? A joke? An admonishment? An essay not good enough to be a poem, or poetic prose which is not quite an essay? It's not a song, because it has meaning but no spirit, it resembles a riddle, but it has no answer. Is it an illusion, no more than the ramblings in an idiot's dream?

(The old man slowly walks to centre stage where there is a piece of rock. He lowers his head and carefully walks around it.)

Woman Is this about him, about you, about me, about her who is that girl, about her but not her, not about you, not about me, and not about you or all of you, just as what you all see is not her, not me, and not you, it's merely the self, but the me you all see is not me, not her, it's only that so-called self looking at her, looking at me, what more can you or I say?

(The old man finally stops in front of the rock and leans on his walking stick. As he is about to sit down, he looks closely at what is in front of him. It seems that he sees a snowflake falling slowly onto his foot. He takes off the hat and makes a motion to catch the falling snowflake.)

Woman What is the self? Besides these words, these empty, hollow words about nothing, what else is left?

(The old man puts on his hat, wobbles along past the rock and exits.)

Woman *(Opens her lips and takes a deep breath as if she is singing a song.)* — *(But she slowly draws back and lowers her eyes and her head. Bending to lie face down on the floor, she no longer says anything.)*

(The stage is only left with the rock and its shadow, which is changing and moving slowly. Afterwards, the rumbling sound of different kinds of tires is heard. Woman, still lying down, looks like a pile of abandoned clothing in the faint light.)

The End

First draft finished 29 January 1991 in Paris.
Second draft, 18 March 1991.
Final draft, 1 April 1991.

(This play is sponsored by the Bureau of Culture of France. Premiere rights belong to France.)

Some Suggestions on Producing *Between Life and Death*

1. The play starts out with the idea of traditional Chinese theatre in pursuit of a modern form of dramatic performance. It has no intention to create "realism" on stage; quite the opposite, it strives to highlight the feeling of performance and theatricality.
2. The play combines tragedy, comedy, and farce, and it does not seek to exclude acrobatics, dance, or magic. If simplicity is pursued, it can be found in the play's uniform style of narration, which remains unchanged from beginning to end.
3. The narrator in the play, i.e., Woman, should not be regarded as the same as a character. She is both in and out of the character, but still preserving her status as an actress.
4. The language in the play should not strive for excessive naturalness. After all, drama is drama, it is not real life.
5. The actors on stage need not pursue excessive realistic details in their acting. If they can, relying on their deliberations, establish their credibility on stage, communication with the audience will ensue.

The above suggestions are for reference only.

Dialogue and Rebuttal

(A Play in Two Parts)

Time and location uncertain.

An empty stage, some clothing, several objects.

Characters:

A young girl
A middle-aged man
A monk
Two heads: one male, one female

Dialogue and Rebuttal. Theater des Augenblicks, Wien, Austria. Directed by Gao Xingjian. 1992.

Dialogue and Rebuttal. Théâtre Molière, Paris, France. Directed by Gao Xingjian. 1995.

Dialogue and Rebuttal. Théâtre Molière, Paris, France. Directed by Gao Xingjian. 1995.

First Half

(The stage is white [if possible], on which one sees a young girl and a middle-aged man. A black overcoat and a travelling tote bag have been thrown to one side; on the other side towards the back, there lies a bathrobe, which has been tossed down in a heap. At front stage on the right, a wooden fish has been placed on the floor.)*

Girl Finished?
Man Finished.
Girl How was it?
Man Quite good. *(Pause.)* How about you?
Girl Not bad. *(Pause.)* Quite good, I should say.

(Man tries to say something but stops.)

Girl So …
Man What?
Girl Nothing much.
Man Nothing much what?

(Girl smiles slightly.)

Man What are you smiling at?
Girl Nothing.
Man Why are you still smiling?
Girl I'm not smiling.

(Helpless, Man stares at her.
Girl avoids his stare and looks away.)

* A percussion instrument made of a hollow wooden block, used by Buddhist priests to make rhythm while chanting scriptures.

Man	Is it over?
Girl	Isn't it better this way?
Man	Are you always like this?
Girl	What?
Man	With men …
Girl	Of course, you're not the first one.

(Man is taken aback, then laughs out loud.)

Girl	You're all the same.
Man	*(Happily.)* Do you mean we —
Girl	I mean you, you men!
Man	*(Corrects her.)* Men and women!

(Both laugh. Girl stops laughing abruptly. Man also stops.)

Man	What's wrong?
Girl	Nothing.
Man	I'm sorry.
Girl	*(Coldly.)* There's nothing to be sorry about.

(Man walks away and puts on bathrobe.)

Girl	If we had known …
Man	Speak for yourself.
Girl	Hypocrite!
Man	But I love you —

(Immediately Girl starts to laugh out loud. Man also laughs heartily. Monk enters slowly from the right side of the stage. He is bald, wearing a kasaya, a Buddhist robe, and a pair of straw sandals. With his eyes lowered and his palms clasped, he is chanting "Amitabha Buddha"!
Man and Girl stop laughing.
Monk walks to a corner at right stage, turns around until his back is facing the audience, sits down with his legs crossed and starts to beat the wooden fish.

Man and Girl restrain themselves. They both look down, listening carefully to the continuous beating of the wooden fish.)

Girl *(Softly.)* She doesn't understand why, why she followed such a man, but she followed him anyway, following him to …

Man *(Softly.)* She understands everything, she knew it very well, it's all very simple and clear, both had the need …

Girl *(Softly.)* No, she only wanted to know if it could happen … She knew it was possible but not entirely unavoidable …

Man *(Softly.)* Things are bound to happen anytime, anywhere in the world, when something happens, you'll just have to go along with it and have some fun.

Girl *(Softly.)* He may look eager and willing, but she knows very well that he's faking it, if she'd only arched her back and held him off, the whole thing wouldn't have happened.

Man *(Softly.)* One minute early or one minute late, it's all the same. Why put on an act? You and I are no different, that's the way it is.

Girl *(Softly.)* Of course she'd been expecting it, she knew right from the beginning how it would end, but she never thought it would be so sudden, so hasty, and the end would come so fast.

(Monk beats the wooden fish twice.)

Girl Forget it! There's nothing worth celebrating.

Man I didn't say anything.

Girl Better keep it that way.

(Man droops his head.
Monk starts to beat lightly on the wooden fish, chanting softly and continually: "Amitabha Buddha.")

Girl	How come you're not saying anything?
Man	What's there to say?
Girl	Anything you want.
Man	You talk, I'll listen.
Girl	Tell me about yourself.
Man	I'm a man.
Girl	You don't have to tell me that.
Man	What shall I tell you then?
Girl	Don't you know how to talk with people?
Man	I'm afraid you won't like it.
Girl	The problem is you've got to have something to talk about.
Man	Except love —
Girl	Don't talk to me about love!
Man	Tell me, what else is there to talk about with a woman?

(Girl stands up to get her overcoat.)

Man	Where are you going?
Girl	It's none of your business.
Man	I can ask, can't I?
Girl	But you really don't want to know.
Man	Why not? I do want to know.
Girl	You only want a woman's body, you don't understand women, not even a tiny bit.
Man	I don't understand myself either.
Girl	Well said. You're such a pig!
Man	And you?
Girl	You think I'm that low-down?
Man	That's not what I meant.
Girl	Your attitude, it's disgusting!
Man	To tell you the truth, I also disgust myself.
Girl	What a wonderful confession! *(Turns and puts on her overcoat.)*
Man	*(Snatches away her overcoat.)* Don't go!
Girl	What more do you want?

Man Don't go! You've got to listen to me.
Girl You don't have the right to stop me. *(Struggles free.)* I've got to agree first!
Man *(Apprehensive.)* Now that you're here, well, of course I invited you, and I'm very glad —
Girl You — you're an out-and-out bastard!

(Man laughs.)

Girl What are you laughing at?
Man Myself, I'm laughing at myself. What is it to you?
Girl Fine then, let me go.
Man *(Blocking her.)* I love you, really I do!
Girl Stop acting. *(Pushes him away.)*

(Monk picks up wooden fish and beats on it while chanting "Amitabha Buddha." He exits left stage as Girl watches.)

Man I don't understand, it's really hard to figure you out. Tell me, what are you going to do? What is it that you want?
Girl *(Nonchalantly.)* Don't ask me, I don't know. I only, only wanted to know …
Man You already know everything there is to know.
Girl What do I know?
Man That I'm a man. Other men, aren't they the same?
Girl Don't talk to me about men!
Man Then what shall we talk about?
Girl Something interesting, cheerful, something which makes people happy. How stupid can you get?
Man Really?
Girl You only think you're smart.
Man And you're a smart Girl.
Girl Not necessarily. Otherwise I wouldn't have come here with you.
Man In fact I prefer stupid women.

Girl	Because they're submissive, gullible and easy to manipulate, is that it?
Man	No, I'm only talking about myself, that way I can be more relaxed.
	(Monotonous beating on the wooden fish. Monk has not yet entered.)
Man	You want to drink something?
Girl	No, I guess I'd better be going.
Man	It's raining outside.
Girl	*(Listening.)* I don't think so.
Man	If I say it's raining, it's got to be raining.
Girl	Who do you think you are, God?
Man	I can hear it raining. I know all the sounds in and outside this place, the wind, the rain, the water heater, and the leaking toilet, every single one of them. I've owned this place for years.
Girl	Leave me out of your ownership, I belong to me, and me only.
Man	Is that very important?
Girl	I don't know, maybe. Anyway, I still haven't found the right person to belong to.
Man	Obviously I'm not that person.
Girl	At last you've said something intelligent.
Man	Thanks for the compliment.
Girl	Intelligent men are a rare breed nowadays.
Man	Most women are also stupid dingbats. Of course you're an exception.
Girl	Do you really think so?
Man	I never lie, don't you believe me?
Girl	Do you say the same thing to every woman you're with?
Man	You know why I said it to you? It's only because you like to hear people say that about you.
Girl	You're — really — very bad.

(Man laughs, and Girl laughs with him.)

Man Are you sure you don't want anything to drink?

Girl Only if you promise not to mix anything in it. Nothing's worse than that.

Man That's to say you must have done it yourself. I'm sure you must've had tons of strange things happening to you before.

Girl I mean when somebody puts something in your drink and you don't realize it even after you've drunk the darn thing.

Man You mean just now, at the bar? If anybody put anything in it, it was definitely not me.

Girl I meant it happened once, in India.

Man But this certainly isn't India.

Girl I'm saying I went on a trip to India once.

Man With your friend, one of your many boyfriends, if I'm not mistaken?

Girl You might as well save that little bit of intelligence you have for something else. Of course I wasn't alone. Travelling alone can bore you to tears.

Man But if I were going on a trip, I'd never coax my female companion into doing drugs.

Girl It doesn't take any coaxing, does it? We're not kids any more.

Man Of course taking drugs is only human. Tell me, what do you use as a regular?

Girl I'm telling you I don't have the habit!

Man But how come you said when you were in India —

Girl I was in this small village close to the Tibetan border. The sky was real blue, I've never seen such a blue sky before. The clouds were real close, and as I watched them dissipating strand by strand in mid-air, I got dizzy, I couldn't climb up any more. My head was aching, my ears were ringing, as if some guy was ringing a bell like crazy next to my ears ... He wanted to take some shots of the glaciers, you know, my friend was into photography, so I took the car and went back alone to a town where there was a small inn. There was this Indian man standing by the door and he asked me if I wanted any marijuana. He spoke some English, and he led me to his house to get some.

Man And you went with him just like that?

Girl Yes, I did, so what?

Man So what? It's the same as your coming here with me, isn't it?

Girl You sell marijuana too?

Man If you really want some.

Girl You don't know how to listen, do you?

Man Go on!

Girl I don't want to tell you any more.

(Monk enters, one hand holding an alms bowl, the other carrying a small bell. As he chants "Amitabha Buddha" in a low voice, he sprinkles some water into the bowl with his middle finger and rings the bell softly.)

Man Did he force you to take any drugs?

Girl No.

Man Did he make love to you?

Girl He was very gentle and very polite.

(Man wants to say something but stops.)

Girl There were these two women in his house, the younger one must have been his daughter, and they both bowed to me. He asked me to sit down and told the women to bring some wine, it was kind of sweet. The women stood on the side waiting on us, they only watched and smiled at me. I drank two cups in one go, and then they brought in some dried fruit and some sticky rice cakes.

(Girl listens attentively to the ringing of the bell.)

Man Go on, go on.

Girl I didn't know why but somehow I felt sleepy. I think for a whole week I was just lying down, not wanting to move.

Man Did you go back to the inn?

Girl No, I was in his room, on his bed —

Man Naked?

Girl Is that important?

Man When you're telling a story, you've got to give details.

Girl Anyway, my body didn't seem to belong to me, my hands and feet were too heavy to move, and my mind was totally blank … But I was still conscious …

Man Weren't you scared?

Girl The two women would come in every now and then, whenever he was not there they would come to give me something to eat or drink. I wanted to speak and scream, but they didn't say anything except to touch and stroke me all the time. Then without knowing it I fell asleep again until he came back and woke me up …

Man Did he rape you?

Girl No, I think … I don't know … Maybe I accepted it, I also, enjoyed … Maybe I wanted it too, there was no way out. Do you find this exciting?

Man Not really, I mean, he ruined you.

Girl Didn't you?

Man It's not the same, under the circumstances, he could have abused you until you died and no one would know anything about it.

Girl He was very gentle from beginning to end, he didn't force me at all, I gave him all he wanted without holding anything back … You know, I gave him everything I had until I became a total void … Except that after one week, I realized later that it'd been a whole week, it was either daytime or at night when I found myself completely paralysed, I didn't even want to move a finger, the room had only one oil lamp and it smelled real bad.

Man Maybe it was burning tallow, or animal fat, a kind of beef oil.

Girl Have you been there as well?

Man I read about it in some travel book on Tibet. Didn't you say the place was right next to Tibet?

Girl Uh-huh …

(The bell stops ringing.)

Man Go on, why have you stopped talking?

Girl What else should I talk about?

Man Talk about the smell.

Girl As I was saying, that was when I woke up for the first time, afterwards I didn't smell it any more, I only felt I was warm all over, I thought, I must have had that smell on me as well. Afterwards I washed again and again but I just couldn't get rid of …

Man That greasy muttony smell?

Girl No, the smell of his body.

Man Stop it! I've had enough.

(Monk has finished sprinkling and bends down as if to splash water onto the ground. He exits, holding up his sleeves with his hands.)

Girl *(Collects her thoughts and turns to look at him.)* Why?

Man There's no why.

Girl You don't like what I said?

Man I'm listening.

Girl What do you want to listen to?

Man It's up to you, whatever you want to say.

Girl You want me to say that I'm horny all the time?

Man You said it, not me.

Girl Don't you want every woman to be horny?

Man Women, they're actually like that.

Girl That's only in a man's imagination.

Man Believe me, men are no different.

Girl Then what's there to be curious about?

Man It's just the sex that's different.

Girl How about between one woman and another, are they the same to you?

Man Can't you change the subject?

Girl Shall we talk about the smell then?

Man To hell with the smell!

Girl You're really no fun!

Man What? Fine, fine, let's talk about the smell then.

Girl I don't want to talk about it any more.

(Monk enters tumbling in the air. He has taken off his kasaya *and is dressed in a casual jacket and pants. He holds his breath and stands motionlessly kungfu style.)*

Man *(Looks towards Monk and speaks softly.)* You can never understand what really goes on in a woman's mind. *(Loudly.)* An interesting story, very interesting. *(Turns to look at Girl.)* How come he didn't kill you?

Girl Why?

Man There's no why.

Girl All you men want to do is to possess, possess, and possess until everything's all busted and gone! *(Sighs.)* Men are so selfish, they only think of themselves.

Man Men this, men that, why do you have to keep babbling on about men?

Girl Aren't you one of them?

Man If anything, I'm still a person, a real, tangible, living human being.

Girl But you haven't been treating me like one. Let me tell you, I'm not just some plaything for venting your sexual desires. And one woman is different from another —

Man When we first started, we were talking in general terms, now it's different —

Girl How different?

Man Now it's you and me, and not men and women in the general sense. We're face to face with each other, we can see each other, and we've had some contact, I don't just mean physical contact, we're bound to have some feelings, some understanding of each other, because we're two living human beings.

Girl Wait a minute. You mean when you made love to me just now, you were treating me like your so-called women in the general sense, in other words, just a plaything.

Man Don't talk like that, because you and I were in the same boat, weren't we? We were like two people possessed —

Girl Let me finish. You didn't even ask me my name, as soon as we entered the door, you ...

Man Don't forget, you didn't exactly refuse me.

Girl That's true, but ...

Man I see, my sincerest apologies.

(Monk successfully completes a handstand. Then he tries to take away one hand to attempt a one-hand handstand, but at once he loses his balance and hurriedly lands his feet on the ground.)

Man *(Softly.)* What's wrong?

Girl *(At a loss.)* Nothing.

(Silence. Monk again attempts a one-hand handstand.)

Man *(Takes a look at her tote bag.)* Tell me, what happened afterwards? How about that friend of yours?

Girl We split up a long time ago.

Man So now you're on your own and you're wandering all over the globe?

Girl I've been looking for a companion, but none lasted.

Man Yes, nowadays it's the in thing to do, like fashion, which tends to change from one year to another, or from one season to the next.

Girl *(Looks around.)* You don't look like you're living alone, eh?

Man Of course I've had, how should I put it, a wife? What's the matter? You don't like that word?

Girl I can't stand being tied down.

Man Well, I guess we're no different from each other there.

(Both laugh heartily. Monk, who is doing a handstand, again takes away one hand and fails once more. He hurriedly lands his feet on the ground.)

Man *(Very carefully.)* May I ask your name?

Girl Is that important? Try to remember it well and make sure that you don't get it wrong.

Man Why? Somebody did?

Girl I hope you're not as bad.

(Both laugh somewhat bitterly.
Monk kneads his hands and attempts a handstand for the third time.)

Girl Maria or Anna, which one do you prefer?

Man The question is which one is your real name?

Girl If I told you it's Maria, then would I surely be Maria?

Man That's a real problem. But if I called you Anna, you'd still be you and not someone called Anna, therefore, you really shouldn't worry too much about it.

Girl *(Dryly.)* I don't want to be a stand-in for somebody else!

Man Of course. A name is just a code, what's important is not the sign itself but the actual person behind that sign. You can call me whatever you like, even if it's some name you're familiar with, or some name that accidentally slips from your tongue, anything, I don't think I'd mind.

Girl	I don't want to waste any more time on this subject. I don't want to know your name either, it's useless to me. And don't bother making up a fake name and then forget about it in short order. When it's over, it's over.
Man	But we've just begun, how could it be over so soon? Now that you've agreed that a name isn't important and that it's a real burden, let's get to the important part: between you and me …
Girl	Between a man and a woman? How interesting!
Man	The whole thing would become more pure, and the relationship more sincere and more real, don't you think?
	(Monk completes a handstand and takes away one hand, but he fails again just when it looks as if he is going to succeed. He exits dejected.)
Girl	You really can't get it.
Man	*(Quite Interested.)* Get what?
Girl	Impossible, it's impossible. I mean, a woman's heart.
Man	If I guessed right, you're talking about love, aren't you? That of course is a very delicate subject.
Girl	I'm talking about emotion, which you can't possibly understand.
Man	Try me, you never know.
Girl	How?
Man	Between you and me —
Girl	We've tried that before.
Man	Try again. If it doesn't work, we'll just try again.
Girl	*(On guard.)* No, you can never have it, you can never have anything!
Man	Just now I was too rushed, really.
Girl	*(Smiles coldly.)* You're always in a rush.
Man	*(Somewhat repentant.)* Can I make it up to you in any way?
Girl	Don't think that because you've had a lot of women … You don't know women, you'll never be loved, it's in your destiny.

(Girl turns around. Monk enters carrying a wooden stick. He looks around for something.)

Man *(Sarcastically.)* What's love? Try to explain it to me.
Girl It can't be explained.
Man There's no harm in trying.
Girl There are things you can explain, and there are things you can't. Don't you know that?
Man Of course I do, but I still want to know about love.
Girl What a fool!
Man Then go find yourself someone who isn't.
Girl Aren't we discussing something? And the topic is love?
Man We just made love, do we have to discuss it too?
Girl Isn't it true that you like to discuss all kinds of things?
Man Well, go find someone that you can discuss with and discuss them all you want!
Girl Why are you so hotheaded?

(Monk finally finds a spot and tries very carefully to stand the stick up on the floor. But once he removes his hand, the stick falls and he at once grabs it and holds on to it. He turns to find another spot.
Man looks at Monk and can't help feeling a bit depressed.)

Girl Answer me, are you or are you not a philosopher?
Man Philosophy can go to hell.
Girl You're such an overgrown kid. *(Embraces his head.)* Be careful, I'm beginning to like you.
Man Isn't that nice?
Girl It's very dangerous.
Man *(Gets away from her.)* Why?
Girl Dangerous for you and for me.
Man As far as I'm concerned, if you want to stay then stay, you won't be in my way. I've got everything here, a bathroom, a kitchen, a bedroom and a bed, of course, there's only one bed, but there's everything that a woman needs.

Girl Do you have shampoo, make-up and a night gown too?

Man Yes, if you need them, except underwear, you know, everyone is a different size. Make yourself at home, as a matter of fact, I won't mind if you treat this place like your own home —

Girl As long as none of your girlfriends is coming?

Man At least none is coming right now. You can stay as long as you like, it's free. When you want to eat something, just go to the fridge and help yourself, and don't bother to pay me.

Girl I can't stay with a man all the time.

Man There's no need to. Anyway, if you want to go, it'll be very simple.

Girl And very cheap.

Man I'm doing this out of good will, you can stay if you don't have anywhere else to go, that is, if you really want to stay.

Girl Thanks, I don't live off men, so you don't have to worry about that.

Man I'm not worrying. I can even give you a key, just leave it behind when you go.

Girl Do you entertain women like this all the time?

Man Not all the time, only sometimes, it's the same with any other single man, there's nothing unusual about it.

Girl What's unusual is — Is there anything that's unusual about you?

Man Well, I do have a strange habit. I can't stand people shaving their armpits in front of me. Don't get me wrong, I'm not against hair or anything. We're born with it, and it's natural and it can be very exciting. And of course, I have no objection to a woman dressing herself up.

Girl For me, I can't stand anyone snoring beside me.

Man Fortunately I'm not that old yet, well, at least I haven't noticed it, and no women have left me because of it.

Girl Why did they leave you then?

Man It's very simple, either I couldn't stand them or they couldn't stand me.

Girl May I ask why couldn't they stand you?

Man I like eating raw garlic.

Girl It shouldn't be much of a problem, as long as you brush your teeth afterwards.

Man Another thing is probably that I don't have patience, and I just can't stand neurotic behaviour.

Girl Well, there's no woman who isn't neurotic.

Man And you too?

Girl It depends on the person and the time. *(Silence.)* What else shall we talk about?

Man *(Scrutinizing her.)* Are you still at school? I'm just asking. What I mean is, you're so young.

Girl You want to see my diploma or something? Are you planning to hire me?

Man Come to think of it, I might. But how shall I put it, I can't afford to pay you.

Girl I don't want to be a maid to wait on people, I don't do cleaning, and I hate washing dishes.

Man I don't entertain at home much, unless it's some young girl like you. What I mean to say is, sometimes I do need to use the desk at night. If you're still at school and you've got homework to do, there could be a slight problem.

Girl Do you write? Are you a writer?

Man *(Hurriedly.)* No, we're living in an age of women writers, every woman likes to write something. All men's books have already been written. And when men write about women it's just not as realistic as women writing about themselves.

Girl Do you read only books written by women?

Man Not necessarily. I've read some. As for women writing about men … How shall I put it? …

Girl Too exciting? Or too neurotic?

Man Too sissyish. I don't mean to criticize, let's leave criticism to the critics, it's their job. What I mean is, women don't understand men, just as men don't understand women.

Girl If I were to write about men —

Man They'd all be bastards?

Girl Not necessarily.

Man Even worse than bastards?

Girl They don't even qualify, they'd just be cowards.

Man *(Hesitantly.)* Actually, it'd be quite interesting if you were to write like that. Have you written anything yet?

Girl I want to write, but I know I'll never be a writer.

Man Whoever writes is a writer, you don't need a diploma to be one. It's as simple as that.

Girl But who's going to support me? I've got to pay my rent first, you know.

Man Of course, you can't live on writing. Nowadays writing has become a luxury and an extravagant habit.

Girl You seem to like literature, don't you? Do you prefer poetry or fiction?

Man Why just poetry or fiction? Only women read those nowadays. Oh, I beg your pardon, what I mean is —

Girl Why apologize? *(Teasing him.)* I'm no poet and I can't write fiction, I'm not any of those, I'm just a woman.

Man Thank God for that. These days men are always busy earning money and making deals. On weekends? Well, they either have business engagements or they can't wait to go away with their girlfriends. Only women can afford to have the leisure and the time to read.

Girl Not all women read, they're also busy living. We only live once, don't you think?

Man I know. Nowadays, anyone who writes a book has to read it himself.

Girl You don't look like a businessman. Tell me, do you write books just for yourself to read?

Man I don't have the luxury. Once in a while, I'll take a look at the books other people have written.

Girl May I ask what kind of books do you read?

Man Books on politics.

Girl Wow! Are you a politician? Are you involved in politics in any way?

Man Thank God no, I think it's better to leave the politicians alone.

Girl Then why do you still read about politics then?

Man I only read political memoirs.

Girl Then you must be studying history, right?

Man Not exactly studying. I only want to see how the politicians can lie with a straight face, cheat on one another, swindle, and play with public opinion as if it were a card game. And you know, they'll only let out a little bit of truth in their memoirs after they've been kicked out. And like you said, we only live once, right? So don't let them take you for a ride.

Girl Please don't talk to me about politics. All men like politics, 'cause they want to show people they have the talent and the intelligence to run the ship of the state.

Man Relax, it's more interesting to talk about women when you're with a woman.

Girl You've got to know how, otherwise you'll just make a real pest of yourself.

Man Of course, flirting is an art, or the art of living even. It's a lot more interesting than playing cards. Cards are dead and people are living creatures, and they're all different from one another, don't you think?

Girl Are you done yet?

Man Yes.

(Monk finally manages to stand the stick up. Man and Girl both look at him.)

Girl What else shall we talk about?

Man We'll keep on talking about women of course.

Girl Generally, or shall we pick a specific one?

Man Why don't you talk about yourself? I want to get to know you, but please don't mention that India thing again.

Girl You wouldn't believe me if I did.
Man Have you been feeding me lies?
Girl Haven't you lied before? Haven't you ever cheated on your wife? Don't lie to me!
Man Of course I did, I never said I was a saint.
Girl Exactly. You know why women cheat? It's only because they've learned the tricks from men first.
Man You mean people cheat on you all the time?
Girl Cheating is a form of self-defence.
Man Does that include cheating on oneself?
Girl Everyone cheats, otherwise it'd be impossible to live.
Man You seem to be living quite painfully, don't you?
Girl Everyone's in pain. You don't look like you're too happy yourself.
Man Can't you change the way you talk?
Girl How? How should I change it? C'mon, tell me.
Man You're always so defensive, it's so hard to talk to you.
Girl The same here. It's really tiring talking to you.
Man You're like that too. Now I've got a headache.
Girl *(Somewhat sympathetic.)* Come on, let's change to a lighter subject, something that'll cheer us up.

(Having completed his previous stunt, Monk rubs his hands and starts to become enthusiastic again. He takes out an egg from inside his robe and tries to stand the egg on the tip of the stick.)

Man What else shall we talk about? Something in praise of women or what? But everything that has to be said has been said already, there's really nothing new left to say any more. Perhaps I should say that you're young and beautiful? That you're charming and attractive? Or that you're sexy? By the way, these are not empty words, and they're not meant to flatter you or to make you feel good, they're all true.
Girl My dear, you seem to be more lovely when you're not

using your brain. For once can't you just honestly talk about yourself? Tell me, how do you spend your time?

Man You mean right now?

Girl Yes, at this very moment —

Man Make love, if someone's willing.

Girl What if there's nobody around? Then what would you do?

Man I dream, when I'm doing nothing I always dream. Dreams are more real than reality itself, they're closer to the self. Don't you think so? *(Lights a candle.)*

Girl Me too, I dream almost every day. Tell me about your dreams.

Man One day, I dreamt that I was sinking into the ground, my whole body was trapped deep inside, there were two extremely high walls on either side of me, or should I say huge crags, no matter how hard I tried I just couldn't climb over them and get out … What are you laughing at?

Girl You made it all up, you're only thinking about women.

Man You can't really tell what happens in your dream, can you? If you're dreaming things happen in no particular order and you're confused, when you wake up and try to talk about it, you'd simply lay it on and fabricate, or you'd deceive yourself, and later when you tell your dream to somebody, you'd add on your own fantasies for self-gratification. In a dream, you're only living in your feelings at the time, that's all. *(Looks at Monk.)* There's no plot, just narration.

(The egg falls from the tip of the stick onto the ground. Monk takes another egg from inside his robe and tries patiently to stand it on the tip of the stick again.
Girl smiles surreptitiously.)

Man It's just wishful thinking trying to tell a dream.

Girl You're an idiot.

Man That's right. You're you only when you're dreaming.

Girl *(Steps back to inspect him.)* Are you saying that at this very moment you aren't real?

Man Who cares if I'm real or not? You're only concerned with how you feel, right? Only feelings can be real.

Girl Now you're beginning to scare me.

Man You weren't scared when that Indian guy raped you, and you're telling me that you're scared now? *(Walking closer to her.)*

Girl Don't even try, I'm going.

Man You're not going anywhere.

Girl Don't try to intimidate me.

Man Just playing. You get scared easily when we play for real.

Girl Because it's not fun.

Man Well then, why don't you tell me how we should play?

Girl It's got to be more relaxing, more cheerful. But you just keep annoying people.

Man All right. Whatever you say, I'm game. Tell me, how do you want to play?
(Puts down the candlestick.)

(Again the egg falls and rolls on the ground. Monk takes out a third egg from inside his robe. He rubs it in his palms and then places it on the tip of the stick.)

Girl Fine. Take off your clothes for me, take them all off! That's what you want, right?

(Monk turns his head as if to take a glance at them.)

Girl I can't stand your bathrobe, don't you think it's ugly? It makes me sick!

(Monk turns back his head to continue with his task.
Man takes off his bathrobe and throw it on the ground.)

Man Okay, now it's your turn.

Girl Can't you put it more gently?

Man How?

Girl Do I have to teach you that too?

Man When you're stark naked you're more natural, and more beautiful.

Girl *(Sighs.)* Your trouble is you're lonely, so lonely that you're dying for someone to give you a little tender loving care.

(When Monk takes his hand away, the egg falls rolling onto the ground as before.
Girl takes off her blouse. Monk keeps looking at the egg, not knowing what to do.)

Man *(At once getting excited.)* You're a real knockout!

Girl You only found out just now? It sure took you long enough. You really don't know how to appreciate what you've got, or how to cherish it.

Man It's still not too late. Come over here … No, go stand over there!

Girl Where?

Man On the opposite side. Look at me, and put your hands down.

(Girl drops her hands and laughs, facing him.
Monk sighs and again takes out an egg from inside his robe.)

Man Spread your arms like a bird in flight. You're a bird, a living and breathing big bird. Spread your arms for me!

Girl What if I don't?

(Monk is persisting, still trying to place the egg on the tip of the stick.)

Man When I say spread, spread. Don't you like birds?

Girl You're a bird, not me.

Man Spread your arms!

Girl No.

(Man and Girl are locked in a stalemate.
Frustrated, Monk cracks the egg on the tip of the stick, and the egg shell finally stands on the stick.)

Girl *(Begging.)* Say something nice to me.

Man I want you … Close your eyes.

(Girl reluctantly spreads her arms and closes her eyes.
Monk rubs his hands and exits satisfied.)

Man *(Man quietly circles to the back of Girl.)* On your knees now. *(Takes a knife from inside his bathrobe.)*

Girl No, you're disgusting. *(Reluctant, half kneeling and half sitting down.)*

Man Put your hands on the floor. We're playing a game, are we not? *(He hides the knife behind him and pulls her hands down on the floor and holds them there with his other hand.)*

Girl *(Frees herself from his hand.)* No, I'm not a dog! You're really sick. *(Gets up.)*

Man Are we playing or not? You wanted it, and you started it first —

Girl That's enough. Can't you just use your imagination?

Man *(Coaxing her.)* All right, then you'll be a fish, now try to imagine you're a fish, a bouncy and jumping mermaid fish dragged out of the water and landed on dry land, okay?

Girl To hell with you. I'm not your plaything, go play with yourself.

Man But you started it first. After you've got people interested, you turn around and say you don't want to play any more. It just isn't fair.

Girl You make me sick! You understand?

Man Has it ever crossed your mind that you make people

sick also? Everybody's sick of everybody! Everyone is sickening!

Girl You're just a log! A rotten log, rotten to the core!

(Man and Girl face each other in silence. Suddenly Girl laughs out loud. Man is dejected. He quietly puts the knife back inside his bathrobe.)

Girl Dance for me!

Man *(Confounded.)* What?

Girl Are you playing or not?

Man Forget it, let's knock it off. I'm not interested any more.

Girl But now I am. You forced me to play when I wasn't interested, didn't you? *(Pleading with him.)* Please, dance for me, just one dance, okay?

Man I don't know how to.

Girl Then what do you know? Or do you only know how to think?

Man Don't talk to me about thinking or not thinking.

Girl Then go and stand over there, you do know how, don't you? Please, please do me a favour, go and stand over there.

Man Where?

Girl There, stand there like Michaelangelo's David, but act like you're thinking.

Man *(Goes to the other side reluctantly.)* You act like one of those woman executives. Do you enjoy ordering men around?

Girl It'd be nice if I could. Listen, David represents man at his best, I'm making it easy for you.

Man You're an unqualified witch!

Girl That's it! Raise your hands for me, just like a Michaelangelo.

Man Michaelangelo was gay.

(Girl laughs heartily. Man reluctantly raises his hands and laughs.)

Girl I like being gay. Nobody asked you to become impotent!

Man Gosh, what a she-devil!

Girl I'm going to hurt you, hurt you real bad! Run, I say run!

(Continuous beating of the cymbal. Monk still has not entered.)

Man How?

Girl Run in a circle around me!

Man Do you want everyone to run around you?

Girl Aren't you the same? You won't be happy until you turn every woman into your slave. *(Very excited.)* Raise your hand now like you're throwing a javelin.

Man *(Screaming.)* I'm not a model!

Girl Why is it that only women can be models? Now try it and see what it's like! Didn't you say this is the age of women? Who told you to lose your sense of imagination? Run! I say run!

Man *(Running and shouting.)* If a woman became God, the world would turn into a pandemonium, much more horrible than it is now. I don't know, maybe it'd be better, but it'd more likely be much worse, like some chick's tantrum!

Girl So what if for once we were God Almighty? *(Blocks his way.)* Blindfold yourself!

Man Stop fooling around, I beg you. Okay?

Girl Oh, so you can fool around but I can't, is that what you're saying? If we're going to fool around, let's fool around together, you and I, until we both can't take it any more!

(Girl takes the chance to strip Man of his clothes. He kisses her, taking advantage of the situation. She wraps the clothes around his head, covering his eyes.
Monk enters beating a gong.
Girl hurriedly takes out a pair of pantyhose from her handbag, ties it around Man's clothes and pushes him away.)

Girl Over here.

Man I'm going to get you! You little devil you!

(Man chases after Girl. Both of them run in circles.)

Man You pigfeet — you dirty little rat — where are you?

Girl Here I am ... *(Quietly picks up the overcoat.)*

Man You won't get away this time! *(Jumps on Girl.)*

(Just as he is about to catch her, she sticks out a leg and he trips and misses her.
Monk is stunned and exits.)

Man *(Yanks off her pantyhose and throws it on the ground.)* What the hell are you doing?

Girl *(Giggling.)* Isn't this what you want? Isn't it?

Man *(Irritated.)* You must be out of your mind. Are you crazy or something?

Girl You're crazy, you're sick, not me! All you want is sex, sex, sex and getting yourself turned on. It's your sexual fantasy, not mine.

Man *(Grabs her at once.)* Now let's see if you can go on bullshitting!

Girl *(Pushes him away.)* Get away from me! You want fantasies, right? Go fantasize yourself! *(Picks up the handbag.)*

Man *(Knocks her to the ground.)* Don't even think of running away! You'll never make it! *(Fishes out the knife from inside his bathrobe.)* I'll kill you first!

Girl *(Startled. She moves back and tries to block him with her handbag.)* What? Are you crazy or something? Stay away from me!

Man *(Forces his way towards her and grabs her handbag.)* Slut! Whore! You want to run? Go ahead and try! — *(Kisses her by force.)*

Girl *(Seizes a pencil case, wallet, underwear, notebook, book, make-up, a set of keys and other unimaginable sundry items from* *her handbag and throws them at Man one after another.)* No, don't! Don't —!

Man Stop — it! *(Grabs her.)* I'm going to make a whore out of you yet!

Girl I'm no —

Man I don't care if you aren't, you still have to pretend once —

Girl No! Get away from me! Let — me — go —! Let me go! Let go! I — don't — *(Becomes hysterical and strikes him again and again.)*

Man *(Letting go of her, stunned.)* I was just fooling around. Didn't you start it first? You started the whole thing, didn't you?

(Man puts down the knife and walks away perplexed.

Monk enters, beating the wooden fish in his hand. He chants loudly:
"A … mi … tabha! Great mercy, great pity, Amitabha! Sympathy … goodness! Virtuous men, virtuous women, purify your hearts! And in your highest voices, recite the Five Wisdoms Sutra! Since the time of the ancients, such a doctrine, this doctrine of thoughtlessness, has been upheld in sudden enlightenment, and in gradual enlightenment. The body is without form, the essence without entity."

Girl covers her face with her hands and crouches down slowly. She starts to sob.
When Man hears her sobbing, he shakes his head and frowns, finally turns around and returns to her side. He stretches out his hand and bends down to stroke her head and neck.)

Girl Don't touch me, I have no feelings … *(Starts to wail loudly.)* No feelings! No feelings! No feelings …

(Man jumps on Girl. She falls onto the ground and wails and cries continuously.

Monk walks slowly to front stage and sits down, his legs crossed. He beats the wooden fish and chants the sutra: "Monks of the Buddha, nuns of the Buddha, and man disciples, woman disciples, and the wise men in all directions, they all subscribe to the Law. The Law is neither long nor short, one moment is ten thousand years. No being is not being, all directions are before your eyes.

"The extremely big is the same as small, all boundaries forgotten; the extremely small is the same as big, all limits disappeared. Presence is absence, absence is presence. Anything that is not so, it is not worth keeping. One is all, all is one. If this could be so, how could any worry remain unresolved?")

Man This world, it's all gone crazy,

Girl *(Mumbling.)* Just because of loneliness,

Man *(Whispering.)* Just because of boredom,

Girl Just because of thirst and hunger,

Man Just because of desires,

Girl It's unbearable,

Man Just because it's unbearable,

Girl Just because it's unbearable to be a woman,

Man Just because to be a man is unbearable,

Girl Just because not only being a woman but also being human,

Man A living human being, a body of flesh and blood,

Girl It's only to have feelings,

Man It's only to resist death,

Girl Just because of the fear of death,

Man Just because the yearning for life,

Girl It's only to experience the fear of death,

Man It's only to prove the existence of the self,

Girl It's only for the reason of just because —

Man Just because of the reason of it's only for —

Girl It's only because just because …
Man No therefore there is no purpose.

(Monk starts to turn the beads of his Buddhist rosary, reciting the sutra in silence. The sound of the wooden fish becomes increasingly lighter, and Monk closes his eyes in meditation. Sound of wooden fish fades completely.)

Girl A sound, sharp and piercing …
Man A greenish grey sun, gyrating in the dark …
Girl Dead at knife-point, dead in space …
Man Motor cars howling ferociously —
Girl And the fingers are very cruel!
Man Zooming past, zooming, zooming and gone …
Girl Void and empty, all over the body …
Man A swollen leather bag …
Girl Flowing from the inside of the body to the outside …
Man Window panes shaking furiously forever …
Girl Up and down and all over, no more existence, no more weight, all shapes have vanished —
Man Only hear something breathing —
Girl Water's dripping, where is it?
Man *(Listening.)* No sound.
Girl Still dripping, and still dripping …
Man Any more troubles?
Girl Not turned off properly … How come it can't be turned off completely?
Man Turn off what completely?
Girl The tap, the tap in the bathroom.
Man Let it drip.
Girl Go turn it off, I beg you.
Man *(Sits up and observes her.)* The doors, the windows and all the taps have been shut off properly!
Girl But I'm still uneasy …
Man You're hypersensitive.
Girl I'm always frightened, always afraid …

Man What's there to be afraid of?

Girl Afraid of death, afraid of dark houses, I've been afraid of staying in a room by myself since I was young, even when I was sleeping, I had got to turn on the light. First I was afraid of growing up, then I was afraid of men, and afraid of becoming a woman, a real woman, of course I'm not afraid of that any more, but I'm still afraid, afraid that someone might just suddenly kill me, just like that, with no particular reason …

Man *(Becoming alert.)* What are you talking about? Who wants to kill you?

Girl I don't know, but I'm afraid, there's always a certain fear, always afraid that … When I was eighteen I was afraid of being twenty, when I was twenty I was afraid of being over twenty, and after twenty I felt that death was getting closer day by day.

Man *(Relieved.)* According to what you said, it's the same with everybody. But you're still young.

Girl When I'm alone at night I'm always jumpy. I'm afraid of weekends, afraid of spending the days by myself. I'm afraid of mornings, afraid that someday crinkles might appear at the corner of my eyes, I'm afraid, afraid that someday I'll suddenly grow old.

Man Tell me, how old are you really?

Girl I'm close to twenty six, I'm not young any more.

Man What is twenty six? I was still a kid when I was twenty six. I didn't even know how to fart properly, let alone knowing women.

Girl But that's you, to a woman, once she reaches thirty it spells death, and that's the truth!

Man According to you, I should have been dead a long time ago, shouldn't I?

Girl For a man, life begins at thirty, but for a woman, the best time of her life is over and done with already.

Man There's no need to worry. You're still in your prime, still fresh as a daisy —

Girl Really? Am I still fresh?

Man When did you first do it? Your first time?

Girl Let me think, sixteen, no, at that time I was … only fourteen.

Man Did you do it with a classmate? Or with a dirty old man?

Girl No, my teacher, a physical education teacher.

Man The bastard!

Girl He told me that I had a good figure, that I had long legs and I was agile, so he would give me special lessons. He invited me to his place and gave me some candies, I was very fond of candies then. He told me to take off my clothes. You see, there wasn't anybody else at his place. Then he told me to demonstrate some movements for him to look at and he would correct me. First he held my waist to help me press my legs down, then … he … raped me.

Man *(Letting go of her.)* You only thought he did?

Girl At the time I felt … I also wanted to know something about my body …

Man And since then you've been going all out to use yourself up, to consume it all. (*Sits up.*)

Girl Aren't you also using yourself up? And you think that's love, don't you? Go pull a fast one on some wide-eyed teenybopper!

Man You're always flirting, has it ever occurred to you that you've got some kind of psychological problem?

Girl Problem? Everyone has a problem, including you, me, everyone. Have you seen how men stare at women? The look in your eyes, the way you whisper, the way you behave, and the way you leer at women's clothing, aren't they all meant to encourage women, so that they'll make themselves sexy for men? The bras, panties, necklaces, jewellery, and perfume, by the way, men also use perfume, only the brand names are different, aren't they all designed by men and for men's excitement? Women themselves don't need these things at all.

Movies, television, fashion, advertisements, pop songs, bars and nightclubs, is there anything that's not meant to turn people on? You men all want to turn women into playthings, and you, you're not much better.

Man I knew it, I knew it. You're a feminist!

Girl You don't know anything. I'm no believer in feminism or any other ism. I'm a living human being, I only want to live life to the fullest as a woman.

Man Wonderful! So why are you still complaining?

Girl I'm not complaining, I'm only saying that I'm afraid, afraid that all these will disappear …

Man That's why you're trying desperately to seize every moment?

Girl Aren't you doing the same thing? Whenever you see an opportunity, you never let it go.

Man *(Stands up.)* Everybody is sick, the whole world is sick.

(Girl tenderly caresses Man's leg, her face leaning close to him.
Monk lifts his head and beat softly on the wooden fish.)

Man *(Looks at Monk and talks to himself.)* We'll all be used up before we die.

(Monk holds up the wooden fish and beats on it. The sounds becomes louder. Monk exits.)

Girl Don't leave me.

Man *(Stroking her head.)* I'm right by your side, am I not?

Girl I don't have anybody to rely on, you wouldn't understand even if I told you.

Man You and I are in the same boat, the world is a desert.

Girl I'm afraid that tomorrow …

Man Tomorrow, tomorrow, it's still early …

Girl No one's coming?

Man Tomorrow, no one.

Girl Do I have your word for it?

Man You're a silly girl.

Girl A silly woman.

Man And a silly child.

Girl Do you deserve to have a child?

(Man is silent. He just holds her head and looks at it closely.)

Girl You must be thinking of something. Don't look at me like that! *(Pushes him away.)*

Man What's wrong with that?

Girl You know exactly what's wrong.

Man *(Letting her go.)* I don't understand you, I just don't understand what goes on in your mind.

Girl Is that important?

Man *(Somewhat troubled.)* I can't decide whether or not I should love you.

Girl It's the same here.

Man You mean you love me?

Girl Don't take it too seriously. *(Sincerely.)* At least, I like you.

Man You've set my mind at ease. I like you too, really.

Girl Since when?

Man In the pub, when I caught sight of you right away. Remember that corner with the light hanging on the wall? You were sitting there, your face towards the entrance.

Girl *(Smiling.)* And you came over to me just like that, without even asking, right?

Man The light was shining on your neck … in the shadow, I couldn't quite see your eyes.

Girl It's not nice to look at other people's eyes.

Man Tell me, what should I look at then?

Girl Anyway, you shouldn't look without asking, it's very rude.

Man I was only looking at a shadow, that soft shadow in between your breasts. And then the old black guy on the stage was singing some jazz song, it was so melancholy.

	When I sat down in the chair opposite you, you didn't say anything, did you?
Girl	For a girl you didn't know, you really shouldn't have looked at her that way.
Man	But you didn't exactly refuse me at the time. You didn't have a date, you were only waiting, waiting for that someone, until he sat down opposite you, weren't you?
Girl	Remember, you just said something very pleasing to the ear.
Man	Good, then I'll keep my mouth shut.
Girl	You know, … today is my birthday.
Man	Why didn't you tell me earlier? Let's celebrate!
Girl	We did already. *(Silence. Then softly.)* Just now.
Man	That was your birthday celebration?
Girl	Yes, my twenty sixth birthday. I was born at midnight, what time is it?
Man	I know now, you just wanted to prove that you're still young, still attractive to men.
Girl	There's no need to prove anything. All women at my age are still attractive. I just wanted …
Man	What?
Girl	To wait for a miracle.

(Girl does not say anything. Man walks away.)

Man	I didn't know. At first I thought …
Girl	I'm exactly what you thought I was, don't you see? *(Pulls up her dress.)*
Man	*(Begging.)* Fine, fine. Stop flirting, please …
Girl	Who's flirting? Tell me, how much were you prepared to pay me?
Man	Really, you devil you!
Girl	No, not a devil, but a cock-teasing goddess! Your idol, your whore. *(Opens her arms to him.)*
Man	Don't abuse yourself.
Girl	You did already. Stop acting like you're a gentleman.

Man All right then. You want a cheque or something? A ring? Or a necklace?

Girl Things that've been thrown away by other women, right?

Man Then how much? Give it to me straight, don't give me the run-around!

Girl I want you to make up for my birthday, I want you to spend the night with me before I turn into a totally incurable slut. You think I'm still sexy, don't you?

Man Wait, wait, calm down. Listen, you're still young, you can start all over again, there's no need to destroy yourself like that.

Girl *(Laughs loudly.)* You're more honest when you're not preaching. Hypocrite, an out-and-out hypocrite!

Man What is it that you really want? Tell me!

Girl (*Looking at the knife on the floor.*) I want your head.

Man That'd be kind of hard. Have you had too much to drink? Are you on drugs or something?

Girl This isn't India.

Man Will you stop making up stories? You just can't quit playing your game, can you?

Girl Isn't making love like playing a game? Either you're playing with me or I'm playing with you. What are you going to say to that?

Man I really should have killed you!

Girl I know. You're only wishing, you wouldn't dare. I've already seen through you ever since I first caught sight of you. You know, the look in your eyes actually gave you away. I'm telling you, you're a piece of crap.

Man *(Becoming very angry.)* Why did you come here then? You stinking whore!

Girl *(Calmly.)* I just wanted to prove something.

Man That you also put yourself up for sale?

Girl All women do, there's no need to prove that.

Man *(Puzzled.)* Then what were you trying to prove?

Girl *(Pauses. Laughs.)* … Do you want to play one last game with me?

Man What more is there to play?

Girl Play with death, a game of death.

Man That's not a bad idea. How do we play?

Girl Let's borrow your head for the time being.

Man Do you really want my head?

Girl *(Giggles.)* I said borrow.

Man *(Thinks for a moment. Goes over to her and lowers his head.)* All right, take it.

(Girl circles to Man's back. Suddenly she seizes the knife and raises it up high. Immediately the lights on the stage darken. Two loud and clear drum beats. Man falls down.

Monk enters, bareback and with a piece of red cloth tied around his waist. He is holding an axe in one hand and a wooden stick in the other, his head lowered.

Girl picks up the black overcoat and quietly covers Man's body with it. Monk bends down to look for a spot. He finally finds it at the other corner of the stage. He supports the wooden stick with one hand and softly bangs on it with the axe.

Man walks to the back of Girl. He is wrapped in the black overcoat with its collar pulled up. His face is cold and grey.)

Girl *(Without turning her head.)* You ... you're not dead yet?

Man *(In a low voice.)* An eye for an eye? It's only fair. *(Raises the knife.)*

(Monk succeeds in making the wooden stick stand up. He raises the axe with both hands and hammers it down. The stick is nailed onto the floor. Monk is stupefied.

In the dark, both Man and Girl fall down quietly at the same time.

Monk picks up an egg from the floor and exits.)

Second Half

(The stage has been cleaned and tidied up. It is empty except for two heads under the beaming light, one male and the other female.
Man and Girl are lying down and resting in the dark.
Sound of a tinkling bell.)

Girl The place is so quiet … as if it would break once you touched it …
Man What?
Girl Listen, how can it be so quiet, like there's absolutely nothing here, nothing has happened …
Man What's happening?
Girl Hush! Don't say a word —

(Girl gets to her feet and listens. The ringing disappears.)

Girl Someone's coming!
Man No one would come at this hour.
Girl Listen! Listen carefully —
Man *(Lifts his head.)* You're too sensitive. *(Lies down again.)*

(Crystal clear sound of bell ringing as if it's unreal.)

Girl Someone's at the door!
Man It's impossible.
Girl There's a knock on the door, I heard it. Someone's right there at the door.
Man Yeah, you heard it, so? Nobody can possibly come in here.
Girl Didn't you give someone the key?
Man That was a long time ago …
Girl How long ago?
Man I can't remember. It must have been years ago.
Girl Why didn't you ask for the key back?

Man	I didn't bother. Anyway, it was ancient history, why mention it now?
Girl	But if that someone suddenly remembered?
Man	Who are you talking about? Who remembered?
Girl	The one you gave the key to.
Man	Remembered what?
Girl	Remembered you. That person can come here any time, right?
Man	Apart from you, is there anyone else who'd be thinking of me right now?
Girl	You're so screwy.
Man	*(Sits up and looks at her.)* Don't worry, no one's going to come any more. There's only you and me. Besides, we're dead already. Who'd think of visiting the dead? Don't be daft.
Girl	Listen, listen, it's right above us. *(Looks up.)*
Man	*(Listening.)* I don't hear anything. Besides, the place is so big, even if there were dead bodies rotting in here our neighbours wouldn't know anything about it, and they won't come knocking at the door unless the corridor smells.
Girl	But we're both dead already, aren't we?

(Man and Girl lower their heads, silently gathering their thoughts.)

Man	It looks like it. *(Looking at the two heads.)* Only you and me, nobody else knows. Besides, you can't tell, I can't tell, and it's impossible, absolutely impossible for anybody to tell the outside world!
Girl	Are we going to be locked up here for ever?
Man	It wouldn't be too bad if this were a desert island, isolated from the rest of the world and without any sign of human habitation. But there's no blue sky to look at, and no beautiful sea to behold. If only we could hear the sound of surging waves from the sea …

Girl And you can't tell if it's day or night.

Man There's no sound, there's no movement, we're left in oblivion and stuck in a forgotten corner, no, an enclosed black box. It's not a coffin, it's not anything. We don't even know the time, is there time any more? Ah, time is no more than a notion, if you think there's time, then there's time. And death, it isn't such a horrible thing, is it?

Girl What's so scary is that you can't die quickly, this fear …

Man Nonsense! What's there to be scared of any more? You and I are already dead.

Girl I don't know, am I …?

Man Are you what? Now you want to change your mind?

Girl I don't know, I don't know anything, is death better than living? I really can't say, everything is so confusing, so elusive … Please, please don't ask me any more questions.

Man *(Delightedly, like a child.)* You and I can't go back any more! Whether you like it or not, ha ha, we are stuck together for ever like a man and his shadow. You and I, we're each other's shadow.

Girl Why are you still gloating now that you've turned into a shadow, a slave at the feet of a woman? I don't get you.

Man It doesn't matter, you and I are in the same boat, nobody can leave anybody. It makes no difference if you're my shadow or if I'm your shadow.

Girl You said it, not me.

Man So? The bottom line is … I love you.

Girl Me too.

Man We can't afford not to, we're inseparable now! Inseparable forever …

Girl *(Moved.)* Stay by me, like a good kid. *(Wants to kiss him.)*

Man *(Moves away.)* I'm tired. I don't have the urge.

Girl It's better this way. Stay by me, as long as I can hear your voice.

Man What more shall we talk about?

Girl	You decide, anything's fine with me. Just say something, for instance, something you're thinking of.
Man	I ... can't think.
Girl	How about your sarcasm, your mockery, and your ridicule? You enjoy doing these things, don't you?
Man	I've said everything I can say ... I really can't think of anything else ... what else can I say?
Girl	Maybe you could fantasize. Let's talk about your fantasies about women.
Man	I've become impotent.
Girl	*(Startled.)* That's no fun, what has become of that little bit of intelligence you had?
Man	I'm really very drowsy ...
Girl	Don't close your eyes. Look at me and say something!
Man	Leave me alone, I'm totally exhausted ...
Girl	How miserable ... How can you be so boring ...
Man	Who? Who's boring?
Girl	I mean it's really boring when a person dies. *(Looks at Girl's head.)*

(Girl crawls in front of the head and stares at it.)

Man	What are you doing?
Girl	Nothing.
Man	*(Sits up.)* Just like a nightmare. *(Also looks at Man's head.)* This is ... is this my head? Do you believe in resurrection?
Girl	What?
Man	Transmigration.
Girl	What did you say?
Man	Nothing.

(The two sit quietly back to back.)

Girl	*(Persistently.)* She asks, what did you say?
Man	*(Wearily.)* You say, you didn't say anything.

Girl She says she clearly heard you say something.

Man *(Without looking at her.)* You ask what did she hear you say?

Girl She says would she ask you if she knew?

Man You say that means you didn't say anything.

Girl Then she says, Oh. *(Turns to face the audience.)*

(Girl sits up straight, then she covers her face with her hands, her head lowered.
Man looks at woman's head.)

Man Then you see a contemptuous face. You say even if you wanted to say something, you wouldn't be saying it to her, and you say even if you actually said something, it wouldn't have anything to do with her, you're only talking about yourself. And the you that you're referring to only means you, which is no more than your self, you mean you, that self of yourself, keep on troubling you.

Girl She says she's afraid of silence, she can't stand people not talking when they're face to face with each other, she finds that suffocating. She's much more afraid of silence than of death, death is more bearable than not talking to each other like this.

Man You say you, you're only talking to yourself.

Girl She says she, she's only left with her memories.

Man You say you, the only way you can get a little bit of comfort is by talking to yourself.

Girl She says she, the only way she can invoke a little bit of fantasy is through her memories.

Man You say you, you can feel somewhat relaxed only when you're talking to yourself.

Girl She says she, she can see herself clearly only when she's fantasizing.

Man You say it's not that you don't want to get away from your self, but you're always talking to yourself, in that way the self will never go away and it'll never stop haunting you.

Girl She says only when she indulges herself in fantasies can she empty herself of her worries, be carefree and recall her past feelings. Even though they may have been scary feelings, they still manage to touch her heart.

(Man stands up slowly and walks in front of man's head.)

Man You have to get rid of the baggage in your mind completely, let bygones be bygones, get away from it all, and get it off your back for ever.

Girl She's falling asleep … It's best to sleep deeply and never wake up, but she just can't sleep well, she's suffering from anxieties all the time …

Man *(Circles around the head and inspects it.)* You've got to find a way to get out of here!

Girl Dreams, one after another, intermittent and disjointed, there's no beginning, there's no end …

Man *(Lifts his head.)* It doesn't matter where you're going, when you've got to go, you've got to go!

Girl Her head is swooning and she's unsteady on her feet, she has no idea where she is …

Man You're groping around, you're trying hard to find a way out, you're afraid that you might bump into something …

Girl A wall, it is collapsing in silence, right in front of her eyes …

Man Finally you manage to find a door, it must be a door, it is tightly shut …

Girl That high wall, the one which has been standing erect in front of her, suddenly collapses just like that, without a sound, nobody has touched it …

Man You must open the door, even if it's only a little crack, as long as you can … squeeze through it sideways …

Girl She actually sees a patch of sky, misty and grey … just like fog …

Man	You carefully walk into a dark and shady long corridor … it's curved and bent … there's no end …
Girl	A big patch of misty grey sky, it's dark and light at the same time, like it's neither morning nor evening …
Man	*(Lowers his head.)* Strange, where did this top hat come from? You don't know, should you or shouldn't you pick it up?
Girl	Then she clearly hears a squeaking sound.
Man	But you're afraid it might be a trap — *(Lifts his head.)*
Girl	She knows that a knife is cutting —
Man	You lift it up — *(Bends down to pick up the top hat.)*
Girl	Cutting open a naked body —
Man	Oh, a nest of ants! *(Immediately retreats.)*
Girl	She sees it now, there's a crowd surrounding a woman, they're cutting open her stomach to dig out her internal organs.
Man	*(Inspecting the top hat in his hand.)* It looks like your own hat, you haven't worn it for a long time, how could you have forgotten about it?
Girl	They're butchering her, they're dissecting and discussing at the same time. There's also a woman mixed in among them, can't tell how old she is.
Man	*(Puts on the hat.)* It actually fits. Only your own hat would fit this well.
Girl	She lifts her head and looks around. A pair of hollow eye sockets! She takes to her feet at once!
Man	*(Pulls down the brim of the hat.)* You can't go without a hat, a man without a hat is like a man without clothes.
Girl	*(She bends down until her head touches the ground.)* Something's flowing down her thigh, she knows it may be blood, she feels awfully embarrassed.
Man	*(Somewhat comforted, he raises his voice slightly.)* You walk down the pitch-dark corridor, at the same time you're groping for a way, you know what you should avoid, as if you've passed through the same corridor once, twice, and even three times before.

Girl She's actually not afraid of bleeding, just that she's afraid of the sight of blood. Once when she was a small girl she went fishing with the grown-ups, she saw them toss a big fish onto the shore, they'd just caught that fish, it was all shiny and glittering, and then they started to cut it open right there on a piece of rock, their fingers became sticky with blood, and the fish was still struggling and jerking up and down. She felt rather sorry for that fish, it hadn't died and yet it couldn't live any longer.

Man *(Wobbles backward rather purposely.)* You know it very well, there is no end, but still you have to keep on going, turning wherever there's a turn. There's no end, you can't stop because you have to go on, even though you know nothing will ever come of it.

Girl She really wants to cry, but she can't, she has no more tears. She knows her heart is hardened and dried, a barren stretch of desolation, just like those naked hills behind the old house she lived in when she was a child. She only went there once, she was alone, after that she didn't dare to go any more, the naked branches in the bushes were shaking, shaking with the wailing wind among those hills.

Man *(Finally he cannot stand steadily.)* You don't know where you should go, should you stop, or perhaps should you turn and go back?

Girl *(Gets up, at a loss.)* She doesn't know how it happened, but somehow she's in this railway station, it's all deserted and empty, there're no signs on the platform. She wants to know where the next train is going, but she can't find anyone to ask. She feels a bit scared, from here to there in this mammoth platform, she can only hear the hollow tapping of her own footsteps.

(Man walks behind her, staring at her back.
She walks away at once and then suddenly stops.
He takes two steps forward and follows her.)

Girl *(Closes her eyes and holds her breath.)* She knows there's someone behind her, she can feel that he's staring at her, her back is cold, she is waiting for that someone to raise the knife, she has no strength to lift her feet — *(Panting.)*

(Man extends his hands towards her, and she runs away as if she is possessed.
Man drops his hands.)

Girl *(Running and panting for breath.)* She says she's terrified, but then she's not really terrified, she knows she's only terrified of her memories of terror.

(Man droops his head.)

Girl Nobody can save her except herself, but she feels too weak even to think of saving herself. *(Dejected.)*

(Man stares at his feet.
Girl looks at him at a distance.)

Girl At last she sees someone in front of her, a man she's long been waiting for, a man who can perhaps save her! She really wants to see his face clearly, but it's just a blur, she can't quite make it out no matter how hard she tries. *(Walks around him and looks at him closely.)* My God, it's only a shadow!

(Disappointed, she retreats step by step, head down.)

Man *(Slowly lifts his head and marches forward.)* Shit. *(Crouches down to tie the shoelace on his right shoe, gets up, and starts to put forward his right foot.)* Shit! *(Crouches down to tie the shoelace on his left shoe, gets up, and starts to put forward his left foot.)* Shit! *(Crouches down to tie right shoelace again, gets up, and puts forward his right foot.)* Fucking shi — *(Turns to look at left foot, takes back right foot, crouches down*

	to tie left shoelace again, gets up, and starts to lift right foot.) Mother fucking shit! *(Lifts his right foot in the air to tie shoelace. Then with his right foot touching the ground, he raises the tip of his left foot.)* Mother fucking sh — *(Frustrated, he takes off both shoes, throws them away and sits on the ground trying to figure out what to do next.)*
Girl	*(Looks at herself all over.)* She has no idea, is she also a shadow herself? *(Looks at the shadow under her feet and turns around again and again on the same spot.)* Is the shadow herself? *(Becoming dizzy.)* Or is she no more than the shadow of this shadow? *(Closes her eyes.)* Who is the real she?
	(Monk enters dancing. He is holding a horsetail whisk to dust himself. He picks up an imaginary leaf from his shoulder and blows on it, making a whistling sound. Then he closes his eyes and chants: "Good men and women, good knowledge, purify your nature, purify your heart, Amitabha Buddha!" Monk exits. *Afterwards Man and Girl's behaviour becomes increasingly abnormal and strange.)*
Man	*(Talking to himself.)* Behind that door, perhaps there is nothing.
Girl	*(Asking herself.)* No memories?
Man	*(Ruminating.)* That door, behind that door, perhaps there is really nothing, do you believe that?
Girl	No fantasies?
Man	That's right, there's nothing behind that door, you thought there was something, but there's nothing.
Girl	And no dreams either?
Man	*(To audience.)* That door, behind that door, there's nothing.
Girl	She can't remember anything.
Man	*(To himself.)* There's absolutely nothing behind that door. *(Giggles.)*
Girl	*(To audience.)* What happened?

Man *(Softly, his back facing Girl.)* That door, behind that door, there is nothing.

Girl *(Softly.)* And no memories.

Man Absolutely, absolutely.

Girl And no fantasies.

Man Absolutely, absolutely. *(Nods his head.)*

Girl And no dreams either.

Man Absolutely, absolutely! *(Becoming contemptuous, his head to one side.)*

Girl *(More softly.)* Can't say.

Man *(Very softly.)* Why?

Girl *(With certainty.)* Can't say.

Man Why can't you say it?

Girl *(Almost whispering.)* Can't say!

(Man is speechless.
Monk enters. Sound of running water.
Monk hastens forward, kneels on one knee, bends down and clasps his hands as if to cup the water. He dips his little finger in the water to wash his ears. After cleaning both ears, he rises and listens respectfully. His mouth opens slowly and reveals a Buddha-like smile. He exits quietly.)

Girl She can't believe that she actually said it, she said something that can't be said, but she said it, clearly this can't be said but why did she have to say it? It ought not to be said it can't be said but she said it regardless, it's her misfortune, it's her disaster, it's her sin.

Man *(Gets up, looks around and speaks loudly.)* And no door! *(Facing audience.)* The door? Where's the door? The door? The door? The door … *(Lowers his head.)* If you think you see it then you see it, if you think there's something then there's something, but what if you think there isn't? The door? Of course it's not there. (*Laughs to himself.*) That door of yours — no doubt it's something out of nothing, you're just being nosy, you just want to find a way out.

What if you can't find a way out? Isn't that just as good? *(Laughs loudly.)*

Girl *(On her knees, murmuring.)* Her sin, well, if she feels guilty then she's guilty. She's afraid of this and afraid of that, afraid of this, afraid of that, afraid, afraid, afraid, but she's not afraid of her, not afraid of herself. But what happens if she's also afraid of herself? Then wouldn't she be not afraid?

Man A way out, a way out, since there's no way out, why go and look for it? You only want to prove you're not trapped, or look at it another way, you're looking just to prove that you're trapped? What if you were to stop looking? Then you're not trapped, and you aren't not trapped? Either you're trapped or you're not trapped, either you're not trapped or you aren't not trapped, isn't it all your own doing?

Girl If she feels she's not guilty, what's there to be afraid of? She's afraid because she feels she's guilty, she feels guilty because she's afraid. And if she's not afraid then she no longer — *(Pauses.)* That's even more horrifying than Silent Extinction …

Man If you weren't you, there wouldn't be the need to prove anything, would it? But if you weren't you, then who are you?

Girl A silkworm, which gets enmeshed in its own cocoon.

Man Do you care who you are? Why can't you put down this you of yours?

Girl Left with only the remnants of a broken wish?

Man You keep on babbling only to show that you are you, that you're not like other people.

Girl A wisp of silk at large.

Man You are you because you're still talking, that's all there is to it.

Girl Wind.

Man Actually you don't know what you're talking about, you talk only because you want to. *(Shakes his head.)*

Girl Hollow.

Man You can't understand the meaning of your own words, you're just the slave of language, but you can't stop yourself from talking endlessly — *(Shakes his head.)*

Girl Tin soldier.

Man You can't free yourself from language's entanglement, just like a spider — *(Shakes his head.)* No, you're not a spider, but you're still a spider. *(Shakes his head.)*

Girl Candle.

Man You're not free to move, being trapped in the web of language of your own making — *(Shakes his head.)*

Girl Sa, send, da, la, wood —

Man Drunk city, mourning, stone statue — *(Listening to himself attentively.)* Why mourn a stone statue? Is the whole city drunk, or is everyone drunk all over the city? Or is someone or something mourning the idol with drunkenness? Stones are heartless, do humans have a heart? Is the city drunk? Does the stone know?

Girl Trap, jump, show, mouth, cut —

Man Hut — sin — grief — chime — bell. *(Tilting his head to think.)* Who's actually grieving for who? Is this the hut owner's death or the instruments' pain? Do the instruments know their suffering? If they don't, how can they mourn? Where is the mourner? How does one know? This one, that one, what are they mourning? What is there to mourn? It's all utter nonsense!

(Monk enters sweeping the floor. He is holding a big broom, his back to the audience. He stops when he comes to front stage and sees the two heads.
The lights on stage gradually darken, except for the light shining on the heads, which becomes brighter. Monk turns to observe Man and Girl.
Man and Girl's movements become very slow.)

Girl *(Murmuring.)* Win — ter …

Man *(Observing her.)* Aha!

Girl Makes …
Man What?
Girl Tea — pot …
Man *(Sarcastically.)* Winter makes teapot?
Girl Teapot …
Man Teapot what?
Girl Makes …
Man Makes what?
Girl Winter …
Man Teapot makes winter?
Girl Makes …
Man And then — ?
Girl Teapot …
Man And then makes teapot?
Girl It is …
Man It is what? Speak!
Girl It is not …
Man It is it is not?
Girl Is …
Man Is it is it not — is it winter makes teapot or teapot makes winter? *(Getting angry.)* Or is it it is not winter makes teapot or teapot makes winter? Or it is it is not is it not winter makes teapot or is it it is teapot makes winter? Or is it winter makes teapot makes winter? Or it is it is not is it winter makes teapot and then makes winter? Speak, speak, speak, go on!

(Monk ignores them, sweeping more earnestly.
Man and Girl move and speak faster with the quickening rhythm of the broom. Their bodies become more contorted, like two strange crawling reptiles.)

Girl Crack …
Man What crack?
Girl A crack …
Man What kind of a crack?

Girl	A crack line …
Man	What crack line?
Girl	A crack …
Man	What's this crack like?
Girl	A crack …
Man	Why a crack?
Girl	A crack …
Man	Where's this crack?
Girl	A crack …
Man	Why is it called a crack?
Girl	A crack …
Man	A crack and a crack!
Girl	A crack …
Man	Why is there just a crack?
Girl	A crack …
Man	A crack is a crack!
Girl	A crack …
Man	Okay, fine, a crack, so? What about it?
Girl	A crack …
Man	To hell with the crack!
Girl	A crack …
Man	Only one crack?
Girl	A crack …
Man	Another crack?
Girl	A crack …
Man	*(Exploding.)* A cr — a — ck —?
Girl	A crack …
Man	*(Laughs bitterly.)* A crack.
Girl	A crack …
Man	*(Talking to himself.)* A crack …
Girl	A crack …
Man	*(Murmuring.)* A crack …
Man & Girl	*(Almost simultaneously.)* A crack —

(Monk coughs and throws the broom on the ground at the same time. He halts.

Man and Girl are stunned by the noise, staring at Monk.
Monk turns to face the audience. He inhales deeply and slowly and then exhales as slowly. All lights go out.
Monk turns to open a curtain, revealing a greyish blue sky. Monk stands motionless and looks outside the door, his back to the audience. Gradually the wind starts to blow.)

The End

14 June 1992, Saint-Herblin, France.

Some Suggestions on Producing *Dialogue and Rebuttal*

1. The play is not intended to narrate a real or fictional story; the emphasis is on how to narrate or on the act of narration itself. Thus there is no need for the director to rationalize the characters or the stage setting, and he should instead focus his attention on the mode of narration and its variations according to the instructions in the script.
2. The two characters in the play need not be sharply defined in terms of character traits. Shunning total identification, the actors playing the parts only have to ease themselves into the situations and pay attention to establishing communication with their partner and the audience. The acting must strive for clarity and simplicity.
3. The key to the dialogue between Man and Girl lies in the use of personal pronouns. There is a distinction between Man's uses of the first person "I" and the second person "you," and between Girl's use of the first person "I" and the third person "she." With the first person "I," the actor is the character; with the second person "you" or the third person "she," the actor is referring to the character he or she is playing. When "I" is used, the acting should be natural; when "you" or "she" is used, the actor is listening closely to himself or herself, and the acting should stress somatic movements or even try to express itself through dancing.
4. The actor playing the Monk will preferably be someone who has had some training in traditional Chinese opera or in the Japanese Noh play. However, as long as he can execute the movements prescribed in the script in a neat and tidy manner and without drawing attention to himself, he does not have to preoccupy himself with stylized movements or conventions.
5. The play's dialogic form is inspired by the *gongan* 公案 style of question and answer in Chinese Zen Buddhism. The play has no intention of promoting Buddhism, and there is no need for the director to devote his time and effort in expounding the meaning of Zen Buddhism. The author only wants to propose that this kind of dialogue and cross-questioning is capable of being dramatized as a form of stage performance.

The above suggestions are for reference only.

Nocturnal Wanderer

(A play in three acts)

Characters:

Traveller
Old Man
Young Woman
Young Man
Man
Train Inspector

(Actors playing the above roles can also play)

Sleepwalker
Tramp
Prostitute
Ruffian
Thug
Masked Person

Act I

(A first-class train cabin is located at front stage left. Light comes from the rear. There are two or three rows of red serge armchairs facing one another. To the right several passengers are sitting by a window with the blinds pulled up. Old Man sits by the door next to a vacant seat in the same row. Young Woman, covered in an overcoat, is resting on a row of seats to the left. Young Man is leaning on the door. There is a sign on the door, on which the words "No Smoking" have been scraped off, leaving only faint traces. The train rumbles along.
Young Man takes out a pack of cigarettes from his pocket. He is going to light a cigarette when the train inspector enters.)

Inspector Good evening, ladies and gentlemen. Tickets please!
Young Man *(Smiling at him.)* Somebody picked my pocket.
Inspector And the ticket's gone too?
Young Man They swiped my money and my bags at the station. Damn it, I didn't even have time to buy another ticket. I've got to hurry to the match, an international tournament, I had no choice but....
Inspector You're an athlete?
Young Man Kind of. Marine sport, motorized sailboat, you know. It's very fashionable these days. We've even got a sponsor. *(Smiles)*
Inspector Any I.D.? That's swiped too, I presume?
Young Man Of course I have I.D. *(Takes out a piece of paper from his pocket.)* And the report issued by the police at the station.

(Inspector takes the report and writes on his notebook.)

Young Man It's not a common last name. A bit strange, isn't it?
Inspector *(Returns the paper. Turns to Old Man.)* Mister, your ticket please.
Old Man *(He is rolling a cigarette. He lifts his head.)* No ticket.
Inspector And no money?

Old Man No.

Inspector Where did you get on?

Old Man *(Mumbles.)* I just got on.

Inspector Where are you going?

Old Man Maastricht.

Inspector Where?

Old Man M…A…A…S…T…R…I…C…H…T. Maastricht!

Inspector This train doesn't stop there. I'm afraid you're on the wrong train. What's your nationality?

Old Man *(With an accent.)* Foreign.

Inspector Do you speak English?

Old Man *(Syllable by syllable.)* Vo…lun…tar…y fo…reign…er.

Inspector Have you got a passport?

(Old Man fumbles in his pockets, fishes out a passport and shows it to Inspector.)

Inspector How come it doesn't show your address, your regular place of residence?

(Old Man looks at him and does not say a word. Inspector gives up, records the information on his notebook and returns the passport.)

Inspector *(To Traveller)* Ticket please, mister.

(Traveller hands him the ticket.)

Inspector This is a second-class ticket, and you're in first-class.

Traveller Where does it say that? There isn't a sign or anything.

Inspector Anything that's red, red armchairs, red carpet, etc., means it's first-class.

Traveller Where's the second-class coach then?

Inspector This is the European Express, which has no second-class coach. With this ticket you should've got on the last train, or the next, in which case you'll have to wait another two and a quarter hours. You have to pay another … *(Checks his price list.)* two hundred and fifty.

(Traveller pays. Young Man opens his eyes wide and stares at him.)

Inspector *(Writes a receipt and hands it to Traveller.)* Thank you. *(To Young Woman)* Lady …

(Young Woman takes out a ticket from her handbag and hands it to him.)

Inspector *(Takes a look.)* This ticket's expired

Young Woman Oh, I'm sorry.

Inspector Have you got another ticket?

Young Woman Of course. *(She gets up to pick up her handbag and puts on her overcoat.)* Excuse me. *(She goes outside and opens the handbag to look for the ticket.)*

(Inspector follows her outside. Young Man comes in, sits down, and lights a cigarette.)

Young Woman Strange, I have absolutely no idea where I could possibly have left it. How come I can't find it?

Inspector Are you like this all the time?

Young Woman Oh no, only when … *(Closes the handbag and pulls her overcoat up high to reveal her thigh.)*

Inspector All right. Good luck! *(Exits)*

(Young Woman comes back inside.)

Young Man *(Stands up and lets Young Woman sit down by the window.)* Excuse me, please. *(Sits down next to her.)*

(Young Woman pays no attention to him but clings to her overcoat.)

Young Man *(To Traveller)* It's funny. You bought the ticket, right? But you still have to pay the fine. *(He takes out a few tickets from his shirt pocket and show them to Traveller. Then he stuffs them back and winks at him.)* Follow the rules and they'll give it to you. You've gotta be tough and know how to play with them. They'll only take this, you know.

(Traveller smiles and picks up a book to read.)

Young Man *(Turns to Young Woman)* Excuse me, are you on vacation? A rendezvous? A very special trip, if I'm not mistaken? You're offended? Sorry, just asking.

(Young Woman leans her head on the window to sleep, her eyes closed. Man enters in raincoat and top hat. He takes a look at the faded no-smoking sign, comes in through the door and sits down. He takes out a cigar. Young Man offers him a light.)

Man Thanks. They give you a sleeping berth and a diner where you can wine and dine yourself. They offer all kinds of services, but they don't give you no place to smoke! Except for this tiny little corner here. At first I wasn't even sure. If you smoke you're not supposed to travel in comfort, right? Tell me, what sort of stupid set-up is this?

(Nobody answers him. Young Woman turns off the light above her seat and closes her eyes. Traveller starts to read a book. The vibrating sound of two trains meeting becomes louder. The light in the left corner begins to darken.)

A voice reading It's night and the rain is drizzling beneath the street lights. You can't remember clearly how long it has been in this city, polluted by the clattering of car engines and exhaust fumes all day, since you took such a leisurely stroll and felt such refreshing rain. The air is moist and fresh; as to whether it's really fresh or not, it's none of your concern. Anyway, the streets are totally deserted: no pedestrians, no cars. Now you can take a stroll any way you like, and without any purpose. There's no need to see anybody, no need to say hello to anybody, no need to be polite, and no need to utter any meaningless words.

In fact, in the middle of the hustle and bustle of the city, you have not been able to live your life fully. You're either in front of somebody or behind somebody, and you're always squeezed and squashed among the crowd. If you missed one step, somebody would surely crash into you, then you'd have to say sorry to somebody or that somebody would have to say sorry to you, even though no one is really sorry. Just like the phrase "How are you?", which you have to say countless times in a single day. But even if you told people you're not well, you think anyone would care and help you with your problems? People suffer from so many nameless anxieties all the time: they turn them over and over in their minds, they worry themselves to death, and they torment themselves mentally and physically, but how could they possibly find a way out?

(The gradually brightening stage reveals a lamppost, on which is hung a yellowish street light. It faintly illuminates the rainy and foggy night. A street corner slowly becomes visible. Sleepwalker's back is seen at the street corner. He has on only an undershirt which almost stretches to his knees. His thighs are bare. On his feet are a pair of thick and heavy shoes. The shoelaces are undone and dangling.)

Sleepwalker You can hear your own footsteps, you can hear your own breathing. When you take a deep breath and the air rushes in from the tip of your nose to your lungs, you feel cold all over.... Only your feet are heated and warm. When a man's feet are warm, he feels snug and comfortable.

These shoes are quite heavy, they're also very sturdy. When you walk on the street and your feet feel sturdy, there's no need to hurry, and no need to look left and right. You can go wherever you want to go, be it on the pavement or in the middle of the road. Walk where your heart leads you, there are no restrictions and no burdens. *(Playfully walking backwards on his heels.)*

Finally you're free of all responsibilities, free of all troubles. You know, man asks for troubles himself. Everyone has to have either this or that problem, if he can't find any problem, he loses all reason for living. But at this moment in time you have absolutely no problems at all. *(Thinking.)* No problem whatsoever, nothing, really nothing! It's hard to say if it's lucky for a man not to have any problems. In the final analysis, you should congratulate yourself somewhat. And because everyone has problems and you don't, you can't help but tell it to the world. But the street is empty, so you can only tell it to yourself: Hear! Hear! You're the only person without any problem in this huge metropolis!

(He kicks and taps his feet, and after a while, he switches into another piece of fancy footwork, finally landing on a pile of cardboard boxes in front of a store which has been closed for the night.)

Tramp What the hell is going on? *(Sticking his neck out from the box.)*

Sleepwalker You say you didn't see ...

Tramp Look, this is a huge cardboard box, not a dinky needle. There's no way you could've missed it.

Sleepwalker Sorry.

Tramp Sorry my ass!

Sleepwalker You say you weren't looking, and you thought that this late at night only the garbage waiting to be picked up would be stored in the cardboard boxes discarded in the street. You didn't think that you'd be resting inside. Therefore you offer an apology.

Tramp You woke me up!

Sleepwalker You say you're really sorry. You thought that you're only relieving yourself inside, and you didn't know that you also slept in there. This calls for a double apology.

Tramp You have a walking problem or something?

Sleepwalker Walk, you say of course you know how to walk. But how should you put it? You don't usually walk like that, it's just that you felt so good that you got carried away, and you bumped into you by accident. You can only say you're sorry.

Tramp You could've walked like you used to, couldn't you?

Sleepwalker You say the problem is you can't go back to the way you used to … You've forgotten how to alternate your feet …

Tramp One foot in front, and the other behind! Didn't your mom teach you how to walk when you were small? You're asking for trouble, aren't you? *(Crawling out of the box.)*

Sleepwalker You say okay you'll walk, like this … *(Slips out one foot to try.)*

Tramp What's wrong with you, blind or something?

Sleepwalker You say your eyes are not blind, but —. *(Thinking to himself.)* You understand perfectly but you can't say it out, once you tell the truth, you're through.

Tramp So you gonna walk or not?

Sleepwalker You say right away, but you're trying to think of a place to go … You don't know where you should go.

Tramp Just follow the street and go straight. If something hits your nose, make a turn!

(Sleepwalker cautiously explores the road with his feet. Tramp retires into the cardboard box.)

Sleepwalker *(Goes to the middle of the road.)* Everybody wants to control you, everybody wants to be God. *(Stops.)* You only wanted to take a leisurely stroll, without purpose and without destination; what fun is there if you're told where to go? People are always telling you to do this, to do that and then when troubles comes it's you who have to bear the brunt. It's like the so-called "purpose." If they let a rabbit go and tell you to chase after it, what are you going to do when the rabbit runs away? *(He turns his head but cannot find Tramp. He shouts.)* You have no purpose, no direction. Just walk on and live with it!

(Sleepwalker turns in a circle, casually points to a direction and walks away.
The roar of an engine approaches then stops. Sleepwalker looks up, and sees a flyover hanging high at the back of the stage.)

Sleepwalker Last train?

(The engine starts again and moves away.)

Sleepwalker Yes, it's probably past midnight.

(Ruffian enters. Sleepwalker stops. Ruffian walks to him, stops, and checks him out.
Sleepwalker hesitates. When he takes one step to the left, Ruffian follows with one step. When Sleepwalker goes to the right, Ruffian follows with another step to the right. The two eventually collide.)

Sleepwalker Oh, sorry!
Ruffian Christ, don't you know how to walk?
Sleepwalker You say you already said sorry. You didn't do it on purpose.

Ruffian A bastard with eyes that can't see.

Sleepwalker You say why are you cursing people for no reason?

Ruffian 'Cause you crashed into yours sincerely.

Sleepwalker You say you have eyes too, why did you crash right into you when the street was practically empty?

Ruffian You want trouble?

Sleepwalker You say you waited until the wee hours to come out for a walk just to avoid trouble. You never expected to crash into anyone.

Ruffian You were in my way!

Sleepwalker You say you heard the footsteps and you were going to step aside. But you suddenly stopped …

Ruffian You said it. You heard me coming, right? Why didn't you listen more carefully when I stopped?

Sleepwalker You say you've come out to take a walk, not to listen to anybody, or for that matter, for anyone's footsteps. You don't have to listen to anybody! You ask him to go away, then each will go his separate way. All you want is just some peace and quiet.

Ruffian I'm really dying to know what it is that you really want! But I'm gonna smash your stinking dog face in first —. *(Raises his hand.)*

(The tapping of high-heel shoes. Prostitute enters, wearing a super-mini skirt and holding an opened umbrella. Ruffian turns and walks away at once.)

Prostitute Hi there!

Sleepwalker Good evening.

Prostitute *(Raises the umbrella and approaches him for a close inspection.)* How's it going?

Sleepwalker Nothing much, just living, that's all.

(Prostitute circles him, lowers the umbrella and walks away. Ruffian comes up at once, walks by her side and whistles. Prostitute turns away.)

Ruffian	The weather, is it hot enough for you?
Prostitute	*(Lowers the umbrella.)* You like it hot?
Ruffian	The broad, she's really something!
Prostitute	Wanna buy me a drink?
Ruffian	Sure, your place?
Prostitute	The pub!
Ruffian	Where? They're all closed for the night.
Prostitute	Some are still open.
Ruffian	Don't you have a pad close by?
Prostitute	How about your place?
Ruffian	Too far, broad.
Prostitute	Doesn't matter. It's only a cab ride away.
Ruffian	Why don't we just pick a quiet corner, eh? Saves a lot of trouble. That guy, you with him?
Prostitute	You want a threesome?
Ruffian	Don't make me sick, babe. Just you will do.
Prostitute	Got any dough?
Ruffian	Can't do without. *(Takes out a cigarette and lights up to inspect her.)* Mm, not bad.
Prostitute	As long as you like it. Alright, where?
Ruffian	*(Lights the cigarette.)* Sweetie! *(Embraces her.)*
Prostitute	How much are you willing to pay? How much, huh?

(Ruffian stretches out his hand towards her.)

Prostitute	Don't rush it — Hold on a sec!
Ruffian	I'll pay you.
Prostitute	Well, pay first.
Ruffian	A fresh one, still not quite used up.
Prostitute	Don't touch! Don't you know the rules!
Ruffian	You want me to teach you something first? *(Cups her chin with his hand.)*
Prostitute	*(Pushes his hand away.)* What an asshole!
Ruffian	Look at you. Don't be so uptight. That's no way to treat a customer. *(Forcibly raises her chin with his fingers.)* Yeah, that's more like it. *(Takes the cigarette from his*

mouth and stuffs it into hers.) Fun, isn't it? You've gotta learn.

Prostitute *(Spits out the cigarette.)* Get lost!

(Ruffian laughs. Prostitute turns to walk away.)

Ruffian *(Follows her.)* Sweetie, where do you think you're goin'?

Prostitute Get away from me, you're sick — *(Forces him away.)*

Ruffian You slut! Don't you like it when men do it to you?

Prostitute Bastard! *(Walks faster, exits.)*

Ruffian All right! (*Takes a glance at Sleepwalker and stamps his foot on the cigarette she threw away. Chases after her in big strides. Exits.*)

(The tapping of Prostitute's high heels moves further away. It becomes faster and faster, then suddenly stops. Silence.)

Sleepwalker *(Screaming.)* Son of a bitch — !

Tramp *(Stretching his neck out from the other side of the cardboard box.)* What are you doing?

Sleepwalker You say you're not doing anything.

Tramp *(Crawling out of the box.)* Then why are you making such a racket at this God-forsaken hour?

Sleepwalker You say over there — *(Silence.)*

Tramp That's also a profession.

Sleepwalker You say maybe she's being raped.

Tramp Well, if you're in the business, it's bound to happen, isn't it?

Sleepwalker Don't you have any compassion, just a little bit of compassion?

Tramp Oh yeah? You're saying that you do, right? But what's the use?

Sleepwalker You say you're pissed off!

Tramp Why don't you go and rescue her then?

Sleepwalker You say you know you can't save her. Even if you gave up your life to save her once, you wouldn't be able to save her the second time around.

Tramp That's the whole point, isn't it?

Sleepwalker You say that's why you screamed!

Tramp If you want to scream, go home, close the door and scream your heart out. Don't do it here and make a pest of yourself!

Sleepwalker You … How should you put it? You have no heart, no feeling! You say you're telling you.

Tramp And you … how about you? You wanna save the world? You're preaching to an old man like me?

Sleepwalker You say, you have nothing to say to you.

Tramp Don't say it then.

Sleepwalker You say you go back to your sleep, and you'll go back to your street.

(Tramp crawls back into the cardboard box.)

Sleepwalker *(After a while.)* You're not going to say anything any more, not even a word. You're not even going to make any sound. You'll only immerse yourself in your own world, you won't make friends with anybody! You can't stand anybody, everything in this world stifles you! You're still alive, you still act like a human being, but only because you're still thinking, more or less. (Stands up motionless like a statue.)

(Faint music is wafted along with the wind.)

Sleepwalker *(Changes his posture.)* You're all by yourself, you're talking to yourself. What are you thinking about? It doesn't matter. What's important is that you're still thinking, that you still have your own thoughts. Never mind if they seem totally worthless in other people's eyes.
(Changes into another posture.) Other people are nothing to you. They're their own business; you are you, and only you. You are a human being, or maybe a worm, a butterfly, or an ant. Why should you worry about what

you look like in other people's eyes? Happiness is only when you're contemplating things by yourself. *(Changes into yet another posture.)* You contemplate and you wander without any worries, between heaven and earth, in your own private world, and in this way you acquire supreme freedom —

(He makes a turn towards the inside and comes to a black doorway opposite to the street, which is littered with piles of cardboard boxes. Suddenly an arm appears and takes a firm hold of his throat. Unable to move, he is dragged into the shadow of the doorway.)

Thug *(In a low voice.)* Freeze! Make a sound and you're history! Pose for me! Keep dancing like you were! Yeah, that's it. You know what's poking you in your back, right? *(Lets go his hand.)* Take one step forward and wait at that bright spot over there. Change your pose, marvellous. Where are you from? Who sent you? C'mon talk to me, I'm asking you a question!

Sleepwalker No … nobody. You say you're … only taking a walk by yourself …

Thug Don't get smart with me! You're playing with your life!

Sleepwalker It's true, you say no … nobody sent you. Really, nobody did. You just felt like it all of a sudden, it just came to you out of the blue, it wasn't planned. You can't help it if you don't believe it. Do what you want, guns haven't got eyes anyway. Whoever gets hit will certainly go down. You can't do anything if it's in your fate.

Thug What the hell were you doing, waiting here all night long? I'm tellin' ya, I've had my eyes on you for more than an hour!

Sleepwalker You say you either lost your sense of direction, or you didn't want to go in any particular direction, so you just decided to take a turn every now and then. You say you probably don't understand it, not that you don't want to understand, but you still might not understand even if you tried to explain it. If you put yourself in your shoes and imagine yourself in the same situation, of course it's quite impossible, but if you did you'd still find it hard to understand why you kept on turning around and around on the same spot.

Thug Either you're a moron or you're an asshole!

Sleepwalker Maybe, maybe both. You say you don't know which is which and why you've become so stupid.

Thug Enough. I haven't got all day to chew the fat with you. You son of a bitch, you wanna play, right? You're gonna play for a long long time!

Sleepwalker *(Frightened.)* Don't — Don't —

Thug Switch, change to a different pose!

(Sleepwalker switches to a strange pose, rather like a suffering Jesus Christ.)

Thug You know that guy? Answer me!

Sleepwalker Which guy? That horny bastard who just went by? You say you utterly refuse to be friends with such scoundrels.

Thug I mean that scum hiding in the cardboard box on the other side.

Sleepwalker You ask, do you mean that homeless tramp?

Thug Yes, I'm asking you!

Sleepwalker You say you don't know anybody, you don't socialize with anybody, in fact you're afraid to socialize with people and that's why you've come out to take a walk by yourself at this hour of the night.

Thug Get him out of there!

Sleepwalker You haven't got the nerve to bother him, you say, after all you're the one who's always being bothered, not the opposite. Besides, it's not that you don't want to bother people, it's that you're unable and you're powerless, you even lack the courage. That's why you're in such dire straits.

Thug Get your ass over there and pull the guy out of the garbage dump for me! And keep on dancing!

Sleepwalker You say your legs and stomach are sore. They won't listen to your commands ... You say you're not a dancer, you really haven't had any training. Would it be possible to stop?

Thug I told you to pose for me! Just like before. That's right. Stay there, you got me?

Sleepwalker You say you're not going to risk your life. Man only lives once, wouldn't you say?

Thug Scram!

(Sleepwalker extracts himself completely out of the shadow of the doorway. Immobilized at the centre of the street, he tries in vain to recapitulate his former movements.
A car zooms by somewhere in the distance. Silence resumes. Prostitute enters, empty-handed and without her umbrella.)

Prostitute *(Approaching Sleepwalker.)* What's wrong? Stomach ache?

Sleepwalker No, just tying my shoelaces.

Prostitute Got any cigarettes? Give me one.

Sleepwalker No, you say, at this moment you have nothing. *(Thinking to himself.)* Except your life, which is also in other people's hands.

Prostitute Oh, forget it. Stay with me for a while!

Sleepwalker You say no problem. You also want to have someone here with you. *(Thinking to himself.)* That way there'd be someone to call the police in case you're hit by a stray bullet or something. *(Looks back at the doorway.)*

Prostitute What are you looking at?

Sleepwalker Oh, you say you're not looking at anything. Talking to yourself has become a bad habit, and you don't even know you're doing it.

Prostitute *(Turns her head and looks at her own leg.)* There's a hole.

Sleepwalker *(Startled.)* You ask, what hole?

Prostitute The hole in my stockings. *(Adjusts her pantyhose.)*

Sleepwalker Oh, stockings. They'll run after some time. There aren't any stockings that don't run.

Prostitute But they're new. I bought them only yesterday.

Sleepwalker That's certainly quite regrettable. *(Thinking to himself.)* It's amazing, she feels no regret for herself.

Prostitute I stumbled and fell.

Sleepwalker You say it's raining and you're wearing high heels, no wonder you stumbled and fell. *(Thinking to himself.)* You didn't want to know whether she did stumble and fall, only whether or not she was raped, but it's too embarrassing to ask.

Prostitute I'm beat.

Sleepwalker Go home then, you say you also feel that you've had enough.

Prostitute I wouldn't dare …

Sleepwalker *(Thinking to himself.)* You feel the same way. You can't go home either, but you don't tell her.

Prostitute I'm scared.

Sleepwalker *(Thinking to himself.)* It's the same with you, you're in the same boat. Apart from the fact that you haven't been raped, you're not that much better. You've taken one step already, but you don't know whether or not you'd be able to take another one. Of course you didn't tell her.

Prostitute *(Whispering in his ears anxiously.)* I'm sure he's still there. He hasn't let go of me and he's still watching me somewhere near by. You see, when I left he was tailing me. I can't let him know where I live and I can't let him know I'm scared of him, I definitely cannot let myself fall into his hands. You got me?

Sleepwalker *(Thinking to himself.)* You understand totally and completely. Your situation is more or less the same as hers. She's already told you, but you still can't tell her yet.

Prostitute *(Loudly.)* You, you're such a lousy yellow-bellied wimp!

Sleepwalker Why? You can't help asking.

Prostitute Ever slept with a woman?

Sleepwalker You say of course you're not a virgin, and you're not a homosexual either. The problem is, you see, at this time you can't pay.

Prostitute We can go to your place if it's not too far, that is, if you don't have an old lady waiting for you at home. But you don't look like you're hitched.

Sleepwalker You say of course it'd be a pleasure, but you don't want to die in the hands of a woman.

Prostitute Do you think women are terrifying or something?

Sleepwalker It depends on what kind of woman.

Prostitute Don't you find them sexy? Or is it because you don't really want to do it?

Sleepwalker Oh, you say, you find them more than sexy. They're so lovely, so vulnerable, and so alive, unlike those dead-pan images on the billboards.

Prostitute That's it, let's go straight to your place! *(Whispering.)* How much? It's up to you.

Sleepwalker Surely it's a dream. *(Whispering.)* A bad dream! *(Loudly.)* You say of course you're willing to have a woman with you, because there'd be a witness in case you're shot by a sniper's bullet. You say you're a lovely girl. It makes one's heart ache.

Prostitute You're a good man, and good men are hard to find. *(Snuggles up to him.)*

Sleepwalker It's difficult to judge whether you're good or bad, you say. You can only say that you've never done anything extremely bad like murder, rape, arson, fraud, or extortion. But you're not completely free from sin either. The feeling of sin is actually quite tempting to you.

Prostitute It's nothing. Tell me, is there anybody who can resist the temptation?

Sleepwalker And you can't help thinking of the hole in her stockings, can't help seeing that dark and hollow muzzle of a gun coming towards you, you seem to be walking towards death one step at a time ...

(Sleepwalker puts his hand around Prostitute's waist and leads her towards the pile of cardboard boxes, smiling.)

Prostitute Is this your home? Seriously.

Sleepwalker *(Beating on a box to get the dirt off.)* Have a seat, make yourself at home!

(Tramp crawls out from the cardboard box.)

Prostitute Hey, this is really fun! *(Feeling happy and laughing.)*

Tramp It's not funny, you little moppet! *(To Sleepwalker.)* You gave me your word. You're not being honest.

Sleepwalker You ask what use is honesty? You may look honest, but who knows what you've got hiding behind your back? You may be as honest as the day is long, but how come you can't even find a decent place to live in? *(Throws himself down and sits on the cardboard box.)*

Tramp You don't sleep, and you're here to screw around so that nobody gets any sleep. Out with it! What is it that you really want to do?

Sleepwalker You say your problem is exactly that you don't want to do anything. Moreover, you can't be sure.

Tramp You want these cardboard boxes? Why didn't you say so in the first place? Don't beat around the bush with me. Take them, take them all and get out of here!

Prostitute Do you really wanna go inside that box?

Sleepwalker It's better to be inside in this bitter cold. Come on ...

Prostitute No! Don't come near me! You're so dirty.

Sleepwalker What, are you so clean yourself?

Prostitute You're even dirtier than that bastard!

Sleepwalker People, they're all garbage!

Prostitute Including yourself?

Sleepwalker All bastards, bastards and sluts, they're all the same.

Tramp Right, a real wise guy.

Sleepwalker It doesn't take too much wisdom.

Prostitute So you're an intellectual?

Sleepwalker Intellectuals stink.

(Prostitute giggles, so happy that her feet keep kicking at the cardboard box she's sitting on.)

Tramp Hey girl, don't knock down my bottle in there.
Sleepwalker You got wine in there?
Tramp You know, man can survive anything, but he can't live without wine.
Prostitute Why didn't you say so earlier? *(Puts her hand inside the cardboard box and gropes around. She takes out a worn-out bag.)* Wow, you really got something there!
Tramp Stop!
Prostitute You got money in here?
Tramp It's very hard to say. *(Takes out a wine bottle and puts the bag aside.)* Life's okay as long as there's wine.

(Tramp takes the cap off the wine bottle and takes a mouthful. He hands the bottle to Prostitute, who grabs it and downs a big gulp.)

Tramp Don't drink it all. You shouldn't drink too much of this stuff, although you can't live without it either. *(To Sleepwalker.)* You want some?
Prostitute He thinks it's dirty. *(Laughs aloud.)*
Sleepwalker Slut.
Prostitute What did he say?
Sleepwalker You say you didn't say anything.
Tramp You look like a happy girl.
Prostitute Why not?
Tramp I'll say. If you want to be unhappy, you'll be unhappy. It's enough to be alive, what more do you want?
Prostitute I really want to have an old father like you.
Tramp Oh, really?
Prostitute You think I'm lying? To an old guy like you? I wouldn't bother.
Tramp Then you've got one.

(Prostitute gives him a loud kiss.)

Tramp That a girl.

Prostitute *(Pulls the bag over.)* Hey, can I open this? Is there anything to eat in there?

Tramp *(Takes the bag and puts it aside.)* Even if there was anything, it wouldn't have lasted till now. And I wouldn't have to be up all night if they hadn't messed up my things.

Prostitute Pa, I'm hungry!

Tramp What am I goin' to do with her?

Sleepwalker Do you trust her? You're asking the old guy.

Tramp I trust everybody, as long as everybody trusts me. *(Smiles.)*

Prostitute Pa, got any cigarettes? I wanna have one.

Tramp Who doesn't want one at this time? But it's a luxury, like women.

Prostitute You think of women too?

Tramp Oh, women, expensive stuff.

Sleepwalker Some are free, you say.

Prostitute *(Giggling.)* You don't believe women have feelings?

Sleepwalker You say anybody does who is human.

Prostitute Are you saying only money can buy a woman's love?

Sleepwalker You didn't say that, you say.

Prostitute You don't believe a woman can truly love someone, and that her love is not for sale?

Sleepwalker You say you believe in everything, including God.

Prostitute In fact, you don't believe in nothing!

Sleepwalker This, you say, is not a bad thing. You ask her, do you believe?

Prostitute I only believe in money!

Tramp Right on! That a girl!

Prostitute *(Pulls the bag to her side.)* What's inside? It's quite heavy, let's have a look.

Tramp *(Smiling.)* Take a guess.

Sleepwalker Not a weapon, you hope, you say.

Tramp I've never stepped out of line, I'm content with my poverty. I'd never rob or mug anybody, and I'd never steal anything.

Sleepwalker You say, maybe you plan to use the thing to defend yourself.

Tramp There's no need. When you have nothing to lose or nothing worth robbing, why do you need that kind of stuff?

Sleepwalker You never know if you'll be hit by an unexpected disaster or something, you say loudly. How do you know if someone'll go crazy, just out of the blue like that? Or if a bullet'll go astray, and ... and who knows what else? Then you'll surely get it! Nothing is certain in this world!

Tramp Everything must have a cause before it happens. There must be a reason.

Sleepwalker Can you be so sure that you won't be hit by a car when you cross the road? You ask.

Tramp You've got to watch the lights. If you keep changing your mind and leap onto the road before you're sure it's clear, can you blame the car if you get hit? *(Smiles.)*

Sleepwalker You don't even have a place to go home to, you say, maybe you, you mean you yourself, are the cause of all of this?

Tramp So you're saying you've got a home, right? Then how come you're still prowling the streets at this ungodly hour of the night? *(Smiles.)*

(All is quiet, then gradually the wind starts to blow.)

Prostitute *(Opens the bag.)* Hey Pa, there's something in here.

Tramp Stop it! Stop it!

Prostitute What does it matter?

Tramp You can't touch it!

Prostitute It wouldn't be fulla money, would it?

Tramp Girl, nobody can say for sure, especially when luck crosses your path.

Prostitute *(Takes no heed of Tramp and fishes out a bundle of paper from the bag.)* Oh, lottery tickets.

Tramp If you say so.

Prostitute Stop fooling around. All of these are tickets people've thrown out, yeah?

Tramp But people had to buy them with money, didn't they?

Prostitute Don't pull my leg no more, old man. They're good for nothing. Why did you pick 'em up?

Tramp We've all got to work, right? We each have our own line of work. Look, those who have nothing to do, aren't they all trying to find some job for themselves? You see, girl, my job is collecting all kinds of lottery tickets. *(Smiles.)*

Prostitute You just wanna find something to do when your belly's full. Gosh, what a waste of time!

Tramp Oh no, don't put it that way. There are people who'd only collect old stamps, and those who'd only collect old cars, old pocket watches, snuff-boxes and so on. Girl, this is called "to each his own."

Prostitute That's because they've got money to burn. Your no-good tickets, can you sell them off for money?

Tramp Of all the wishes people have made, tell me, how many of them have actually come true? But people still make them anyway. It's difficult enough to live from hand to mouth and from day to day. For me, my life is sustained by my wishes, or by wine. Girl, what kind of wish have you made for yourself?

Prostitute Old man, I bet you don't even know how to make a wish.

Tramp That's true. Actually there's nothing to wish for. I live by the empty wishes made by other people. That's why I've been picking these waste papers for a living.

Prostitute Don't preach to me like you're God Almighty himself. I wouldn't trust your funny business! *(Casually throws away a bundle of tickets.)*

Sleepwalker You say bravo! Well done! Check out his bag and see if there's any other stuff. Go on, turn it upside down, shake them all out!

(Bundle by bundle, Prostitute takes out the tickets from the bag and scatters them in the air.)

Tramp Have you two gone nuts or something? *(Picks up the tickets hurriedly.)* I've spent days, even months gathering these tickets one by one, hunting for them everywhere …

Sleepwalker Throw them away! All of them! You shout.

Tramp You've ruined them all! *(Looks helplessly at the tickets, which have been strewn all over the ground.)*

Prostitute Old man, don't you get tuckered out carrying this bag fulla crap around? *(Throws the bag away. Laughs.)*

Tramp That's right, mess them up, mess them all up. You've both gone out of whack, haven't you? *(Picks up the wine bottle.)*

(Sleepwalker looks towards the doorway. Tramp picks up the bag and exits slowly.
The wind blows harder and harder.)

Prostitute *(Quietly approaches Sleepwalker.)* Shall we go too?

Sleepwalker Where? You say.

Prostitute *(Tenderly embraces him from behind. Whispers in his ear.)* How about your place?

(Sleepwalker still has his eyes on the shadowy doorway.
Somewhere a window slams again and again in the wind.)

Prostitute *(Loudly)* What are you doing?

Sleepwalker Nothing, you say.

(Prostitute moves towards the doorway. She turns her head and sees that he is still staring at it.)

Prostitute *(Loudly.)* What are you looking at?

Sleepwalker I'm not looking at anything, you say. *(Still looking at the doorway.)*

(Prostitute approaches the door gingerly.)

Sleepwalker You want to say something, but you have nothing to say. You didn't stop her, you let her walk in there, getting closer and closer with each step. You hope that something will happen ... but then again you also hope that nothing will ...

(Prostitute goes to the doorway and peeps in. Suddenly she retreats and screams. Bang! It sounds like a monotonous gunshot, or a window slammed shut by a sudden gust of wind. At the same time it appears that she trips on something, and she slowly bends down and falls into the shadow of the doorway. Immediately all lights are out.
The sound of a tooting train rushes across the stage.
On left stage, a soft light gradually brightens up the coach on the train. Traveller is dozing on his original seat, his head lowered, and his face not in clear view. All the other passengers have left, except for Young Woman. Wrapped in her overcoat and with her face to the wall, she is resting on the opposite side, occupying the whole bench. One of her high heels is lying on the floor. The slight vibration of a moving train is heard.)

Act II

(The stage gradually becomes brighter with a bluish grey light. A strong wind is blowing, scattering waste paper around. It is an extremely desolate scene. A high heel shoe is found where the woman fell.
Sleepwalker stands motionless in front of the shoe.)

Sleepwalker A shoe, *(Picking it up.)* only a shoe.
Each woman's shoe represents a story.
A discarded shoe. When it is discarded, it is discarded, nothing more.
There has to be something fishy about a discarded woman's shoe.
Women discard their shoes like garbage,
But a discarded woman's shoe naturally invokes many associations,
About the woman who wore this shoe, about the shoe that the woman wore,
About the many unimaginable speculations on the woman who wore the shoe,
About the men behind the woman, who usually number more than one,
About how a certain man involved with the woman used her, manipulated her, and buried her alive.
Was it murder, or was it extortion? Suddenly you are a bit frightened — *(Immediately he puts the shoe down where it was. He walks away, but he can't help looking back at the shoe.)* If you called the police, you'd be causing trouble for everybody, to say the least. And if you didn't, well, you wouldn't exactly feel right either, as if you're guilty like the others. You were just walking on the street, you could have ignored this discarded shoe and what happened to the woman wouldn't have concerned you at all. But you chose to pick it up and put it down, so no matter how you look at it, you are involved one way or

the other. That little whore has caused you worries to no end … *(Hesitates.)*

(Sleepwalker lifts his head. Thug appears in the doorway, holding a box.)

Sleepwalker You ask, can you go now? You've finished what you've been told to do.

(The two look at each other face to face. Thug puts the box down, his hand still tucked inside the pocket of his wind breaker.)

Thug Nobody told you to kill her.

Sleepwalker No way you killed anybody! You say if she was killed, it was you who killed her! Your hands are clean. *(Opens his hands.)* Why would you kill her for no reason?

Thug It was you who pushed her in front of the gun.

Sleepwalker Don't wag your tongue. What are you shifting your weight for? You say you didn't touch her at all!

Thug Everybody saw you picking up her shoe!

Sleepwalker You picked it up, but you also put it down. You say, how could this prove anything?

Thug Why did you pick up her shoe?

Sleepwalker Just curious. It's purely accidental. You say, there could be many, many other explanations, and they all clear you of any involvement with her.

Thug Why'd you have to take only her shoe and not anyone else's?

Sleepwalker Anyone else? You say you're not interested in anyone else!

Thug That's it, isn't it?

Sleepwalker What is it?

Thug The fact is: you killed her.

Sleepwalker Yeah? But for what reason, you ask?

Thug You've gotta ask the killer, and the killer is you!

Sleepwalker You say you had absolutely nothing to do with her, you didn't even know her! You only heard something like a gunshot and she tripped and fell down.

Thug Who fell down?

Sleepwalker That whore!

Thug If you were not her customer, how'd you know she was a whore?

Sleepwalker You — who are you? Are you the police?

Thug *(Laughs.)* Buddy, you're a real prick, y'know!

Sleepwalker You say you're not your buddy, and you're not anybody's slave!

Thug Let's say you're a friend of hers. What happened was that when you were finished with her, you killed her.

Sleepwalker That's only your hypothesis. Unfortunately, it's not a fact.

Thug What is fact?

Sleepwalker A fact is something that's real, something that's irrefutable evidence!

Thug Evidence? *(Takes out a handkerchief from his shirt pocket and wraps the shoe in it.)* The shoe is evidence, complete with fingerprints. *(Stuffs the shoe into his wind breaker pocket.)*

Sleepwalker Don't try laying it on others. You're the killer! You say, accuse all you want, but you're not the least bit scared. You won't take this blackmailing shit!

Thug How come your fingers are trembling like hell, huh? Which means, my friend, you're scared shitless, aren't you?

Sleepwalker *(Looks at his fingers.)* You say you're angry, 'cause you've been accused of something you never did! And one more thing, you absolutely don't have a friend like you!

Thug Not a friend, then what? A bad guy?

Sleepwalker You say you're not trying to cause you any trouble, and you don't have any axe to grind.

Thug Then are we partners?

Sleepwalker You say there's no secret that you can't tell no one! And you don't need no one to be your partner!

Thug You really think you're clean? You got your leg over her, even if that little whore did really make the first move, which she couldn't have unless you were horny yourself. In a word, you're her john, and together you two made good this filthy business —

Sleepwalker You say you didn't do anything with her!

Thug Are you sure? Think again!

Sleepwalker You did many times already, so what? Even if you did do it with her, so what? It's not murder!

Thug *(Sneers at him.)* A whore and her john, was it just hot nuts or was it also cold-blooded murder? It's hard to tell. And now my friend, who besides the whore can prove if you're guilty or not guilty?

Sleepwalker *(Shouts.)* You say you —

Thug Don't you yell at me. Besides, it's no use blowin' your cool like that. Nobody can prove you're clean now! You had this shit going with her, and after it was over, you killed her. Only you will know for sure what made you do it.

Sleepwalker You go to hell!

Thug I'm telling you, you'll be in deep shit when the cops come!

Sleepwalker You say it's obvious you're the killer! Not you!

Thug How can you prove that?

Sleepwalker You say you were passing through the scene of the crime, and you saw it with your own eyes.

Thug What'd happen if somebody else said the same thing about you? You've gotta have evidence, my friend. Make no mistake about it, it's better to settle this kind of thing between ourselves than blowing it all out into the open.

Sleepwalker You ask, what in the world do you want?

Thug Me? Buddy, I just want to help. I'm gonna be helping you all the way, and of course you won't forget to pay me handsomely afterwards.

Sleepwalker Helping you to do what, you ask?

Thug Come here.

Sleepwalker You say what if you don't?

Thug You'll be dead just the same.

Sleepwalker *(Hesitates.)* You say at this time you can …

Thug You can certainly try. If the worst comes to worst, we'll have to see if lady luck is with you.

Sleepwalker Then, you ask what exactly do you want to do?

Thug Come on in first, through the door.

Sleepwalker *(After some thoughts.)* You say, let's lay down all the cards on the table. What's in it for me? You get what you pay for, right? That seems to be the rule of the game these days. What's the deal you have in mind?

Thug Okay, now listen up. This is the deal: If you can carry this suitcase through that door and across the road over there safely, we'll split what's in the suitcase, fifty, fifty.

Sleepwalker There's only one suitcase. You could very well carry it yourself. Why do you have to pay somebody else to do it for you? You seem to be getting the short end of the stick in this deal.

Thug You're certainly no pushover. Let me repeat it for you: the suitcase is worth at least two heads, yours and mine. The high price I'm offering is for insurance! We've got no time to waste. Either you skip out of here with me or you'll end up like the whore! I'm goin' to count to three: one, two —

(Sleepwalker steps into the shadow of the doorway.
Thug pulls out his gun and takes off his wind breaker.)

Thug Put this on! Pick it up and go!

(Sleepwalker puts on the wind breaker and steps out of the doorway shadow, carrying the suitcase in his hand. He stops, his body swaying left and right.)

Thug Move it! Go straight ahead and cross the street!

(Step by step, Sleepwalker walks gingerly towards the opposite side of the street.

Thug leaps out from the doorway. As he starts to walk away leaning against the wall, there comes the sound of a gunshot. Sleepwalker is stunned. He thinks he has been shot and his body becomes stiff and motionless.
Thug falls down with a loud thud. Sleepwalker runs for his life.
Ruffian enters, blocking his way.)

Ruffian Hey, buddies!

Sleepwalker *(Immediately explains.)* You say you're not with him. He is he, and you are you. You say somebody put the squeeze on you —

Ruffian I meant you and me, we two are buddies —

Sleepwalker You say you're on nobody's side. You're going to pretend not to see whatever you did. You'll just go in peace, and don't you worry. You're clean, both of you.

Ruffian We're on our own separate paths, but I'm sure we're working on the same deal.

Sleepwalker You say you're unable to work on any deal. Besides, you didn't do anything at all.

Ruffian Stop wagging your tongue. Just hand over the goods!

Sleepwalker You ask what goods? Which goods does he mean? You can't pretend to know when you don't.

Ruffian Put down what you're holding in your hand!

Sleepwalker *(At once puts the suitcase on the floor.)* You don't want any dirty money. Just take it. You say you were forced to carry the thing, and now is a good time to get rid of it. *(Backs off.)*

Ruffian *(Stretches out his hands, which have on a pair of black leather gloves, to take the suitcase. He opens it and closes it back at once.)* You butthead! You scare me! What's in it?

Sleepwalker You say how would you know? You really have no idea! Isn't it gold, silver, jewellery or money?

Ruffian Son of a bitch, you're no do-gooder either! *(Tries to corner him.)*

(Sleepwalker turns and tries to run away.)

Ruffian Freeze! *(Takes out his gun.)* Where do you think you're goin'?

Sleepwalker You say you only want to hurry home. You're not going to the police. It's been like a bad dream, and you'll pretend to be deaf and dumb whoever asks you. *(Forces on himself a smiling face, as if he's smiling yet not smiling.)*

Ruffian Good dream or bad dream, you've gotta finish it. Turn around!

(Sleepwalker turns around quickly, his hands up in the air. Ruffian searches Thug's body, finds some money and fishes out a gun from his overcoat pocket. He takes out the bullets, raises the gun and inspects the barrel.)

Sleepwalker *(Turns his head away.)* Don't —

Ruffian *(Tucks the emptied gun back in Thug's wind breaker pocket.)* Drag him over there!

Sleepwalker Where?

Ruffian Dump him, chuck him into the cardboard box. The garbage men'll take care of him when they come. No littering the city and no disturbing the public peace either. Afterwards you can sleep all you want, and we'll both be in the clear. How about it, eh? When you start something, you've gotta finish it, right? As long as you don't leave any mess behind, nobody's gonna see or smell anything, absolutely no one. I mean the whole thing'll be airtight, like a perfect circle.

(Sleepwalker drags Thug in front of the box, picks him up and stuffs him inside. At the same time, he also hides Thug's gun inside his shirt.)

Ruffian Another one over there, get her in the box as well!

Sleepwalker Where?

Ruffian Inside the hole, that bitch.

(Sleepwalker goes over to the doorway. He hesitates and draws back his hands.)

Ruffian What the hell are you waiting for? Haven't you touched a woman before?

Sleepwalker It's gone.

Ruffian What's gone?

Sleepwalker The body.

Ruffian How could it be gone when she's already dead?

Sleepwalker It's really gone.

Ruffian The hell you say! Cut the crap, will ya? I haven't got all day!

Sleepwalker See for yourself if you don't buy it.

(Ruffian enters to inspect the doorway with the gun in his hand. Sleepwalker fishes out Thug's gun from his shirt and whacks the killer's head from behind. Ruffian falls. Sleepwalker bends down to listen, rises.)

Sleepwalker Thank God you've gotten rid of that swine. You didn't mean to kill anybody, but under the circumstances you were forced to do it, you had no choice. You were driven against the wall, anyone would have done the same if they were in your shoes. *(Grabs Ruffian's feet and drags him in front of the cardboard box.)* That was a real nightmare. At the time, you really wanted to swear at somebody or something. You'd rather kill someone first than waiting for that someone to kill you. Better kill than to be killed. Only now did you realize that there's also pleasure in killing. Your brain was pounding up and down and your blood vessels were bursting, you were so excited. It's amazing, face to face with that vicious brute, you were equally as vicious. They say evil for evil and goodness for goodness. Well, who cares if it's true, the point is you actually managed to get away in one piece.

(Drags the body and stuffs it into the cardboard box.) In your heart you're actually congratulating yourself, because you're so calm that you can carry on with your life as if nothing has happened, and this hand, it is still your hand, *(looks at his hand)* it bears no trace of murder....

(Leans on the cardboard box with a sigh of relief.) Of course you should feel lucky. At the same time you can't help wondering: the world is full of evil, you're surrounded by evil, but you don't feel at all strange about it, you even experienced a certain vague feeling of pleasure when you were at it. Nobody saw you, nobody will tell, so you too can carry on with your evil deeds like the others. If everyone acted the same way, we could all live in peace and harmony, couldn't we? As long you keep away from disasters, as long as you can escape punishment, and as long as you can overcome your own cowardice, you'll be able to continue with your game, feeling happy about other people's misfortunes. *(Drops his hands.)*

(The light contracts and concentrates on Sleepwalker, then gradually dims.

On the left of the front stage, a light shines faintly on the train coach. Traveller is asleep, his head in his arms and his feet stretched out. The book he was reading has fallen onto the floor. Young Woman and the high heeled shoe, which was on the floor, are gone.

The monotonous roar of an engine gradually fades.)

Act III

(Sleepwalker stands motionless at centre stage. The lights shine vertically from above and are focused on him. Everything around him has faded into darkness, except for the suitcase, which stays in the lit circle.)

Sleepwalker You can't find the way from which you came.
How can you go back if you've forgotten how you came? You were innocent all right, but you can't say for sure if you're totally innocent.
At any rate, evil is all around you, and the more you struggle to be free, the deeper you're trapped, and you can't get away from it.
Watchful eyes, they're here, there and everywhere. You've become a prey waiting to be preyed upon. You're besieged by all kind of traps, there's no way out.
It's better to await judgement than to run away. You're waiting for the time when the pop of a gunshot will come, any time, from any direction in the dark — that's the trick, like a sword hanging dangerously over your head. *(He stops in front of the suitcase, his head lowered.)* Is this a well-laid trap? *(Lifts his head.)* You've had this strange habit ever since you were a kid: you always wanted to open all kinds of boxes, cupboards and doors which couldn't be opened, just to take a peek at the secrets you weren't supposed to see, the secrets you weren't allowed to see. But once they were opened you'd always discover that there was nothing worth seeing inside. The real feeling of mystery was in between the times when they were unopened and opened, that's when your heart never stopped pounding. The mystery resided not in the boxes but in your mind.
(He circles around the suitcase with caution and then walks away, but he cannot help looking back.) Certainly you did peep through a door crack or behind a curtain, ogling at the secrets of a girl who'd just been awakened to desire,

a desire which also tormented you.... Then the whole thing became commonplace after a while. Satisfying a desire is nothing more than having a good meal. Now only when you're face to face with evil, is the excitement enough to satisfy the evil in your heart, you're that close to death and you're playing a death game. You know it well, over there on the side of death there's nothing, nothing can possibly exist. You're merely toying with death, and at the brink of death you more or less have a feeling of apprehension ... *(Returns to the suitcase and opens it carefully.)*

(A woman's head rolls out. Stunned, Sleepwalker backs off, stops and looks down.
It becomes gradually brighter behind the opened doorway, revealing a silent night sky. There are no clouds. The moonlight is clear, but the moon is not seen. The caws of seagulls can be heard faintly.)

Sleepwalker *(Looking back at the door.)* And then you heard the tide and the rumbling of the waves, and you saw the moonlight galloping on the sea and on top of the blue ripples. Before the full moon rose, there came wave after wave of blue radiance, and they swam and danced amid the dingy sea water like slithering snakes. The waves, glittering and breaking at times, disappeared before your bare ankles, which were now immersed in the ice cold sea water. And your young self of a long time ago, overawed and surprised, couldn't help walking deeper and deeper into the water in unhurried steps ...
(Walking towards the big door.) You felt the temptation of death for the first time.
(Stops.) You've been afraid of death ever since you were small, afraid that one day you'd disappear from the face of the earth once and for all.
At one time you shot and killed a bird with plumed

feathers. It was cut up so badly that its insides all spilled out. Only an indigo plume remained, which you kept … *(Keeps walking.)* Your life is in fact an enigma, you've not been able to walk away from desires, including sleeping with women, getting married and getting divorced. You're still afraid of death, even though not as much as before. If one day it arrives, your life will be over and that's that, there'll be no need to think about it any more. But you're still trying everything possible to avoid its coming; apart from the instinct to survive, there's no other meaning you can think of, no other reason for you to keep on living. Even if you cried out loud or blew a whistle as hard as you could, the whole thing would still be nonsensical, a laughable nonsense even today.
(Walks in front of the door.) You can't walk in through this door, it's in your destiny, once you cross the threshold, everything here will vanish, no more.
You know very well that there's nothing behind the door, all is but your imagination, even your childhood memories are shadowy, they'll only come back to you slowly and reveal themselves after you've ransacked your brain, but they remain blurred, the only thing that's clear is the effort you've put in. You've made the effort, trying in vain to sketch an outline of your memory, but it's like this door frame, you can't be sure what's inside.
(Turns around.) You can't map out the border between memory and imagination, if memory is real and imagination is mere fantasy, how can you tell how much reality actually resides in memory, which has already been processed by imagination, and how much of it is not mere fantasy? In the final analysis you can't return to the reality which has elapsed, and you're destined to live in the here and now.
(Leaves the door.) You know that right now you're sleepwalking, living in a world between dream and reality, and you can't be sure whether the reality you're in is

merely your memory or imagination. You don't even have the courage to disturb your dream, is it because such a disturbance would mean the death of your self? There's no way to detect whether you, your self, are real or fictitious. You're like an illusive shadow, perhaps that's why you want to have a woman, the tangible body of a woman, so that you can prove your existence, and it is not important who this woman should be. At this time, you need only a woman who could share your carnal desire with you — something like that. *(Droops his head.)*

(Prostitute appears behind the door with the moonlight on her back. Her face is cold and pale.)

Prostitute You just want her to submit herself to your desire, is that it?

Sleepwalker *(Turns around.)* You say isn't she dead already?

Prostitute It's you, you're the killer …

Sleepwalker You say it's obvious that the Thug did it, or it could have been the other bastard. Who knows? The stray bullet could have come from the front or from behind. They were shooting at each other, unfortunately she was caught in the middle and she became the victim. Anyway, what good can you expect when you've fallen into the hands of gangsters?

(Prostitute snickers.)

Sleepwalker You ask what is she laughing at?

Prostitute *(Moving with the moonlight, she steps in through the door and walks slowly towards him.)* Unfortunately it's you who pushed her inside. You're so forgetful!

(Sleepwalker hurriedly slips the head inside the suitcase.)

Prostitute She was killed by your imagination. You abused her in your imagination, and then you killed her. It's so typical of men.

Sleepwalker You say you're not with them, you're entirely different!

Prostitute But you're a man, all men are the same, they're so egotistical.

Sleepwalker You say more or less you've got to have a bit of ... *(Hides the suitcase behind him.)*

Prostitute A bit of what?

Sleepwalker A bit of compassion ... a bit of apprehension ... a bit of conscience —

Prostitute Don't talk about conscience!

Sleepwalker What then?

Prostitute The small bit of conscience you had has already vanished a long time ago. That's right, there's only a little bit of cowardice left in you, which is the difference between you and them, of course you know what's meant by "them." You don't have the courage to act, to do anything. Only in your imagination or in your fantasy can you let yourself go, being ever so wild and unruly, but you're an absolute coward when it's for real.

(The door behind Prostitute gradually closes until it is half shut.)

Sleepwalker You say you can admit the difference, but you're certainly not a coward.

Prostitute Don't worry, she's not saying you're impotent. She's only referring to your so-called "thinking." You only talk to yourself, and you've been using your brain too much to know how to make love to a woman. That's why you haven't been able to get your woman, the kind you've been dreaming about.

Sleepwalker What kind of woman?

Prostitute Don't you know? A whore, one who can fulfil all your sexual fantasies.

Sleepwalker *(Hesitates.)* Sure I do, the question is whether or not she can do it.

Prostitute There's no way you're going to find her.

Sleepwalker Why not?

Prostitute Because even hookers are human beings and sex to them is only a way of making a living. Isn't it the same with you? You've got to have an occupation, you've got to work whether you like it or not. So you're also putting yourself up for sale, aren't you?

Sleepwalker *(Retorts.)* You say you're talking about her, and you're asking if she enjoys her work.

Prostitute Are you talking about her flesh trade? Or the body she makes a living with? Hookers are like ordinary women, they're not necessarily cold or frigid, nor are they necessarily not wanton. The key is whether you can turn on that special nerve.

Sleepwalker You say then she's after sensual pleasure, isn't she?

Prostitute Maybe it's just the opposite.

Sleepwalker You ask is she going after emotional gratification but thinks that you're in it for the pleasure?

Prostitute You said wrong.

Sleepwalker You say she also has spiritual needs, and she's not doing it just for money?

Prostitute Wrong again.

Sleepwalker You say then you don't understand.

Prostitute You're so pathetic.

Sleepwalker What do women consider sexy then? Is it money? Or is it violence?

Prostitute You're really out of it, aren't you? It's tiring talking to you. You don't know how to listen to a woman, you don't know how to listen to her voice, you'll never be able to understand a woman.

Sleepwalker Maybe it is so. *(Feels frustrated.)*

Prostitute *(Strokes his head.)* In fact she still likes you, you're such a big kid.

Sleepwalker But one who can't arouse her desire.

Prostitute That's not important, as far as a woman is concerned.

Sleepwalker What's important then?

Prostitute Make sure that she has no troubles.

Sleepwalker To flatter her, tell her that she's pretty, sexy, and attractive? And tell her that she's alluring, titillating, a cheap, lowly, and raunchy piece of meat, just like a whore who'd sell herself to the highest bidder?

Prostitute If she can find a customer, why not?

Sleepwalker *(Startled and speechless.)* Is it true … you ask … you say you … could also pay to …

Prostitute *(Moves away.)* It depends, if she accepts the offer.

Sleepwalker You ask her why did she accept the bastard's offer?

Prostitute It doesn't concern you. Even if she did, it's her decision to make. It's her body, her own body! It's none of your business!

Sleepwalker You'd pay! You say you'd pay!

Prostitute But she has to agree first. *(Walks away.)*

Sleepwalker *(Catches up with her.)* You ask did she agree to do it with that rascal? You demand her to say it!

Prostitute *(Steps back.)* Say what?

Sleepwalker Say it, you want her to say — *(Moves forward and forces her.)*

Prostitute There's nothing to say.

Sleepwalker You must have her say it! When that rascal did it with her, did she feel any pleasure?

Prostitute Yes, *(Lifts her head up high.)* so what?

(Sleepwalker is dumbfounded.
Prostitute laughs out loud, bending her waist.
Sleepwalker approaches, and she keeps him away with her hands.)

Sleepwalker You ask what's the meaning of this?

Prostitute Because, you're not a big, bad rascal. *(Turns to move away.)*

Sleepwalker You say she covets the devil!

Prostitute And you're so far from being a devil, right?

Sleepwalker You say there's a devil in everyone's mind. The question is whether or not you set it free.

Prostitute Your problem is not whether you want to, or whether you're willing to, it's that you're incapable.

Sleepwalker You say she's only in it for the pleasure.

Prostitute Don't you also want your life to be wild and crazy?

Sleepwalker You say she is virtually as bad as a broken shoe.

(Prostitute immediately takes off the only shoe she has on. Holding it high above her head, she moves far away from him.)

Prostitute What more have you got to say? She can't stand men wearing undershirts.

(Sleepwalker takes off his undershirt and approaches her.)

Sleepwalker A stinking whore!

(Sleepwalker throws himself at her, but Prostitute turns and gets away.
A frosty looking Ruffian appears in the dark, carrying a gun in a holster attached to a belt on his back. His top is bare. He stops Prostitute and holds her in his arms. He grabs the shoe from her hand, pushes her down and throws the shoe on the floor. Nodding his head, he signals to her to pick up the shoe. As she picks up the shoe, Ruffian stamps his foot on her hand and crushes her fingers. She goes down on her knees.)

Sleepwalker You say, is this the kind of freedom she's after?

Prostitute She asks you, what's the meaning of freedom?

Sleepwalker You say, was freedom the reason why she didn't try to escape? Why did she put up with it? Why didn't she cry for help?

Prostitute She asks where could she have escaped to?

Sleepwalker To where she's no longer under anybody's control! Come, run away with you!

Prostitute Does freedom mean running away with you?

Sleepwalker Freedom means not being under anybody's control!

Prostitute What's the difference, she asks, between being under your control and under other people's control?

Sleepwalker You say at least you wouldn't force her to do things! You can't stand it, seeing her being tortured like this —

Prostitute She says she doesn't need anybody's pity!

Sleepwalker You say you really don't understand —

Prostitute She tells you to get the hell out of here!

(The door gradually closes, leaving a small crack.
Sleepwalker is puzzled and picks up his undershirt.
A bald Thug appears in the dark. He is dressed in a suit but without his wind breaker. He takes Prostitute's hands and dances with her, paying no attention to Ruffian.
Ruffian retreats into darkness.
Sleepwalker turns around and puts on his undershirt.)

Prostitute Poor guy.

Thug Who?

Prostitute The guy over there.

Thug *(Takes a glance at Sleepwalker.)* Oh, the guy carrying the suitcase.

Prostitute What's in the suitcase? It shouldn't be secret.

Thug It's a head.

Prostitute A what?

Thug You know, that gadget's called thinking.

Prostitute Oh, how disgusting. Why put it inside a suitcase?

Thug Otherwise it'd be too hot to handle. That small thing, it tends to roll all over the place.

Prostitute Can't he just dump it somewhere?

Thug My darling, where's he gonna dump it, huh? Tell me, now.

Prostitute Never mind, just don't try to dump this little darling here.

Thug Oh no, how can that be? She's right here, safe and sound. *(Embraces her tightly.)*

Sleepwalker *(Walks further away.)* You can't understand the relationship between you and her, whether she sells and other people buy, whether people consume her or she consumes people, whether she consumes herself, or whether people consume her and consume themselves. But what has all this got to do with you? Maybe you also desire her because people consume her and then consume themselves? Or you're angry or lustful because she sells sex or you're tormented or satisfied because she is abused or she abuses herself and these are all but masochism. And all of these things have nothing to do with her, or do they?

Prostitute He's still there.

Thug Are you scared of him or something?

Prostitute No, but he's a real pest.

Thug Let's get rid of him then.

Prostitute Don't. Let him be. *(Holding him tight.)* Are you happy?

Thug Yeah, I'm happy.

Prostitute If you're happy, I'm happy.

Thug That's swell, darling.

(Thug lifts up her hands and leads her to turn around in circles.)

Thug He says she's a cunning little kitten.

Prostitute She says no, a lazy kitten, lazy and greedy. *(Giggles.)*

(Thug lets her turn again and again, and then with a swing of his hand, Prostitute disappears into the dark.)

Sleepwalker This is a boring world. You think, but only because you're masochistic. You're equally as boring, and you know it very well, you know you're unsalvageable!
(Walks away.) You say you don't like strawberries, they're too mild and too tasteless. You'd rather watch other people eating them, especially a young woman: one by one she puts the voluptuous and red strawberries into her mouth, a mouth which is even redder

and more voluptuous than the strawberries themselves. For you, watching is infinitely more relishing than eating.
(Speaks loudly.) You see a bat falling down — *(Extends his hands and opens his palms to reveal a bat.)* Yes, a bat! You haven't seen any in this city, and no centipedes and no swallows either, just cats and dogs. Even rats are very rare. The streets are all covered with dog shit!

(Thug stares coldly at Sleepwalker.)

Sleepwalker You ask him what does he want?
Thug He says you're his slave.
Sleepwalker You say you're not for hire.
Thug He says you're a worm.
Sleepwalker You say go take a hike! *(Throws the bat at him.)*
Thug He says you're a steer driven by other people.
Sleepwalker *(Sleepwalker picks up the suitcase.)* You say he can't bulldoze you any more.
Thug *(Thug reveals a smile from the corner of his mouth.)* He says you're his dog.
Sleepwalker *(Picks up the suitcase.)* You say he's already dead.
Thug *(With disdain.)* He says your fate's still in his hands.
Sleepwalker *(Lifts the suitcase up high.)* You say he can't do anything to you, he can't control you any more!
Thug *(Makes a weird hand gesture.)* He says you've already done all that he's asked you to.

(Sleepwalker lifts the suitcase and hurls it at him.
Thug calmly picks up the suitcase, without saying a word. At the same time the door, which has been left open with a crack, is closed tightly.
The moonlight disappears completely. Thug vanishes.
There is only a faint and greyish white light on stage.)

Sleepwalker You say you have no compassion, and you have no pity.

When you see others suffer, you feel happy instead.
You say you want to destroy everything,
You say you know that you are vicious,
You can kill without turning a hair.
You say you find evil more exciting than good,
You might not be any less evil in comparison with other people.
You say it's only because you don't have the supreme power,
Otherwise, the world would have been destroyed a long time ago.
You say you want to scream and cry out loud —
But you have lost your voice.
You say all men are like worms,
They squirm all over the world,
Why? You have no idea why,
Just like the quiet sea bed,
Where massacres and devouring carnage
Are carried out in utter silence.
Fire is spreading all over ... *(Looks at his feet.)*

(The streetlight gradually brightens to a dark red colour.)

Sleepwalker A sun,
It has light but no heat,
Falls on a dried up tree. *(Lifts his head to look at the lamppost.)*
Time has already stopped
Why do you still have to run away?
Jesus Christ, a lonely traveller,
Nobody can save anyone. *(Stops and stands under the lamppost.)*
You're not the saviour, you're not a disciple,
You're sick and tired of the game of death.

(Prostitute enters, barefoot and carrying the suitcase. She

sits down and crosses her legs. With the suitcase between them, she opens the suitcase and starts to remove her make-up, paying no attention to what is around her.)

Sleepwalker You've already said enough.

Prostitute *(She rubs her face with a cotton ball, using the opened suitcase top as a mirror.)* She asks you what's the meaning of enough?

Sleepwalker You say enough is enough, enough is a word.

Prostitute She asks, *(Wipes away her eye shadow.)* what is a word?

Sleepwalker A word is a word. Originally it has no meaning, but it could be given countless meanings. It's all up to you, depending on how you want to explain it. But in the final analysis, a word is still a word, it has no meaning. Take for instance black, white, eat, make love, saviour, suffering, and baloney, no matter how you mix these words, using combination as the principle or process, or dismantle them and mess them up again before regrouping them once more, the resulting eloquence is still only a repetition of nonsense.

Prostitute Then she asks, *(Closes left eye.)* what you've just said, is it all nonsense? *(Wipes away left eye shadow.)*

Sleepwalker Whether nonsense or not, it's not important. The important thing is that you're still saying them. You are you only because you can still say the words.

Prostitute She asks, how about you? *(Closes right eye.)* Are you also a word? *(Wipes away right eye shadow.)*

Sleepwalker Maybe, maybe not.

Prostitute *(Pours some lotion on her hand.)* Maybe what? *(Closes both eyes.)* Maybe not what? *(Wipes her face.)*

Sleepwalker Not anything!

Prostitute It's over. *(Her hand lets go the cotton ball, which she uses to take off her make-up.)*

Sleepwalker What's over?

Prostitute Over is over. *(Takes a tissue to wipe her hands.)*

(Prostitute lifts her head. Only a bright red mouth is visible on her face.
Sleepwalker stares.
From the suitcase Prostitute takes out a man's head which bears an extreme likeness to Sleepwalker. She holds it with both hands and inspects it. After a while, she lets go of it carefully and the head starts to roll on the floor. She gets up nonchalantly. The streetlights are off, and Prostitute disappears.
Sleepwalker approaches the head, bends over to scrutinize it and pokes at it with his foot.
Tramp enters with a wine bottle in his hand.)

Tramp It's almost daybreak, why are you still dawdling out here?

Sleepwalker Oh! *(Quickly stamps on the head with his foot and squashes it. Looks back.)* Sorry. You ask him is the head still there?

Tramp *(With disdain.)* Head? Sooner or later everybody's got to lose his head. There's always a time to lose one's head, and there isn't a head which can't be lost.

Sleepwalker That's right. But you're asking is your head still there?

Tramp *(Raises his eyebrows.)* You want to drink some more?

Sleepwalker *(Takes the bottle and immediately takes a gulp. Laughs.)* You say you can't be sure whether it's you or your head that's drinking the stuff.

Tramp It's all the same. *(Raises the bottle to check out the wine inside.)* Whatever we drank, it's gotta be wine anyway. *(Throws away the bottle.)*

(Both laugh heartily and loudly.)

Sleepwalker It's all the woman's fault. If that whore hadn't flashed her legs, wearing only a pair of nylon pantyhose in this freezing cold night, and if she hadn't walked around coming on to people, you'd have had a good night's sleep. You say you're really sorry.

Tramp Women. They never change.

Sleepwalker No mistake about it! If there's got to be a mistake, you say, it's that you got involved in her stupid business, something you really shouldn't have done in the first place. But she said there was a hole in her stockings —

(Tramp gives a guffaw.)

Sleepwalker You say your mistake was to take up her conversation!

(Tramp gives another guffaw.)

Sleepwalker You say you were wrong to have asked her questions.
Sleepwalker It'd have been alright if you hadn't said anything!

(Tramp gives yet another guffaw.)

Sleepwalker *(Laughs as well.)* You say but you did ask her.

(Tramp laughs again.)

Sleepwalker You say you didn't expect to get involved like that …

(Tramp laughs once more.)

Sleepwalker You ask is he laughing at you?

(Tramp laughs yet again.)

Sleepwalker What's so laughable about that?

(Tramp keeps on laughing.)

Sleepwalker You ask is he laughing at you or laughing at the hole in her stockings?

(Tramp still laughs.)

Sleepwalker You ask can he stop laughing?

(Tramp still laughs, blinking his eyes.)

Sleepwalker You ask what does he mean?

(Tramp carries on laughing.)

Sleepwalker It's absolute nonsense!

(Tramp still laughs.)

Sleepwalker You laugh just because it's meaningless.

(Tramp still laughs, his mouth open.)

Sleepwalker You won't say anything any more. *(Walks away.)*

(Tramp still laughs, turning towards him.)

Sleepwalker *(Turns towards him.)* You ask can't he stop his silly giggle?

(Tramp keeps on laughing, his mouth open.)

Sleepwalker *(Yells.)* Okay, you old geezer! *(Approaches him and grips Tramp's neck with his hands.)* You can't stand this kind of taunting any more, you've got to let him know that you're not such a coward. You're alive and kicking, you're not a shadow of other people, you're real and you really exist. You may be equally as meaningless as this meaningless world you're in, but your meaningless resistance against this meaningless world more or less proves your meaningless existence! *(Lets go his hands.)*

(Tramp falls on the floor. The laugh still lingers on his face, as if it is frozen)

Sleepwalker *(Startled.)* You've strangled him to death? That's impossible!
(Shakes him.) Stop fooling around, you old geezer! *(Slaps his face but there is no response.)* You didn't mean to kill him, you just couldn't stand the way he was taunting you ...
(Steps back.) You say — *(Looks around.)* There is no one you could talk to about this, even though you're sure

that everywhere there's always a pair of inquisitive big eyes, and you're constantly being spied upon. You really can't get away from this trap they've laid for you, either someone'll push you down or you'll fall down there yourself. It's a futile struggle, you've tried to pitch evil against evil, anger against brutality, you've tried destroying others to save your own skin, but in the end you still can't help falling into their trap. No, in a dangerous situation like this, you've got to pretend that you haven't done anything wrong, you've got to get this dirty business over with. It doesn't matter who's the instigator, cases like who did what to whom first are never resolved, and you still have to cover your tracks whether you're guilty or not guilty, but how can you possibly be not guilty? Anyway, the verdict is not for you to decide.
(He picks up the old man and pushes him into the suitcase, tucking in his hands and feet. Then he gives a good hard jump on the suitcase and finally manages to close it. He sits on top, panting.) You are on top of evil, no, you're outside the realm of evil, no, evil is in your heart, you have to eliminate the feeling of evil in your heart!
(He stands up and treads on the floor with his feet, making a screeching sound. He halts suddenly and takes off his shoes, which he then holds in his hands.) You're born with this feeling, you can't eliminate it, everybody has it, there's no way you can be innocent, but it'll be alright as long as you don't think about it!

(Dawn breaks over the flyover.)

Sleepwalker Before it becomes light, and before the garbage truck comes along, you'll have to return home. Your neighbours will be hurrying to catch the morning train. As long as you manage to avoid them in the corridor, sneak in through the door and close it without making too

much noise, you'll be able to relax and set your mind at ease. Then you'll take a beautiful hot bath, you'll be clean all over, and you'll lie in your bed without a single worry in the world. You don't need to think about it any more, your nightmare will be over and gone for good.
(He goes back to get the shoes and walks towards the flyover.)
You'll be able to sleep late. When you wake up afterwards, you'll turn on the radio to listen to the news, or you'll go downstairs to the street corner to buy yourself a newspaper, and then while you're enjoying your breakfast and sipping a cup of tea, you'll take a casual look at the newspaper to see if there is any mention of murders, prostitutes, gangsters, or tramps who were drunk or who were frozen to death in the cold —

(A masked man wearing an undershirt similar to Sleepwalker's appears on the flyover. He blocks sleepwalker's way.)

Sleepwalker Who are you? What do you want? You want you to step aside and let you pass! You ask what in the world do you want? You want you — to let you — pass —!

(Neither of them is willing to yield, and they grapple with each other in silence.
The sound of a subway train approaches while the two are still grappling.
The train rushes past. The stage light darkens. There is a loud and coarse scream.
Front left stage gradually becomes light. There is no one in the train coach, just an open book on the floor.
Conductor enters. He picks up the book and exits.
Curtain.)

The End

18 November 1993, Paris, France

(This play was commissioned by the Beaumardrais Foundation of France. Premiere rights belong to France.)

Some Suggestions on Producing *Nocturnal Wanderer*

1. The play's subject matter is a nightmare. Naturally it should avoid real life situations and a naturalistic presentation; on the other hand, neither should it resort to the bizarre. The pursuit of psychological reality and that of theatricality are not mutually exclusive; in fact they are to be equally emphasized for the reason that their interaction also contributes to the tensions in the play. It is hoped that the actors can first build up their neutrality on the stage before they start to listen, narrate and play the roles. This kind of actorial neutrality also helps them to achieve a balance between experiencing the characters' inner feelings and their awareness of being performers on the stage.
2. The props in the play, apart from being objects on the stage, are also partners interacting with the characters. Once the actors make the shoes, the suitcase, the cardboard boxes, the heads, and the doors come alive, the performance will be enriched and the longer monologues will not be relegated to the status of mere recitations. Stage designers should pay attention to highlighting the props so that they are not buried in the set.
3. The play makes frequent use of magic. Its many tricks and uncanny transformations bring about surprises for the audience and help to enhance the play's dramatic effect. The magical tricks are easily adaptable to different stage and lighting designs. Their execution should be clean and tidy; there is no need to overcome the audience's feeling of disbelief.
4. The play attempts to arrive at an explanation of some traditional themes such as the relationship between God and Satan, man and woman, good and evil, and salvation and suffering, and modern man's concerns for language and consciousness, as well as the relationship between the individual and the Other. When the play is performed in Chinese, the characters may be sinicized and endowed with Chinese cultural traits. For instance, Tramp may model himself after the image of *Jigong* 濟公, the Living Buddha in Chinese folklore and not the image of God in Western culture. Other characters can also be sinicized in the same manner: Thug may become the leader of an underworld gang, and

Ruffian may become an assassin in traditional Chinese stories. As for costumes, all the characters may wear modern day street clothing. Prostitute should avoid wearing the Chinese *qipao* 旗袍, and it is better for Sleepwalker not to wear a tie. When the play is performed in Western languages, costume design is discretionary.

The above suggestions are for reference only.

Weekend Quartet

Early summer, cherry season.
A lazy weekend, an old house in a country farm.

Anne, a rather sluggish woman.
Bernard, a painter in his twilight years.
Cecile, a coquettish girl.
Daniel, a middle-aged writer who has run out of things to write about.

Quartet No. 1

Bernard

That afternoon, you're both in the garden, the sunshine is very good, the sunshine is gorgeous, she says. She chooses her words carefully, if you said the sunshine is gorgeous, she'd pick another word to correct you, correcting you has become one of her hobbies. She doesn't do anything, all day long she just holds a book in her hands and then picks up some words and throws them at you. She wants to write, if a woman wants to write, well, let her write. That's a matter of course. The problem is she never actually writes, she just wants to write. Just try it, try spending a whole day with a woman who aspires to be a writer! You've got to discuss things with her all the time, she's not there to be your company, to wait on you, oh no, instead you've got to wait on her. The fair sex, well, their temperament is as fickle as the weather. If you tried arguing with her, just one word out of you and she'd be up in arms against you.... That afternoon, you and she are in the garden, and the sunshine is very good, originally —

Anne, Bernard

The sunshine is gorgeous.

And there's no war!

What did you say?

You said there's no war, what's wrong with that? Then when you see her frowning, you can only force a smile on your face as if you were begging her not to throw one of her tantrums at you. She's still quite a charmer despite her age, well-preserved no doubt, and if time could be turned back twenty years, she'd have been quite a dish, a young and beautiful dish. And look at you, you're left with just a baggy and moldering face. On the other hand, no frowning woman is a beautiful woman, no matter how young or beautiful she is; believe it or not, the more beautiful the woman is, the more you'll feel the pain. Of course when that happens, you've just got to turn your face away and pretend not to see anything.... The door bell is ringing, the guests have arrived. You go and open the door, ah, he has brought his girlfriend along with him, you've invited him to spend a quiet weekend in the country, but now it's more apt to say that you've invited him and his girlfriend. Yeah, the guy never runs out of babes, a lady-killer just like you were in those days.

Anne, Daniel, Cecile, Bernard

Anne.
Daniel.
Cecile.
You can call me old Bern. I'm a bit older than all of you.

Daniel, Bernard

The sunshine is so good!

The sunshine is gorgeous, you immediately correct the guest, or rather, remind the guest, and when you turn around, you suddenly discover that her kneaded eyebrows have disappeared, she's welcoming the guests, all smiles, of course it's directed towards him and only him, and not that radiantly perky kiddie girlfriend of his beside him. She's really out of line with her meanness, you know it yourself. When you're at your age, so advanced in years, you're able to understand yourself perfectly, if nothing else.

Cecile, Bernard, Daniel

What a huge garden!

It goes all the way to the pasture over there, originally this was a farmstead, you could keep horses here if you wanted to.... Look at you, you've made it big, haven't you? And what a beautiful young companion you have here. I'll give you a tour of the place later. In the meantime, you might as well enjoy the place while you're here, hey, do whatever you want, make yourself at home. You want to drink something before we go? Wine or tea?

It's so quiet here, not a bit of noise, you can even hear the bees humming.

Bernard, Cecile

There's only one country road that leads to the house, it's really far away from the highway.

Look, Daniel, you can take a bath while looking at the garden!

See this glass door here, it can be opened completely. In the morning, the sunlight goes right through and shines straight into the bathtub, that is, if you like tanning yourself while taking a bath.

Where's your studio, sir? May we please look at your paintings as well?

Over there in the stable. And don't call me sir. Once you step through the door, there's no need for ceremony, and don't respect me for my age either.

Okay, I'll call you old Bern then, I like that.

Why not? I may be old, but I still have to live, and live happily I will.

Daniel, Anne

This is like paradise on earth.

There're lots of rooms here, nobody'd bother you if you wanted to write, it's totally quiet.

You write too?

Sometimes, just for fun.

Cecile, Daniel, Anne

I envy you. Daniel, let's buy a house in the country, okay?

Sure, if we can afford it.

It wasn't that expensive when we bought it, but we renovated the place afterwards. He was his own designer.

It's not too difficult, is it? You just have to write a best-seller.

A love triangle, better yet, add one more angle and make it a quadrangle, and spice it up with something juicy, you know, cops and robbers, political scandals, sex changes, exotic places, and things like that.

Got to have sex.

Daniel, Anne

Are you writing about sex? Is that what you plan to write about?

I only write about myself, and I'm the only one to read it.

A kind of private writing? Not for publication?

Cecile, Bernard

Look at these, Daniel. Wow! What a life!

Let there be wine! A beautiful weekend, a friend from the city, and the company of a charming young lady to boot, this is the best time to get drunk, wouldn't you say? What a beautiful sunset, and there's no war, what more could we ask for, eh? People, what music shall we put on? Take your pick, but not those crazy teenyboppers' rocking and rolling stuff, you're too old for them. Not that you haven't been crazy before, from self-obsession to revolution, or to be more specific, from subversive art to the art of subversion, you've tried your hand at all of them. In the final analysis, art is still art, and revolution, where's it now? Anyway, you're lucky to be still alive! Here, let's propose a toast to all of them!

Wow, cherries!

That's right. You can pick one off the tree whenever you feel the urge to, and they're grown without pesticides.

I just adore cherries.

Go pick them, don't be shy. Anne, give her a pair of scissors.

Where are they? I'll get them myself later!

Daniel, Bernard

An early summer afternoon.

A weekend.

God has given us one day.

And men think it's not enough.

So that we can take it easy and enjoy life for a while.

If all men were like birds on a tree, far away from all their troubles, wouldn't life be just wonderful?

If there were no earthquakes, no car accidents, no pollution, no frauds, no unemployment, and no Aids, kidnapping or assassinations.

Got to have no justice, no ideals, no sympathy, and no compassion.

And naturally no morality, can you imagine how wonderful the world would be? Who needs them anyway?

No matter what, right now we have this wonderful weekend to ourselves.

This is the Garden of Eden on earth, God isn't the only one who can afford to have a garden.

Bernard, Anne, Daniel, Cecile

Hear, hear! And the sunshine is very good also —
The sunshine is gorgeous.
No wars, either racial or between the sexes.
Wars, wars, forget about wars, they're so annoying.
What do you want to drink?

Cecile, Bernard

I'll have a small martini first.
Ice?
Thanks.

Daniel, Bernard, Anne

Have you seen the papers? You know, Sarajevo.
Everything is happening there.
Can't we talk about something else?
And in Italy, the Mafia —
They're everywhere, aren't they?
At least they're not here yet.

Bernard, Cecile

Oh, sorry, did I make a mess of your dress?
Just a little, don't worry about it.

If you want to take a bath —
In front of the garden?

Anne, Bernard

He designed the whole layout himself, he considers it his *chef d'oeuvre*.
But you still need a young lady who's willing to perform.
Let's talk about something more interesting!

Daniel, Cecile, Anne

One day …
Go on.
Right, go on.
A fable.

Anne, Cecile

What do you mean?
It doesn't mean anything.
Why?

Daniel, Cecile, Anne

A fable which is unspeakable.
That's not funny.
Well, it still means something, doesn't it?

Cecile, Bernard

What does it mean? Tell me!
How sweet!
Somebody says I'm stupid.
Who?
Go ask him.

Anne, Bernard

Can't we talk about something else?
Wow, it's so nice out.

The sunshine is gorgeous!
And there's no war.

Daniel, Bernard, Cecile

Let's drink to our health!
Cheers! Cheers!
Can I, sir, oops, I beg your pardon, can I see your studio?

Bernard, Anne, Daniel, Cecile

Of course, you're most welcome.
She's so full of zest.
And hot air, there's never a moment of quiet when she's around.
Will I be in your way?
So typical of today's younger generation.

Cecile, Bernard

I just adore paintings.
And cherries?
That's right, it's like when I was small, in our place there's also a … Dan —
Let them go, Anne's like a lazy cat whose only love is to bask in the sun.

Anne, Daniel

You like his paintings?
I saw them, you know, those in his albums and in the museum …
You haven't answered my question.
I like him as a person, he's so hospitable.
You slick devil, you.

Cecile

Come quick!

Daniel, Anne

In a minute. Furthermore, he's a straight shooter.
He's straightforward all right, I dare say.
Shall we go together?
You go ahead, I've seen them countless times.

Cecile, Bernard

He's always like that, like his head's in the clouds or something. He tells you to meet him on a certain day, and then he's got the nerve to get the date wrong!

Of course he wouldn't get it wrong if it was his girlfriend, oh, I beg your pardon.

Daniel, Anne

Why not look at them again?
I should go and prepare dinner.

Cecile, Bernard

What do I care? But it's like he's senile without even getting old.
It's not easy living with a writer.

Daniel, Anne

Can I help?
Thanks, I've put them into the oven already.

Cecile, Bernard

To hell with writers, I've got my own stuff to look after. Anyway, it's not like I'm his secretary or something.

Of course, of course, we've all got our own dates to keep, especially a beautiful girl like you.

Anne, Daniel

You certainly know how to please people.

No, it's just good manners.

Cecile, Daniel, Bernard

Daniel!

Coming.

Give me a hand, we rarely open the front door, usually we just use the passage upstairs.

Wow, you've even got a second floor? Gosh, this is such a huge place!

We've divided it into two studios, a big one and a small one. They used to keep a herd of horses here, you know.

(*Music*)

Cecile

Oh, a cherry tree!

She says she's got a soft spot for cherry trees, especially one that's full of red, ripe cherries, all of a sudden she's reminded of her childhood. She's talking about the time when she was small and there's a tree just like this one in their yard. At that time her parents had not yet split up. She had a home, a home with a garden. She also had a father, but she can't remember when she last saw him. Once when she was dashing out of a man's house, rushing down the stairs and across the street, a car suddenly halted right beside her and she was so scared that she began sweating all over. In the car was an old man, he just stared at her and didn't say a word. The street was empty, there were no pedestrians, and then the car just drove away. She suddenly thought if only she had a father …

She says she tried to look for her father and found his number from the phone book. For a long time she was thinking it over whether she should make the phone call. Eventually she did.

She says a woman answered the phone.

She says she left the woman her phone number. Later, her father phoned her back and they were to meet at a cafe. She thought the baggy-eyed bald man sitting in the corner by the glass door must have been her father, but he was so different from the father in her memory, according to her memory, but who knows if it's all just a figment of her imagination …

He said, she says her father said that if she needed money for something urgent she could go to him, but he also added that he didn't have very much money, he was living with this woman, and he had to look after their little girl. But still he wrote her a cheque.

She says, she hasn't tried to find him since, she hasn't tried to find her father.

Bernard, Daniel

Quite a charming young lady.

Of course.

How old is she?

Twenty.

So young.

She always says she's twenty.

She's still in the prime of her life. Still at school?

Sometimes, sometimes not. She doesn't know what she wants to do with herself.

Well, at her age, and a beautiful girl at that, she can afford to pick and choose.

Cecile, Anne

Sorry, I'm a bit nervous.

Why?

I feel strange.

Why's that?

I haven't had my period this month!

Go check it out, it's not that difficult.

You think I'm pregnant?

Do you want to have a child?

He doesn't want one.

Well, you're still young.

Why don't you have a child with him?

Him? He's too old.

Don't say that.
You don't know.
Of course I don't. But he still looks like a ball of fire, and so witty —
But he's a diabetic.

Bernard, Daniel

It's so touching when she's talking about her father ...
She hasn't got a father.
Well, she talked about this cheque —
She told you that?
In any case, it's a very touching story.
She tells everybody, once she meets them.
Must be some kind of incubus, it's understandable. Lovely girl though. You're so lucky.
Lucky or not, it's hard to say, but it's like a godsend that I met her.
Where did you meet her?
At the railway station.
Really!

Cecile, Anne

Shouldn't there be some kind of symptom if I'm pregnant?
I don't know, I haven't had a child before.
I really want to have a child with him.
That's easy enough.
But what if he says it's not his?
Are you involved with some other men as well?
Don't say that, I only love him.
And he?
Of course.
Then you should marry him and have children.
Are you married? Oops! Don't mind me, I was just asking.
I was divorced once.
How about him?
He was too, and we decided not to get married.

Bernard, Daniel

No kidding, the railway station, it's a wonderful place!

To be more specific, it's the café at the railway station.

It's too far from here to the station. At any rate, it's such a small place that it doesn't even have a café. We only have a country pub here, a hang-out for old folks. Young people have all gone to the cities to find work.

Cecile, Anne

Is he famous? I mean as a painter.

Painters have to put in time, they have to grind it out for years, how else can you get yourself known? Do you aspire to be a painter?

Oh no, I like paintings, I mean, I like looking at them, except that I don't quite understand them.

It doesn't matter if you understand them or not, it's how you feel that counts.

Sure I've got feelings, if they're landscapes or nude paintings, but his kind of painting … I wonder how I'd feel if I were his model.

Bernard, Daniel

Go on.

What should I say?

The cafe at the station, I haven't been there for at least ten years, you don't believe me? It's true.

Of course it's true. She came to me and asked me for a cigarette, I gave her one and lit it up for her.

That's pretty much to be expected, doing a little something for a young lady.

And then she sat opposite me at the table.

Was she also waiting for the train?

Yes. She asked me what time it was.

The same train?

The same train.

Well, obviously when you're at the station cafe, you're either waiting for somebody or waiting for the train.

Anne, Cecile

Has he asked you to be his model?

Oh no, he hasn't.

Don't worry about it, he hires models all the time.

And he's got to have models when he paints?

He paints everything.

Nudes too?

He did that a long time ago and then he stopped, and now he's starting to paint them again.

Daniel, Bernard, Anne

What … is something burning?

Anne — the roast! It's all burnt —

Oh, I'm awfully sorry!

(*Music*)

Bernard, Cecile

How about this?

Any way is okay.

Can I tell you something?

Go ahead.

But I don't know how to put it.

Say whatever's on your mind.

It's somewhat embarrassing. I don't know what to say.

Whatever you say, it's bound to be interesting.

Really?

Of course, for example, when you talked about that cherry tree, I found it ever so touching.

Oh that, that's just meaningless kiddy talk, I feel … with you around, I feel like I still haven't grown up. Do you think I'm childish too?

Oh, I'd love to have a daughter like you!

So that I'd be your model and you could paint me?

Have you ever heard of a daughter modelling for her father?

I haven't, but that's why I want to do it. People always want to do things no one else has done before.

To tell you the truth, I wouldn't mind having a father like you.

Is that so? Then I'd have a daughter to model for me all the time.

Anne, Daniel

Please light the candles.

Gladly.

Do be careful with your hands. Don't get them burned.

How seriously can my hands get burned by a candle?

You can't be too careful with fire.

That's true. You always sit by candlelight?

I like candlelight, especially when I'm engaged in a casual conversation with my guests.

It creates a mood, a warm and intimate mood, but if you're sitting alone by candlelight, wouldn't it make you feel even more lonely?

I enjoy being alone, he's the one who's afraid of loneliness, he invites all the guests.

The older you get, the more afraid you are of being alone, isn't that right?

Age has nothing to do with it.

Is he afraid of being forgotten?

Not quite, his paintings are in the museums already.

Then what's he afraid of?

He's afraid of boredom.

Bernard

The slightly open lips, so full, so moist, and so clearly defined. Those tender shadows at the corners of her mouth, the beautiful outlines of her neck and her shoulders, ah, and the two little cherries, so daintily puffed, you can't help but caress them with your eyes, to make her moan softly and feel your touch all over her body. You also admire her delicate hands, her fine and nimble fingers. A wicked little nymph she is.

She loves to flaunt her fine and pearly white teeth, and when she breathes in and wiggles the sides of her nose, or when she takes in her saliva, the veins on her neck will start quivering, pulsating up and down. You like the downy creases on her fair and glowing skin, you like her silky body hair, you like her laughter. Deep inside you there's a feeling of happiness, a happiness which is more than bodily lust. Of course you'd like to have a daughter like her. You want to have a vivacious *femme fatale* like her in front of you, behind you, and all around you, then you could look at her and admire her to your heart's content. But after all you're also a man, and you want to be more than her father.

Daniel, Anne

What else is there to talk about?

She says she's listening.

You say you'd rather hear her talk.

She says she has nothing left to talk about.

You say why doesn't she talk about the book she's going to write.

She says she only thinks about writing, but she hasn't written anything yet. Since you've written so many books, why don't you talk about them.

You say since your books have been written already, all that's left to do is to read them, there's no need to talk about them.

Then talk about those you still haven't written, or those still in the process of writing.

You say the problem is you don't know what you're going to write. Furthermore, what more is there to write about?

Cecile, Bernard

What are you looking at?

Nothing.

You're looking at me, aren't you?

You're looking at her, your daughter.

Then go ahead and look, she won't stop you.

Of course she's not your daughter, that's why it's possible for you to keep on ogling her at will.

Are you still painting?

Of course, of course. Of course you know that painting is just an excuse to keep her by your side, and she also enjoys being admired and looked at, doesn't she?

Do you want me to pose this way, or that way?

Any way will do. A wild kitten she is, of course she can show off all the wares in her possession and in any which way she wants.

Which do you think is better?

Play with her, make her throw all her caution to the winds, make her reveal her womanhood in all its grandeur.

Anne, Daniel

Then talk about yourself. A writer is infinitely more interesting than his work.

Not necessarily, I dare say.

Are all your books fictional? Created from your imagination?

Well, there's got to be real feelings in a book of course. That's something every woman is capable of, as long as she expresses her personal and deeply felt feelings in her, she could, to say the least, produce an interesting book.

Why just women?

If a book's only about men, nobody would want to read it.

Including yourself?

Yes.

In that case your books must be only about women, if I'm not mistaken.

Women and men, or to put it in another way, men and women.

Men and women, women and men, they're people all the same.

Because people have to be either men or women, their feelings are entirely different.

What other differences are there besides sex?

Of course there are, for instance, you and me.

Let's not talk about you and me.

I'm only interested in people who are alive.

But I'm dead already.

Really?

Almost.

Bernard, Cecile

A door …

What did you say?

Nothing. Once it's opened ...

What's opened?

You say you're talking about a door ...

May I ask what are you painting?

Oh yes, a door, once it's opened ...

I see.

Total darkness, so dark that you can't see things clearly.

Shall we turn on all the lights?

There's no need. Don't attempt to do anything. See that gleam of light? Where does it come from?

You're asking me?

No. It's spreading, it's slowly saturating the place, an illusion, a shadow ...

Are you talking about your painting?

You say you're talking to yourself.

I understand it now.

You say you don't need to understand, just see.

Right.

Anne

They didn't even bother to close the door. If she closed the door now, they'd certainly know that she's been here. And if she left it open she wouldn't think it's proper either, because at this hour of the night anything that happens in there would definitely be heard outside.

She's doing this for them, at least, for him, she must close the door quietly.

Maybe he left the door ajar on purpose when he left a crack open like that. But of course she wouldn't exactly barge in there right now, it'd be so embarrassing for everybody. Why should she do anything? Let them turn off the light in the corridor and just walked away quietly.

Bernard, Cecile

A shadowy image in the middle of flickering candlelight, it's the back of a woman. You quietly approach her, hoping that she'll turn around, but she lowers her head lazily and covers her face with her hands. So you softly put your hands on her shoulders. She turns sideways and tilts her head to face you. Oh, no, an old woman's dry and crumbling face! The candlestick falls onto the ground.... Once more you find yourself sinking into darkness, you try to pick up the candlestick, you grope around but you can only find some broken pieces.... You want to see if this is a dream, so you clutch the broken glass pieces in your hands, squeeze them as hard as you can to see if you'll bleed, and the blood keeps oozing out.... Your feet feel cold, as if you're not wearing any trousers, you bend down to touch your foot — It's not real! It's made of plastic!

No kidding?

What's so funny?

She says she didn't laugh. Are you not real? She's just asking.

You say you're talking about an illusion you had.

And what about her? Is she an illusion as well? Is she not real?

What a charming little nymph.

That's right, everybody is charmed.

And charming everybody.

Will a cat walk away from a fish? ... How come you've stopped painting?

Anne

She doesn't know if she loves him or not.

She doesn't know if it's because she's jealous.

She's not his wife, so there's no need to interfere. They haven't signed a contract or anything, so there are no restrictions. A little tramp, and she offers herself to him. His days are numbered, might as well let him do whatever his heart desires.

The bottom line is she's not a Madam. It's a matter between the two of them, the giver is willing and the taker is just as willing, the feeling is mutual, what's that got to do with her?

But she can't understand why she's feeling a bit uneasy, as if she's done something wrong. She only saw that the corridor lights were still on, so she came out and turned them off, that's all there is to it, isn't it?

Daniel, Anne

Sorry, you say you're looking for some matches. Your lighter, you can't remember where you put it.

She says her books are in the sitting room, she usually reads for a while before sleeping.

Of course, books can make people sleepy.

It has to be an interesting book, or she wouldn't read it in bed.

You say you usually sleep late, and before you sleep you've got to smoke a cigarette, you've had this bad habit for years.

She says if she can't sleep she'd drink a small glass of whisky, you want one?

You know that it's only a game, but it's the kind of game which excites you no end.

She acts as if everything was so natural, she doesn't think there's anything wrong in just wearing a lingerie.

Nothing happens by chance in this world, there's got to be a cause, a motivation. Of course, you can say that you're looking for matches or something, but you know, one always finds a way to say whatever he wants to say.

She's not particularly interested in him, no man can steal her heart any more, she knew perfectly well what'd happen even before she drank that glass of whiskey, but she still drank it anyway.

That's right, a woman tired of living still has to live on.

A man will never give up the chance to seduce a woman.

You can't be sure who's seducing whom, but you never change, you just want to have some fun.

She says, stay away from me, don't!

Daniel

You can't go forward
  and you can't go back
Go left
  go right
    you still fall into the trap

Therefore you
only think of enjoying yourself
the decadent pleasure of the moment
Afterwards
you still can't be sure
if there is
an afterwards ...
So there's no need to pretend any more
to act the part
it'll be more true
more relaxing
No more disciples or messengers
your body
is still quite real
Men
are destined
not to lead their lives
in any other way
A joke
a game of sex
just like gambling
you consume yourself
or gamble yourself away
When thinking stops
listen
Mozart
is he also comforted?

Quartet No. 2

Anne, Cecile

How are you?

Very well, thank you. It's been a long time since I had a weekend like this. It's so comfortable living in the country.

You've chosen a good time to come here, it wouldn't be as nice if it were in the winter.

Can't you light a fire or something? I just adore sitting in front of the fireplace.

The studio is so big, it wouldn't get much warmer lighting a fire.

I like space, I feel good whenever I step into a spacious room, no matter what I do.

What are you doing now?

I'm a model, haven't you noticed? He hasn't finished his painting yet.

I mean what do you do for a living?

Anything, as long as it's a job. But what I'd like best is to have my own home, then I could stay there and do nothing. You know, just like you.

You have everything now, haven't you? You and your friend?

Him? He's a writer alright, but he can't support me, I'm not as lucky as you are, I've got to work.

What kind of work do you do?

Whatever I can lay my hands on, it's hard to say, it isn't easy to find meaningful work.

Do you model as well?

Oh no, it's my first time, it's quite fun, don't you think?

Don't you think it's too much trouble? When you're posing you have to remain motionless for a long time, you can't even move one bit.

No, he let me move around, sometimes I could even walk to where he was and watch him paint.

That's true, all his models are very happy working with him.

He's got many models, yeah?

Of course you won't be the last, he changes them frequently, he paints all kinds of women.

Does he paint you often?

He likes young girls.

But I think mature women are more feminine.

That's exactly what's wrong with old men, the older they get the more they like to be with young girls, as long they don't make it difficult for them.

Me? I'm easy. I like older men, they're so gentle, and they look after you.

It's good if you feel so easy towards the whole thing.... In fact why don't you go outside and take a walk in the woods? You don't have to lock yourself up in the studio all day, you know. You're here to enjoy yourself, if you'd come here to work, he'd even have given you some money for it.

I didn't come here for the money! I like to watch him paint, to see how I'd look on canvas, how I'm transformed into a woman who looks like me, and yet a woman I hardly know —

Be careful, don't get him too excited.

I know —

No, you don't, he has high blood pressure.

Excuse me, I'm going out to take a walk in the woods.

Anne, Bernard

How's it going?

Fine. I had a good night's sleep.

I mean your work, you're happy with it?

A vivacious girl, a little vulgar though.

As long as you're still interested.

Sure, sure.

Is everything going smoothly?

Yeah, not bad.

Maybe we can keep her here for a few more days.

Perhaps. But it depends —

She doesn't look like she's working and has to get back when the weekend's over, as long as her boyfriend doesn't say anything.

How about him, do you find him interesting?

What? Oh, him, he's quite intelligent, but somewhat arrogant.

Every writer thinks he's the one and only.

Aren't you the same?

Of course. But only few writers are interesting.

He sure knows how to flirt.

Really? As long as you don't think it's too much trouble. I don't feel right if you think my guests are a bother.

It's all right, they aren't, at least up to now.

Then tell him to stay for two more days, if that's not too much trouble for you.

And his girlfriend stays too?

Of course. Just let me know if you find them unbearable.

You're the master in this house.

And you're the mistress.

I'm not so sure about that, I'd better not play mistress.

Why not?

It'd be easier for all of us.

Why don't you go and take a look at my painting?

I don't want to be in the way.

Well, she's quite patient, and of course she's also a blithe spirit. She likes paintings too, she's curious. She's never modelled before, you know.

That's even better for you, isn't it? You must find the whole thing refreshing.

Of course, also very exciting.

Cecile, Anne

What are you looking at?

A cloud. There's something strange about this cloud.

Why do you think that?

It expands and spreads, and expands and spreads again, then it rolls out, and the middle gets puffed up and spreads once more, it's all happening so fast.

It's going to rain.

Like an overgrown cauliflower.

You sure know how to talk good!

Not really, there's pollution everywhere, even in the clouds.

You want me to make you some toast?
The toaster's on top of the oven, the coffee's still hot.

Daniel, Anne

Oh, it feels great after a cold bath!
Did you sleep well?
Excellent, it's so quiet, I'd still be sleeping if it weren't for the birds singing. Did you get up early?
I love to listen to the birds.
Same here. Outside the windows, at the crack of dawn … It's raining a bit, do you like listening to the rain as well?
When I'm listening to the rain I'm at peace with myself.

Cecile, Bernard

I hate it when it rains, you can't go anywhere.
This rain won't last. As soon as it stops you can go sunbathing in the pasture or by the river, or you can go pick some mushrooms in the wood. We're very easy here, just do whatever you want.
How about messing up things?
What's on your mind, you little devil you?
(Softly) I want to smash something, is that allowed?
Smash all you want, as long as you feel like it!
Can I call you daddy too?
Of course, I should count myself lucky with a daughter like you.
Luck doesn't come easily, it'll slip away if people don't know how to take good care of it.
(Loudly.) Did you hear that?

Daniel

How can you not hear it when it's that loud?

Cecile, Bernard

Never mind him, he's a little hard of hearing.

Are you kidding me?

He always pretends he's thinking.

Anne, Daniel

Is that right?

I'm watching the rain now. You see, when raindrops flow on the window pane, the scenery is immediately transformed, just like a mirage …

In the winter, if there weren't any footprints after a snowfall, it'd be just like a graveyard …

The feeling towards death comes exactly from the desire for life —

Cecile, Bernard

Oops, I'm so sorry! I've broken the teacup …

Something new, something old, you won't have any new things if you don't get rid of the old.

It broke while I was washing it.

Exactly, things do get broken after you've used them for some time, there's no exception, let alone a teacup.

Men too?

Of course, men are like things, after a while they tend to have this problem, then that problem. They just can't seem to help it. Never mind, it's only a teacup.

And the heart?

What heart?

A man's heart —

That's even more of a problem. What's wrong, babe?

Nothing much is wrong with this babe, except that I just cut my hand.

Let me have a look, don't let it get infected, you've got to put a dressing on it! Do we still have any bandages?

Anne, Daniel

A cunning cat.

A butterfly, she attracts all kinds.

Bernard

Follow me, let's put a bandage on it.

Daniel, Anne

He's so full of energy though.

It's still early and you're here, and on top of that, there's a young girl with him. Normally he'll start drinking at noon, and when evening comes he'll be totally exhausted, and the only sound you can hear in this big house is the sound of his snoring. I keep my door open all the time, and if I don't hear his snoring when I get up at night, I get scared. That's how my father died, he also drank ...

You can't go on like this.

What? Like what?

For example, you two could go out sometimes —

He drinks wherever he goes! If he takes the car by himself, who knows when ...

And you plan to go on watching over him all your life?

The situation is not as bad as it looks. I do need a shelter, and if nothing else, he's still a loyal old dog.

Bernard, Anne, Daniel

Have a look at the books in here, and take whatever you want, just as long as it's not anything she likes. At my age, there's nothing worth reading.

Have you had too much to drink or something?

He's just telling the truth. Any book that's worth writing has been written already.

Then why are you still writing?

It's just a habit. In fact, whatever I want to say has already been said.

Hear! Hear!

Then how come you're still saying it?

Because I'm still alive.

Can't we talk about something else?

Sure, right now I'm going to listen to the news to see if there's a war going on. I certainly know what a goddam war means!

All right, all right. Go paint your paintings.

She's driving me crazy.

Women, what can you do with them?

Cecile

Daniel!

Daniel

Coming.

Anne, Bernard

What happened to her?

Don't worry, just a small cut. I've put a bandage on it, she's okay.

Don't go too far!

Just look at you!

I don't really care, it's between you and her. I just want to remind you not to put me on the spot.

Daniel, Cecile

What happened to you?

I cut myself.

Where's the cut, is it serious? Let me see!

Not really, I've put a bandage on it.

What were you fooling around for?

I wasn't fooling around, I was behaving, and very careful too. A tiny little mouse, and cats are everywhere.

Who's the mouse? Who're the cats?

You don't know? You really don't know?

Don't go smashing up things! You're not a kid any more!

I can't help it —

Man is different from animals.

What if he was an animal?
You've got to understand, this is not your home, you know.
I understand. I understand everything.
That's good.
Then it's over.
What's over?
You've been with so many women, don't you know?
No, I really don't know.
All right, I promise I won't fool around no more.
It's a deal. *(Kisses her.)*
Don't you worry! *(Pushes him away and turns around.)*

Anne, Cecile

Are you all right?
I'm fine. It's just the finger, I've got a bandage on it already.
Don't let it come into contact with water. I'll clean up the kitchen later.
Sorry, I was a bit uptight just now.
It's no big deal.
My worries are over, I'm having my period.

Bernard, Daniel

Would you believe you can never truly possess a woman?
It's quite true, so you'd better give up the idea.
But tell me honestly, can you really give it up?
You've got to admit that you can't.
You see, women, not art, are the most exquisite creations in the world.
Then why are you still painting?

God can't be surpassed, no matter how hard we try. Man craves immortality, so he ransacks his brain to manufacture all kinds of illusions, and art is no more than an illusion created by man to be his plaything. And women, they're always beyond your reach, you can't truly possess them. You can only possess illusions, something you label as art.

I guess that's why you've turned to painting women now that you've finished with your abstracts, despite the fact that they're all illusions, right?

And there's no way you can someday say that you've painted them all, I mean women and illusions.

Cecile

A fickle lover whose heart is not there,

An old man who's crazy about her, but who is old enough to be her grandfather,

And she dances and shuffles her feet between the two, tick tap, tick tap!

Making a face at this one, forcing a smile towards the other.

Better be a bird than a butterfly,

Hopping from one branch to another, nobody can get a hold of it.

She's cunning like they say she is, if she wasn't, how could she keep a hold on her men?

Why on earth do they have to be men? Why on earth did she have to be born so pretty?

Where there's a garden there're birds.

Tick, tick, tap — tick tick tap — tick tick tap tap!

Bernard, Daniel

What's she singing?

Who knows? Whenever she's happy she tends to run off at the mouth.

She's a happy little girl.

Exactly, as happy as a dog with two tails.

When you're my age, you'll find out that's the hardest thing to do.

Anne, Cecile

You have a really exquisite voice.

Thank you, but I haven't had any training or anything.

You're still young, you can learn.

It's not something you can learn in two or three days, you've got to train your voice every day and take lessons.

You look like you have plenty of time, don't you?

It takes money, and the fees can be very high. You know, I met this old man once, he said I was born with a great voice, and he wanted to give me free lessons.

Just what you wanted, right?

But on one condition.

What condition?

To sleep with him.

He said it right out?

He didn't need to, it was quite clear what he was aiming for, wasn't it?

If you liked him, why not?

He was too old! Why should I let him feel me up with his hands?

Of course not.

He said he'd take me on a world tour and make me a pop star, and he'd be my manager.

Surely you didn't believe him?

Why should I sleep with him for nothing? Anyway, he didn't exactly teach me anything.

But did you take any lessons with him?

He only taught me how to get into his bed …

(Both of them laugh wholeheartedly.)

Daniel

You're a stranger, destined to be a stranger for ever, you have no hometown, no country, no attachments, no family, and no burdens except paying your taxes.

There is a government in every city, there are officers in every customs station to check passports, and man and wife in every home, but you only prowl from city to city, from country to country and from woman to woman.

You no longer need to take on any town as your hometown, nor any country as your country, nor any woman as your wife.

You have no enemies, and if people want to take you for an enemy to raise their spirits, it's purely their own business. Your only opponent — yourself — has been killed many times; there's no need to look for enemies, to commit suicide, or to do battle in a duel.

You have lost all memories, the past has been cut off once and for all.

You have no ideals, you've left them behind for other people to think about. At this time you wish, for example, to be a leaf wafting in the wind, or better yet, a bird flying at an angle from a tilted rooftop, watching the warped horizon floundering with you. You're moving freely in the air, atop cities and oceans, and without a destination, if suddenly there comes a gun shot or if your heart fails, would you leave any trace once you've fallen from the sky?

You, you wander between one word and another, between one phrase and another, there is no end, how could language or freedom of speech mean anything to you any more? The same language was once like a clattering steel shackle, impeding you and weighing you down, but now it has become as frivolous as this little slut here …

Anne, Daniel

She doesn't know why she keeps on dreaming of a black leather bag. No matter how much it's squeezed, mauled or pounded upon, it still remains so solid and intact.

That's easy enough, for instance, if I had an awl …

There's no need.

It wouldn't hurt to try —

But it's useless. She also dreamed of a tree on fire, it was just standing there, alone in the deserted wilderness, and she just stared at the raging fire with a blank expression on her face, unmoved, and not hearing any sound.

Because you're too far away, try getting closer.

She did, but she still had no feelings, because she's been burned up already. All that's left of her was just a shadow, a shadow belonging to someone else.

Shadow or not, she's got to be a woman.

Just a ghost.

Interesting, a daytime ghost. Did she rise from the dead at night?

She'd be even more fearful at night.

Was the night fearful or was it just your own fear of the night?

Nobody could have resurrected her anyway.

Did you try? There's no harm in talking about it if nobody's going to get hurt.

You're the writer, aren't you? Try to think and imagine it for yourself.

It's just that the images of my imagination have become feelings. If it were the other way around, then maybe the ghost could be resurrected.

So what? She couldn't be anything more than one of the living dead.

It remains to be proven.

Just leave her alone.

Just trying to see if she would respond.

She's poison, better leave her alone.

Bernard

You must prove that you haven't grown old, you don't want to admit that death is creeping up to you step by step.

You have to scream once more, feel once more, and then scream yet one more time, you're not going to allow them to close that dark and secret door behind you once and forever.

You want — you want to exert the strength left in your already weakened body to do battle once more, to struggle once more, and to …

You want — you've already got all you wanted. When you were young, you wanted to have your own car and speed away. Later you wanted to have a huge and classy studio, and now you've got a big farm.

You want to have fame, not power. You oppose every kind of authority, all power suffocates you. You tried rebellion and you succeeded, and now those not-worth-a-fart juvenile urchins are telling the world that you're already *passé*, but you don't need to chase after their passing fancies, because you know that their fads will cease to be even before you die.

You don't need more money, you're not that greedy, you've already got everything you wanted, and that's enough for you. In that case, what is it that you actually want?

You can't bear to say it, you can't say it right out that you crave immortality! Sooner or later your overtaxed body will be consumed, burned out. As for posthumous fame, only Heaven will know. For the time being, you're using up all your energy, the little energy that's left in you, to battle against death. It's a futile struggle, death is waiting quietly by the dark and secret door —

Anne, Daniel

Don't come over here!
What if he does?
Are you crazy?
He's as sane as ever.
Then stay where you are.
Just stand here and do nothing?
Keep talking, go on!
About what?
Anything, whatever you want to say, for example, fantasize —
For instance, a little indulgence —
How?
All women know how.
And men don't?
Men are more direct.
And they don't fantasize?
How?
For example, try fantasizing nakedness, a naked desire … *(softly, and then retreats.)*
But you need feelings to fantasize.
What's wrong with your eyes?
In the arms of a stranger?
No, in a strange place.
Like a trained and obedient animal.
No, rather like a wounded animal,
And then it starts moaning?
It's not making any noise, it's only licking its wounds. *(Retreats further, smiles and disappears behind the door.)*

Quartet No. 3

Anne

This dress suits you very well, don't you think? Walk around, that's right, do your stuff and show off that figure of yours! Pull up your skirt, show your legs, good. Show your tits, a bit more ... that's too much ... that's it! Just like a little tart, not the slightest bit of shame, and no hang-ups whatsoever! See that casual look on her face? It's a real killer. Come on, walk around, move your bum, just like in a fashion show ... turn around, do it again, you've got to turn smoothly, haven't you tried modelling before? Don't laugh! That's right, show your teeth, you little bitch. Good, lean on the door, no wonder men all have the hots for you. Watch it, someday you'll get sick and tired of all of these, you'll feel so tired, would you believe that? Your heart will die all of a sudden, leaving only a body which can't feel any longer. This is not to scare you, what else is there when you've wasted your youth? Nothing lasts forever, except for a tiny bit of memory, like a book which has been read or a story made up by other people, it's worse than a patch of emptiness in the dark. You don't understand, at your age you can't possibly understand. All right, go!

Cecile

I have nothing, I'm a bit sad.

I still have a pair of tits, they're so firm.

My lips are pouted, like a small animal looking for things to eat.

I also have a pair of nice round legs, every woman has them.

And I have a figure which is every woman's envy, all my measurements are just right.

I have no fears, in the past I was afraid, but I'm no longer afraid now.

I have no father, I was brought up by my mother.

I don't go around picking up men, I did, but not any more,

No, I drool all over them now, I didn't do that before, men like to hear this sort of things, don't they?

What more should I say? Oh yes, I also want to write a little something ...

I don't write poetry, I just want to write songs, rock and roll or jazz, or stuff like that.

I play the music myself while I sing, but my voice is not good enough, and I've got no money to take lessons.

I want to find a rich man, a roof over my head, free rent.

I also want to have a garden, I'll just lie there on the grass soaking up the sun, doing nothing.

Look at the clouds in the sky, gosh, even the clouds are polluted.

It's just some empty talk which nobody understands, like trying to chat with men about art.

Daniel

You are not sure
if it's to pursue excitement
Or it's to prove
you're as frivolous
Or you just want to see
what's going to happen?

Anne

She buries herself under a thick layer of make-up, only she herself knows,

Her face, her look, it's all fake from her eyelashes to her lips.

Cecile

She's a sinking ship, an overripe apple, a song sung too many times.

She hops left and right, she breaks out into laughter for no reason, she only wants to turn people on.

Bernard

You go up the stairs and others come down, it wouldn't be too bad if there's a heaven above and a hell down below, you're only afraid that there's absolutely nothing, a big mass of nothingness.

Anne

She's a dead fish, stiff, cold and smooth as glass,
A staring round eye on each side, sparkling but unable to see anything.

Cecile

She's an open book, you can read it whenever you want to.
She's a deep and shadowy abyss, it swallows herself up.

Daniel

You want to have a woman
  and a woman comes
You thought she'd be pretty
  and she's whorish
You thought she'd be glamorous
  and she's frivolous
If you have anything to say
  say it
If you have nothing to say
  feed them a load of boloney

Anne

She's not a fast food dish ready to be consumed,
Once the buttons are undone, you know how it'll all end.
It's all in the game,
There are no miracles.

Bernard

What's happening? Your eyes are too old to see, they're old, unquestionably old! Old age spares nobody, how can you hold it off? You've put up a struggle for nothing.

Cecile

In your eyes she's a little whore. Okay, she's an out and out whore, so what? She hates all of you from inside her heart. But when she's making love, she uses every part of her body, the upper and lower parts, you name it. What more have you got to say?

Bernard

"The partridge stays not for long." Whose poem is it? To hell with it, your memory is deteriorating. The books you've read, the titles and authors have all become a muddle. The ultimate goal of life — can't remember who said it, the essence of life, only a bit of scum is left.

Cecile

But she's not going to die with you,
It's your own business to die.

Anne

A footprint, over another footprint, is still just a footprint. (*Lowers her head.*)

A footprint, over yet another footprint, leaves only a footprint. (*Lifts her head.*)

When you walk over one footprint after another, you'll become … (*Laughs.*)

Daniel, Anne

A witch?
Might as well say a spirit.
Don't go!
What for? To watch you smoking a cigarette?
It wouldn't hurt just to chat.
But you've got to have something to chat about.

Of course. How about dreams?

But you've got to have the dreams first.

Anyway, it seems … And there's also this tiny secret light, it's not really hope …

Why did you stop?

Daniel

All is enveloped in obscurity. In the fuzziness, one could barely see. Among strand after strand of hazy lights, a dead city stands in a bottomless abyss, nestled in block after block of bare and desolate mountains. He looks up from below. It's like wandering at night, and the city itself looks like it's drifting and wandering from the top of the mountains. It's all very clear: the temple, the bell tower, the pavilions, the mansions, and the crisscrossing streets and alleys, except for the square, the road surfaces and the lower halves of the buildings, which remain invisible …

Anne *(Softly.)*

Go on.

Daniel

The low and level clouds are airy and effervescent, they shape themselves into a thin, even layer and drift along at a certain altitude increasing in speed, these are all below him. He seems to be riding on the top of a mountain, his hands have to hold on to a crag so that he will not slide downhill, not far away is the abyss, and he can't help being scared. Drifting with the mountain gives him pleasure, but nevertheless he can't help being a bit apprehensive.

Anne *(Closes her eyes.)*

She feels it too …

Daniel

He knows that he is looking at a forgotten ghost town, he is stunned by its exquisite planning, he strains his eyes to see it more clearly in the haze, to commit it to his memory, but the buildings and their orderly layouts are too intricate for him to comprehend in such a short time. He wants to identify a pattern so that at least he would have a general idea of the layout, but everything is drifting, the low clouds, the city, and the mountain he is riding on are all revolving at the same speed but in different directions. This stunning scene is accompanied by absolute quietude. There is not a single shred of light, but the outlines are so clear, so well-defined to the smallest details. This city of huge and crowded buildings is entirely constructed of wood, it gives out the unadulterated greyish black colour of lumber, the doors and windows are all shut tight.

Anne

She says she can see it all ...

Daniel

In these blocks of buildings and their innumerable rooms, there are many, many people, eating, drinking, loving, lusting, again and again, and again and again, repeatedly and re-repeatedly, they're struggling, troubled and anxious to the point of rendering their lives meaningless, then all of a sudden they die off, unknown to the world. This is becoming somewhat scary, so scary that he feels cold all over, and yet he still can't stop himself from drifting away, any time now he could stumble and plunge into the dark abyss under his feet. He is drifting, he has become weightless, but his eyes are still staring and watching, he feels dizzy looking down from above, and he is attracted by the pitch black abyss, he can't help leaning forward. He tries his best to ward off the temptation to plunge down, keeping his eyes away from the darkness under his feet as much as possible. When he looks to the front, he can still see the ghost town standing erect on top of the abyss on his left side. The mountain he is riding on is like an elephant, or any huge animal, it's squirming up and down as if it's going to lose control, he quickly closes his eyes.

Anne

And then?

Daniel

And then he wakes up, it was only a dream, it only lasted an instant, and only in dreams could one see a miracle like this one, he wishes that it could have lasted for a while longer, so that he could remember it more clearly. He is holding his breath, and he manages to hang on to a shred of its past self, but eventually he's unable to prevent it from disappearing altogether. He is quite moved, as if it's some kind of apocalypse, yet he feels like he has lost something. At the time he knows there are things he can do, and there are things he can't. But what is it that he could have done? He doesn't have the answer any more.

Anne

Then don't talk about it.

Bernard

Gosh! My foot is busted! This foot, it doesn't listen to your commands. Oh, a wooden leg! Only devils have hoofs, and you're not a devil. But there's a devil in every man's heart, the question is whether or not it's set free, if it got out, you'd be the happy one, though other people would have to suffer for your happiness. You have sinned deeply, you should have left that young girl alone, but how would you know if she's a little dove or a little whore if you haven't tried?

One foot is light, and the other one heavy, it's like riding on the clouds — *(Bang!)*

Anne, Daniel

He's calling me! (*Wind blows.*)
No, it's the wind.
I'll go and look.

Cecile, Anne

You scared me!

Sorry, let me close the door.

Where is he?

I don't know, maybe he's in the living room, or in the study.

Thank you for your dress, but it doesn't suit me. I've already put it back into the closet outside the bathroom. I look terrific wearing jeans, I don't want any hand-me-downs. I also want to tell you, I don't want to come here any more, I don't want to see you, you and all the other people. I'm not that stupid, I'm not your plaything! I want to cry, but you won't see my tears. I hate you! I also hate myself, but that's got nothing to do with you. When I cry I'm only crying for myself, and it's nothing for you to gloat about. I don't have to stay around a crappy old man all the time, that you can rest assured. It's a big world, I can go anywhere, I don't need to stare at the same man all the time!

Daniel, Cecile

What's the matter?

I've got nothing to say to you, go and talk to her, you've got a lot to say to each other, haven't you? You're all smart people, cultured, well-bred, and I'm just a little whore, I know you see me like that. Don't try to explain! I don't want to hear it! I'll be leaving in a moment, drive me to the station, I'm going to take the bus home.

What am I going to tell them? We're their guests.

They invited you, not me, I didn't even know them.

Tomorrow, let's go home tomorrow. Listen to me, okay?

I can't wait until tomorrow. It's your home anyway, not mine.

Where are you going at this hour of the night?

— Don't worry about me! I don't need you to pay for my bus ticket!

Daniel

— Okay, this is obviously a comedy, but it's all but ruined because you're in it. Should you try to put on a smile, or should you make a funny face and bear with it? You're not such a good actor after all, you just wanted to play along, you don't know the tricks. You've brought this embarrassment upon yourself.

You're not an expert in the game of love, and that tiny bit of intelligence of yours has already vanished into mid-air. So you'd better leave and become a ball boy outside the court.

Cecile *(The wind blows hard.)*

The sky is a dark grey, and the clouds are whirling high above. She knows that once she stands on the side of the highway and sticks up a finger, some car will stop and its window will open, and there'll appear a man's smiling face. Life is so simple when you see through it, close your eyes and let it take you anywhere.

She wants all the men to be infatuated with her, waiting for the intimacy that comes unexpectedly.

And then she'll dump them one by one, first she'll cry and then she'll laugh out loud, but that's only a joke, just one more joke she's playing on herself.

You know she's not lonely, but she wants to have a dog, it'll follow her anywhere, any time. As long as she blows the whistle, no matter how softly, the dog will happily go to her and circle around her, in front of her or behind her, running and jumping.

But all she wants to do right now is to smoke a cigarette, sitting on the concrete block by the roadside and gazing at the billboards by the entrance to the railway station. She's got no need for the laced bras in the windows, the pair of cupcakes on her chest by themselves are enough to turn them on. She wants to say it to everybody: Here's a whore! Just like everybody says "Hello."

She hates women who put on airs, when she sees their new shoes stepping on dog pooh, she can't help cracking up inside. She's not a kind person, what's the use of being kind anyway? Besides, her mother never taught her anything like that.

She wants to tie fast knots on all the neckties and smash all the vases into pieces. Just like her dreams, one by one they've been shattered, all gone.

Daniel

You grabbed your hair and tried to levitate yourself, but in the end you only gave yourself a painful scalp. You laugh at the world, but in the end it's the world which is laughing at you. If there were no opponents to meet your challenge, life would have lost its meaning. To find meaning where there's no meaning, to find love where there's no love, all are driven by lust and desire. Everything is void and meaningless after all, and that includes yourself.

Afterwards, and afterwards, you're bewildered, you stare at the door, it has been blown open by the wind, everything you've ever done on this side of the door is futile, but no one is willing to enter the door with you, to see whether there's a greener pasture on the other side.

Bernard *(Sound of blowing wind and driving rain)*

Anne! Can you hear me? Oh, my bones … I don't know if any of them's broken. I just had a fall. Help me to the armchair, O … O … My waist, I can still bend my waist, it's not busted yet. It's a good thing that these old bones are still good and sturdy!

Anne

All right, all right, lie down, you really gave me a scare.

Bernard

It's so windy. Remember that year when I just finished renovating the house and I gave a party? The whole house was full of people, the place was so alive! We drank a lot of wine. It was as windy as it is now, and the rain was pouring down, the guests all decided to stay and spend the night here. They slept everywhere, I gave the rooms and the beds to those sleeping in pairs. It was after midnight, and I was resting on this chair when you sneaked in, at that time the chair was still in the studio, remember? Then you decided to stay …

Anne, Bernard

Afterwards I left.
Then you came back. How many years ago was it? At that time …

I was exactly like her?

Right, a vivacious bimbo!

And stark naked …

I was standing in front of a painting, all around us were loud and bright colours, you said that these colours turned you on, remember?

Forget it. Besides, it's already twenty years ago.

Will you ever leave me?

Who knows?

Listen! Is something leaking?

It's raining outside.

You've closed all the windows, haven't you?

Yes.

Ah …

What did you say?

(Sound of snoring.)

Anne

Her bare feet are soaked in the cold water, her skirt is dripping wet, it's dirty and it sticks to her legs. The entire sitting room is immersed in water, and it's still rising, flooding in from the porch, the garden, the forest over there, the former cattle range, the river bank which can't be seen, and from heaven itself. She can't do anything, she just stands in front of the glass door in the living room, she can't prevent this houseful of water from rising further. There's no place to hide, not a corner, not anywhere. The water is all over the carpet and is rising to the first step of the stairs, everything is floating, books, T-shirts, glasses cases, cardboard boxes, jeans and cushions are all stained, swollen. Even the chairs are wobbly. It's hopeless. There's no need to go and look at the studio, which is even lower, the paintings on the floor, surely they're all finished, only the sofa stays immovable in the water, and she, like a bitch in heat, is lying on it, stark naked …

Quartet No. 4

Cecile, Bernard

A ball's fallen to the floor!

Where?

It nearly broke into pieces.

Oh, it's a marble made of ivory. It's harder than a log. You can play with it.

Like this? (*Rolls the marble.*)

Naughty, naughty. I win! (*Takes marble and holds her.*)

All right, I'll let you kiss me once, on the left side.

Daniel, Cecile, Bernard

She really knows how to make people happy.

Now on the right side, also just once. I can't let you kiss both sides, otherwise I'll have none left. Anyone who wants it will get it, but he'll have to do a handstand for me first!

How can this be possible? It's too much to ask at my age.

It's got to be something people can do.

Then do a somersault, that's easy enough, even kids can do it.

This girl, she surely knows how to make life difficult.

Is it okay like this?

Are we playing or not? We're playing a game 'cause we're bored, right? Just listening to you people popping off to no end, don't you think other people should have some fun too?

Daniel, Cecile

Why do we have to play this game? It's so childish.

I want to play, but you don't know how to; I want to go out, but I can't either.

But it's not raining.

Bernard, Cecile

Now tell me, what else shall we play? I'll go along, I'll die if I have to, okay?

How about hide and seek? It's such a big house and there are so many rooms. You've got to do some exercise, both of you, running up and down will do you good!

How charming!

Daniel, Cecile

But still a child.
It's no fun at all, I'm getting old just being with you!
Okay, you win. Out with it, how should we play?
Go tell Anne to play with us!

Bernard, Cecile, Daniel

Leave her out of it, she's too lazy to move even one finger.
All right, take off your shoes, one each!
I don't know what to do with her.
I know.
(*Music*)

Daniel

No door
make a door
You're inside the door
he's outside the door
You want to get out
he wants to get in
To avoid a collision
therefore
you close the door again.
No key
can't go in

No umbrella
it's raining
you're wet all over
No God
create one
No savior
do it yourself
No story
don't tell it then
What if no soul
when there's none there's none
And bad luck is like a toothache
nobody
can be exempt
What if no play
perform it yourself
No applause
clap your own hands
No drummer
play it yourself while you sing
No audience
see it yourself
No nothing
then it's nothing
You build the world
and then destroy it
If you don't build one
better not to build
then you don't need to destroy
you can't destroy
You believe in ghosts
then there are ghosts
If you don't believe
then don't believe it
You want to go in circles
the circling won't end

You don't want to go in circles
  who can order you to?

Cecile

Close this door, open that one. I'm — over here! *(Sneaks behind the door and hides.)*

A Cinderella carrying her crystal shoes. Look at them, so busy running up and down and panting for breath. See how they stumble and fall! *(Bang! She can't help laughing.)* Did you break a bone? Oh … God! *(Covers her eyes with her hands.)*

Bernard *(Getting up from the ground.)*

What happened? *(Sees Cecile behind the door.)*

Cecile *(Pretends to cry.)*

I didn't do it on purpose.

Bernard

It's better to break it once and for all. It's okay, I'm too old, that's all. Even if I broke it I'll go at it again. Break it! Break it once more! … Why are you crying, little girl? Daddy's going to buy his little darling a big doll when he comes home — I'm still your good old daddy, am I not?

Cecile

She's nobody's little girl, small daddy, big daddy, they're all fiddle-faddle! She's sick and tired of playing mistress or model, pretending to be this and that.

Daniel

You say you
  love her

She also says
  she loves you
If you don't love her
  she won't love you
Love is like truth
  they are no different
She says she loves so painfully
  and she actually gets a toothache
She wants to indulge herself and to have fun
  nobody loses
You say everything you've said
  is the real truth
Truth or lies
  they're no myths anyway

Cecile

She's not a plaything, she's not anybody's puppet,
Sexy or not sexy, she's still got her feelings.
You're all looking for excitement, you're all using her to seek emotional release,
That sorrow in her heart, who can dismiss it for her?

Daniel

Everybody says
  whoever
    raises up high
      the big banner of justice
He will
  find
    a reason
Just like
  a married man
    complaining about his wife
      to his mistress

If he wants no trouble
  he should have known
    not to get married
You lift up high
  a foot
    to see how high you can lift it
When you can't lift it any more
  then just
    stop lifting it
If you think you're
  a worm
    then you're a worm
If you think you're
  a tiger
    you have to know
      the tiger
        except
          in cages
            is already extinct

Bernard *(Tiptoeing, his hands at his back.)*

The little whore, where did she go? *(Stealthily pushes the door open.)*

Anne *(Embraces Daniel and kisses him. Bernard approaches and bends down to look.)*

Bastard!

Bernard

I didn't say anything, did I?

Anne, Bernard

You scared me! *(Pushes Daniel away.)*

Sorry to interrupt, please continue! *(Daniel walks away.)*

What are you holding in your hand?

(Extending left hand.) Nothing.

The other one.

(Switches and extends the right hand.) Nothing, it's really nothing.

What's that you're hiding behind your back?

(Shows a pistol.) A toy. *(Pulls the trigger, tick tack.)* See, didn't I tell you it's a toy? A stage prop.

You gave me a real scare … *(Chokes and cries.)*

I'm sorry, I was only kidding. We said we'd play a game, didn't we? It's just a special effect to make it more fun.… It's all right, come on, stop crying — *(Approaches to embrace her.)*

(Backing off.) Don't!

It's just a game, don't take it so seriously.

No, it's not a game. You killed me.

What are you talking about?

You wanted to kill me!

It's not for real, it's just for fun, okay?

No, I can't live with you any longer!

Are you sure? Are you kidding me or something?

I can't go on with you like this!

Right, an ageing bastard whose days are numbered …

Please stop your play-acting, I can't stand it any more! I just can't! You understand?

I understand, I understand everything. That's it! You want to be with him, if this old guy can still think straight.

I don't know. Anyway, I can't go on living with you.

As you wish, it's not that you haven't left me before. For you, this here is always a port you can come back to, as long as this old dock still exists. *(Tosses the pistol away and walks off.)*

What a nightmare. *(Covers her face with her hands.)*

Bernard *(Opens another door.)*

Strange, how come it's snowing?

(Daniel turns around, embraces Anne behind Bernard and kisses her as he did before.)

Bernard *(Still looking outside the door.)*

It flew away.

Anne *(Pushes Daniel away as she did before.)*

What flew away?

Bernard, Anne

(Without looking at them.) Look! There —
What did you say?
It's gone.
What's gone?
It was right there, now it's not there any more.
You're seeing things!
Look, over there!
What did you say?
(Turns around and smiles.) Now there's absolutely nothing.

Daniel, Bernard

Are you fooling me?
Just for the fun of it.
You're fooling me.
It's only a joke, nothing more.
You're fooling me!

My dear friend, you don't have any sense of humuor, do you? You know why I don't like to read the stuff you've written? It's exactly because they're so heavy.

You've invited me here just to make a fool out of me, haven't you? What'll you do if you can't let off your steam?

What are you talking about? This is my house and you're here as my guest. It's true that I invited you, as a rule I only invite people I consider worthy. But my house is not a fun park, not a pub, and I hope people won't mistake my house for a pub or some place where they can do anything they want. Don't I have the right to have some fun in my own house? If you don't have any respect for me, please take your leave! *(Daniel walks away.)* What did I say? *(Shakes his head and walks out of the door. Anne covers her face with her hands as she did before.)*

Cecile, Daniel

Daniel!
(Turns around.) Right here.
Don't touch me.
Why?
'Cause you're a shadow!
What are you talking about?
Well, I just had this dream. I tried to call you but you didn't answer. You were lying on the sofa in the house and I tried to touch you with my hand, but there was nothing, there was just a shadow. You gave me a real scare.

Anne *(Drops her hands.)*

He's dying.

Daniel, Anne

Who's dying?
Him. Just now he walked past me and went out …

(The three of them look outside the door.)

Bernard

It's a wide stretch of snowiness, so white and dazzling that it blinds his eyes, but it doesn't feel cold, it only makes him dizzy. All around him is dead silence, he wants to make sure if it's a dream. In the distance, the dark blue forest and the greyish brown tree trunks are all covered with layers of snow, so solid and so heavy that the branches are all arching downwards. There's a whisk of sound wafting along the lead-grey sky, it's long, it's here and there, it's piercing like the cold, there seems to be a feeling of sharp pain in his ear drums. Along the edge of the forest a few black dots are moving, they could be birds, he seemed to have seen them from inside the door, he tries to make out what colour they are, they're not entirely black, not like the crows. He keeps on going forward, hoping to find out whether those bouncing dots are birds or something else. They look as if they're searching for food, but then they stop moving. They also look like pieces of stones not totally covered by the snow. He can't help feeling a bit puzzled. It is all so quiet, so clear, just the birds, or the few pieces of stones, they are moving in the haziness, but when he looks again they have stopped all their movements, all this make him feel disoriented. He must find out once and for all whether they are birds or stones. If they are birds, are they crows? He stares at them, trying to concentrate his thoughts, and the few black dots become increasingly blurred. Is he too old to see things clearly? *(He closes his eyes and rests for a while, then he strains his eyes to take a closer look.)* The world has not been this clear before, the dividing line between the sky and the snow accumulated on the tree tops, the few dots of bright green leaves half buried under the snow, the greyish brown tree trunks standing there in a row, all the outlines are very well-defined, so sharp and clear that they stun his senses. The shadows have been obliterated, probably because the reflection of the snow is so bright, the depth of field has disappeared too, all is motionless, there's not a breath of wind. When he tries to look at the birds or the stones once more, the dividing line between the sky and the snow accumulated on the tree tops, and the bright green leaves and the greyish brown tree trunks is beginning to disappear all of a sudden and unstoppably. The more he opens his eyes, the more quickly the colours are fading, and the more the outlines are becoming blurred. So he just stands there facing what is set before him, the ashen sky, the greyish black forest and the pure white snow. He stares at the birds or the stones, the only possible signs of movement around. They're still there, they have become more blurred, more intangible, but he must find out whether they are birds or stones. And if they're birds, are they crows? (*Step by step he approaches quietly.*) The pristine white and snowy ground suddenly splits and reveals a crack, gradually separating him from

the crows or whatever birds or stones in front of him ... (*He turns around.*) Surprisingly he sees no footprints behind him. He's not afraid, just a bit alarmed, striving hard to remember from which way he came. While he is deep in thoughts, a crack also appears in the snowy ground behind him, he watches it widening rapidly, then he sees a pool of darkish water under his feet. (*He holds his breath and stands still.*) He's not afraid and he's no longer alarmed, he has no thoughts of any kind, he is just eyeing this fault slowly expanding and creating new faults, expanding ... He is feeling unsteady, maybe it's because he's standing on a piece of floating ice, he allows himself to drift away, he feels relaxed, and he is losing his weight, he no longer cares whether those dots are birds or crows or stones on the snowy ground, he just watches the darkish water under his feet extending further and further. He is sinking slowly, he can't stop it, there's no need to. Oh, he's still holding a hat in his hand, an old hat he hasn't worn for a long time. He's cold and wet all over, he's worried that he might catch a cold, he'd better put the hat on ...
(*Music*)

Anne, Cecile

You look as if you're very happy.
Why not? You're happy too, aren't you?
Look, a blue sky.
Everything is so clear now, isn't it? *(Smiles.)* He told me everything.
Who? What did he tell you?
Don't you know? What's happened between you and him.
Can't you find something else to talk about?
He volunteered to tell me, we're playing a game, you know.
I just don't know what to do with you.
You two certainly know how to play games.
What games?
Everybody knows.
You're acting like a little whore.
But men like it that way!
That's the main thing, I suppose.
You don't smoke?
I quit a long time ago. It's not good for your skin.

I don't care, I still have lots of time.

But sooner or later you'll find out, and when that happens it'll be too late. You want some sour milk?

Thanks, I'll get it myself. Do you people fool around like this all the time?

Surely you jest!

I didn't say that.

Are you through or not?

He told me you said it.

He was lying through his teeth. Don't listen to him!

I don't believe in anybody. *(Opens her mouth and laughs.)*

Are you going to leave soon?

I'm free to stay. Go ask him.

Bernard, Anne

It's a beautiful day. Oh, I beg your pardon, the sunshine is gorgeous!

Go away!

Just kidding. Her nerves are always on an edge.

You're the one who's got something wrong with your nerves, not me.

Bernard, Cecile

Why don't you stay for two more days?

And be a model again?

No, just as a guest. Anne likes you very much, really.

Anne *(Rising.)*

He's afraid of being lonely. *(Walks away.)*

Cecile, Bernard

I like it here too. I'll come again for sure. I'm a good cook, you know.

That's terrific, I like gourmet food.

I can make pastries as well, I'm very good at making cherry cookies.

An excellent idea. Next time you come I'll pick some cherries and you can bake the cookies.

Daniel! Where are you?

Daniel

Can't you see I'm coming?

Bernard, Cecile

That's it, babe, let's make it a date!

Where's Anne?

Daniel, Bernard

She's outside watching the sky.

It doesn't look like it's going to rain. Pity, you haven't taken a walk in the forest. You still have time to go there for a while, you know.

I can't. I'm going to meet my publisher. I'll have to be there this afternoon.

It's an opportunity not to be missed. That novel you're writing, would you consider it a good novel?

It's more like a laughable and meaningless yawn.

It doesn't matter. Sign the contract first!

Only if they accept it.

And if they don't? For instance, they might want you to cater to this or that kind of readership. When people spend money to buy books, they certainly don't want to read page after page of troubles. Of course you know perfectly well what those booksellers want from their books.

If they tag on any extra conditions, they can just forget about the whole thing.

My friend, this is exactly what I like about you, not your books. You know, I have given up reading books. Babe, do you read his books?

Cecile, Bernard

I just look at him. That's enough, isn't it?

Bravo! You've written a book even a girl wouldn't read. Your contract's definitely going down the drain!

Daniel, Bernard

Then I'll write a play.

What if no one's going to perform it?

Then don't.

Isn't that suicide? You're not like me, I've already got one foot in the grave, you still have lots of time left.

Who knows whether it's suicide or not? I'll just have to wait and see, I'll cross that river when I come to it, and I wouldn't mind getting my feet wet either.

Okay, how about a play about suicide?

Why kill yourself when you're alive and well? Might as well write a play about the big Finish.

What Finish?

Everything is finished, finito.

What a wonderful subject to write about! Hey, babe, what do you think?

Cecile, Bernard

Believe it or not, I want to finish myself off!

Oh no, you're so young. Don't imitate this old fellow, just try to live long and well!

This is the life, isn't it? *(Puffs a ring of cigarette smoke.)*

This isn't exactly a happy play. Who'll perform in it? Huh?

Daniel, Cecile, Bernard, Anne

The four of us. It'll be just right, eh?

I don't want to do it. I've had enough.

What are we going to do if the women refuse to play the parts? Anne, you probably didn't hear him, he was talking about a play.

What play?

Taborsky's father is called Taborsky.

Very funny.

Exactly, anything else?

There's an island in the Pacific Ocean, it never sinks no matter what happens. *(Plays some music.)* Don't you want to dance?

Cecile

Sure, why not? Gentlemen, let's dance!

Daniel, Cecile, Bernard, Anne *(Dancing the waltz.)*

Taborsky's father
He is called Taborsky
He eats breakfast every morning
Roosters never lay eggs

An island in the Pacific Ocean
It never sinks no matter what
He lays a trap
And he traps himself

One day the war breaks out
Nobody is alive
And this house exists no more
The sun still shines over the lawn

Mozart is dead
Some people still play the quartet
It would not be so sad
There's no sugar in the coffee

Tea is always bitter
Some teas are sweet
A left-handed person
A fable that is a parable but not speakable

One day he lays a trap
And this house exists no more
Taborsky's son
He is called Taborsky

He eats breakfast every morning
There's no sugar in the coffee
The sun still shines over the lawn
It would not be so sad

An island in the Pacific Ocean
Some people still play the quartet
A left-handed person
It never sinks no matter what

When the war breaks out
Tea is always bitter
Mozart is not dead
Some teas are sweet

A fable that's a parable but not speakable
Roosters never lay eggs
Speakable but not a parable
A parable but not speakable

The End

10 January 1995, France.

(This play was commissioned by the Bibliotheque Municipale de Joué-Lès-Tours and sponsored by Le Centre National du Livre de France.)

Some Suggestions on Producing *Weekend Quartet*

1. The play can be used as a recitation text, a radio drama or a stage performance. The text, combining drama, poetry, and narrative, can easily be accompanied by music.
2. During the performance the four characters are on stage at all times except during the breaks; it is as if they are members of a quartet playing at a concert.
3. Each character has his or her own point of view. As there are four characters, there will be four points of view. In case of the same incident being enacted in different scenes, the director should alter the angle of vision, change the positioning of the characters, or rearrange them in a contrasting manner.
4. The same character should distinguish between the first, second, or third person point of view while he is engaged in a monologue, dialogue or in a conversation involving three or four speakers. This awareness provides the performance with new possibilities. The actor could choose to play the role (when speaking in the first person) or not play the role (when speaking in the third person), or he could also take on the image of his character in the eyes of other characters. There are many options, and the overall design may require the coordination on the part of the director.
5. When an actor has mastered the three different points of view in the dialogues, he will not find it difficult to clearly define his own character and the characters of others and play his part among them. When the dialogue is in the second person, the actor adopts the identity of a neutral actor, and he can address the character he is playing or address the audience directly. When the dialogue is in the third person ("he" or "she"), the actor, taking on the identity of a neutral actor, can explain the character he is playing to the audience or to his addressee in the play.
6. The play has appropriated some structural elements of musical composition, thus logical development and chronological sequence of the plot elements are not its major concerns. Changes in mood are more important than the unfolding of the story. It is essential, more so than any other stage techniques, that the different scenes should be accorded corresponding time span and tempo during the performance.

7. A realistic stage design should be avoided because there are many shifts between reality and imagination, memory and dream, and thought and narration in the play. As for set design and spatial arrangement, it is advisable to use only a few movable doors, chairs, and tables in different combinations. This can be coordinated with changes in lighting or by switching the lights on and off. The actors' costumes and props can be changed behind the doors; there is no need for exits. In this way the tempo of the performance is quickened and the structure tightened.

The above suggestions are for reference only.

Appendix A

Plays Written by Gao Xingjian

1982 *Absolute Signal*《絕對信號》

1983 *Bus Station*《車站》

1984 *Modern Shorts*《現代折子戲》:

The Imitator《模仿者》

Hiding from the Rain《躲雨》

Tough Walk《行路難》

The Pass at Mount Habala《喀巴拉山口》

1985 *Soliloquy*《獨白》

1985 *Wilderness Man*《野人》

1986 *The Other Shore*《彼岸》

1987 *Hades*《冥城》

1989 *The Story of the Classic of Seas and Mountains*《山海經傳》

1989 *Exile*《逃亡》

1991 *Between Life and Death*《生死界》

1992 *Dialogue and Rebuttal*《對話與反詰》

1993 *Nocturnal Wanderer*《夜遊神》

1995 *Weekend Quartet*《周末四重奏》

Appendix B

Selected Criticism on Gao Xingjian's Plays

Chinese

Barmé, Geremie. "Bufang huangdan yixia — Jieshao Gao Xingjian he tade zuopin *Chezhan*"〈不妨荒誕一下 — 介紹高行健和他的作品《車站》〉(It Does not Matter to be a Bit Absurd — An Introduction to Gao Xingjian and His *Bus Station*). — Trans. by Zhang Zebo 張澤波.《香港文學》, 9 (1985).

Beijing Renmin Yishu Juyuan *Juedui Xinhao* Juzu 北京人民藝術劇院《絕對信號》劇組, ed. "*Juedui xinhao*" *wutai yishu tansuo*〈《絕對信號》舞臺藝術探索〉(Explorations into the Dramaturgy of *Absolute Signal*). Beijing: 中國戲劇出版社, 1985.

Chen, Fangzheng 陳方正. "*Lingshan* zhiwai de shengsijie — juzuojia Gao Xingjian yinxiangji"〈《靈山》之外的生死界 — 劇作家高行健印象記〉(The Boundary Between Life and Death Beyond *Spiritual Mountain* — Impressions of the Dramatist Gao Xingjian).《信報》(Hong Kong), 26 Oct. 1993.

Chen, Ganquan 陳敢權. "Cong *Shengsijie* kan Gao Xingjian de xiju lilun"〈從《生死界》看高行健的戲劇理論〉(A Look at Gao Xingjian's Theory of Drama from the point of view of *Between Life and Death*). *Dramatic Arts*《戲劇藝術》(Hong Kong: 香港演藝學院), 9 (1995).

Chen, Liyin 陳麗音. "*Shengsijie* yu Gao Xingjian de xijuguan"〈《生死界》與高行健的戲劇觀〉(*Between Life and Death* and Gao Xingjian's View on Drama). Paper presented at the "International Conference on World Chinese Playwriting" held at The Chinese University of Hong Kong, December 1993.

Chen, Shouzhu 陳瘦竹. "Tan huangdan xijude shuailuo ji qi zai woguode yingxiang"〈談荒誕戲劇的衰落及其在我國的影響〉(The Decline of the Theatre of Absurd and Its Influence in China).《社會科學評論》, 11 (1985).

Da, Yong 大勇. "Gao Xingjian xinzuo *Yeren*"〈高行健新作《野人》〉(*Wilderness Man*, A New Play by Gao Xingjian).《劇本》, 7 (1985).

Ding, Yangzhong 丁楊忠. "Tanlu — *Juedui xinhao* ji qita"〈探路 —《絕對信號》及其他〉(Asking the Way — *Absolute Signal* and Other Opinions).《劇壇》, 2 (1983).

Ding, Yisan, Qu Liuyi, Tong Daoming, Su Yu, and Zhao Huan 丁一三、曲六乙、童道明、蘇予、趙寰. "Dui you zhengyide huaju jubende zhengyi — Zhongguo Xiju Wenxue Xuehui zhaokai you zhengyide huaju juben taolunhui fayan jiyao"〈對有爭議的話劇劇本的爭議 — 中國戲劇文學學會召開有爭議的話劇劇本討論會發言紀要〉(The Controversy Surrounding Controversial Drama — A Summary of the Speeches Delivered at the Seminar on Controversial Drama Organized by the China Society of Studies on Dramatic Literature).《劇本》, 7 (1985).

Du, Qingyuan 杜清源. "Huajude tezheng yu huajude biange"〈話劇的特徵與話劇的變革〉(Drama: Its Characteristics and Changes).《文藝通訊》, 11 (1984).

"Dui wutai zhenshide zhizhe zhuiqiu"〈對舞台真實的執著追求〉(The Earnest Pursuit of Realism on Stage).《作品與爭鳴》, 3 (1983).

Fengzi 鳳子. "Kan *Yeren*"〈看《野人》〉(On *Wilderness Man*).《光明日報》, 13 June 1985.

Gao, Wo 高臥. "Xiaoyi *Juedui xinhao* xiao juchang yanchu"〈小議《絕對信號》小劇場演出〉(*Absolute Signal* Performed in a Small Theatre: A Preliminary Discussion).《戲劇報》, 13 (1982).

"Guanyu *Chezhan* de zhengming"〈關於《車站》的爭鳴〉(The Controversy Surrounding *Bus Station*).《戲劇論叢》, 3 (1984).

"Guanyu jige huajude zhengming (*Juedui xinhao* he *Chezhan*)"〈關於幾個話劇的爭鳴(《絕對信號》和《車站》)〉(The Controversy Surrounding Certain Plays [*Absolute Signal* and *Bus Station*]).《劇本》, 2 (1985).

He, Yan 何閻. "Huaju *Chezhan* guanhou"〈話劇《車站》觀後〉(Written After Seeing *Bus Station*).《文藝報》, 3 (1984).

He, Yangming 何養明. "Huaju yishu xingshide kegui tansuo — wu changci huaju *Juedui xinhao* guangan"〈話劇藝術形式的可貴探索 — 無場次話劇《絕對信號》觀感〉(A Valuable Exploration on Artistic Form — *Absolute Signal*, A Play Without Act Divisions).《老人天地》, 4 (1985).

Hu, Yaoheng 胡耀恒. "Yi yanyuan wei zhuzhoude xiju — lun Gao Xingjian de xiju yishu" 〈以演員為主軸的戲劇 — 論高行健的戲劇藝術〉 (Actor-Centred Theatre — On Gao Xingjian's Dramaturgy). 《中央日報》 (Taipei), 23 Dec. 1995.

Hu, Yaoheng 胡耀恒. *Bainian gengyunde fengshou* 《百年耕耘的豐收》 (Plenitude of a Hundred Years of Cultivation). Taipei: 帝教出版社, 1995.

Huang Mei-hsü 黃美序."Gao Xingjian xijuzhong de fodao renwu" 〈高行健戲劇中的佛道人物〉 (Buddhist and Taoist Characters in Gao Xingjian's Plays). Unpublished paper, delivered at "The Second Chinese Drama Festival, Hong Kong, 1998" held at The Chinese University of Hong Kong, November 1998.

"Huiyu buyide huaju *Yeren*" 〈毀譽不一的話劇《野人》〉 (*Wilderness Man*, A Play of Divided Opinions). 《作品與爭鳴》, 11 (1985).

"*Juedui xinhao* zuotan jiyao" 〈《絕對信號》座談紀要〉 (The Forum on *Absolute Signal*). 《文藝評論報》, 15 Aug. 1983.

Ma, Jian 馬健. "Cong xianshi dao moxuyou de bi'an — ping Gao Xingjian de xiju *Bi'an*" 〈從現實到莫須有的彼岸 — 評高行健的戲劇《彼岸》〉 (From Reality to the Other Shore of Nonexistence — On Gao Xingjian's *The Other Shore*). 《明報》 (Hong Kong), 18 Apr. 1995.

Ma, Wenqi 痲文琦. "Shuiyue jinghua" 〈水月鏡花〉 (The Moon in the Water and the Flowers in the Mirror). In *Houxiandai zhuyi yu dangdai xiju* 《後現代主義與當代戲劇》. Beijing: 中國社會出版社, 1994.

Li, Shuoru 李碩儒. "Xuezhehua yu duchuangxing" 〈學者化與獨創性〉 (Being Scholarly and Being Unique). 《光明日報》, 16 June 1985.

Lin, Kehuan 林克歡. "Doupo" 〈陡坡〉 (Steep Slope). 《戲劇報》, 7 (1985).

Lin, Kehuan 林克歡. "Kenhuang dao bi'an" 〈墾荒到彼岸〉 (From Pioneering to the Other Shore). In Lin Kehuan, ed. *Lin zhaohua daoyan yishu* 《林兆華導演藝術》. Harbin: 北方文藝出版社, 1992.

Lin, Yinyu 林蔭宇. "Dui *Yeren* daoyan yishude shizheng fenxi" 〈對《野人》導演藝術的實證分析〉 (A Positivist Analysis of the Art of Directing in *Wilderness Man*). In Lin Kehuan, ed. *Lin zhaohua daoyan yishu* 《林兆華導演藝術》. Harbin: 北方文藝出版社, 1992.

Liu, Zaifu 劉再復. "*Shanhaijingchuan* xu" 〈《山海經傳》序〉 (Preface to *The Story of the Classic of Seas and Mountains*). In Gao Xingjian 高行健. *Shanhaijinchuan* 《山海經傳》. Hong Kong: 香港天地圖書有限公司, 1993.

Qu, Liuyi 曲六乙. "Xishou, ronghua, duchuangxing"〈吸收、溶化、獨創性〉(Absorption, Assimilation, and Uniqueness).《戲劇報》, 12 (1982).

Qu, Liuyi 曲六乙. "Ping huaju *Chezhan* ji qi piping"〈評話劇《車站》及其批評〉(*Bus Station* and Its Criticism).《文藝報》, 7 (1984).

Run, Sheng 潤生. "Guanyu huaju *Juedui xinhao* de taolun zongshu"〈關於話劇《絕對信號》的討論綜述〉(A Summary of the Discussions on *Absolute Signal*).《作品與爭鳴》, 3 (1983).

Shan, Jia 姍佳. "Guanyu huaju *Chezhan* de taolun zongshu"〈關於話劇《車站》的討論綜述〉(Summing Up the Discussions on *Bus Station*).《北京劇作：徵文專號》(1984).

"Shehui zhuyi xiju bixu zhongshi shehui xiaoguo"〈社會主義戲劇必須重視社會效果〉(Socialist Drama Must Emphasize Social Effects).《北京劇作：徵文專號》(1984).

Song, Luman 宋魯曼. "Yibu you mingxian quexiande zuopin — ping huaju *Chezhan*"〈一部有明顯缺陷的作品 — 評話劇《車站》〉(An Obviously Flawed Play — On *Bus Station*).《北京劇作》, 2 (1984).

Tang, Sifu 唐斯復. "Yige yinren zhumude xinhao"〈一個引人注目的信號〉(An Eye-catching Signal).《文匯報》, 21 Nov. 1982.

Tang, Sifu 唐斯復. "Huiyu canbande huaju *Yeren*"〈毀譽參半的話劇《野人》〉(*Wilderness Man*, A Play of Divided Opinions).《中國青年報，星期日刊》, 19 May 1985.

Tang, Yin, Du Gao, and Zheng Bonong 唐因、杜高、鄭伯農. "*Chezhan* Sanren Tan"〈《車站》三人談〉(A Three-Man Discussion on *Bus Station*).《戲劇報》, 3 (1984).

"Tuozhan xiju siwei"〈拓展戲劇思維〉(Expanding the Modes of Thinking in Drama).《戲劇電影報》, 26 May 1985.

Wang, Xiaocong, Tao Xianlu, Pan Xinxin, and Xia Fan 王小琮、陶先露、潘欣欣、夏幡. "Xingfen zhihou de sikao"〈興奮之後的思考〉(Thoughts After Excitement).《戲劇報》, 7 (1985).

Wang, Yusheng 王育生. "Kanguo *Yeren* huo de jidian zhiyi"〈看過《野人》後的幾點質疑〉(A Few Questions After Seeing *Wilderness Man*).《文藝報》, 13 July 1985.

Wen, Tao 聞濤. "Zhanxinde xiju xingshi — huaju *Yeren* guanhou"〈嶄新的戲劇形式 — 話劇《野人》觀後〉(A Totally New Dramatic Form — After Seeing *Wilderness Man*).《工人日報》, 12 May 1985.

Wen, Yuhong 溫裕紅. "Wo kan Gao Xingjian de xiju lilun"〈我看高行健的戲

劇理論〉(My Opinions on Gao Xingjian's Theory of Drama). *Dramatic Arts*《戲劇藝術》(Hong Kong: 香港演藝學院), 10 (1996).

Wu, Geng 武耕. "Gudude xunmei xinling — ping Gao Xingjian de *Bi'an*"〈孤獨的尋美心靈 — 評高行健的《彼岸》〉(The Lonely Heart In Search of Beauty — On Gao Xingjian's *The Other Shore*).《信報》(Hong Kong), 12 April 1995.

Wu, Jicheng, Xu Nianfu, and Yao Mingde 吳繼成、徐念福、姚明德. "*Yeren* wu wen"〈《野人》五問〉(Five Questions Concerning *Wilderness Man*).《戲劇報》, 7 (1985).

Xi, Yan 溪煙. "Pingjia zuopinde yiju shi shenme — Qu Liuyi Tongzhi wenzhang duhou"〈評價作品的依據是甚麼 — 曲六乙同志文章讀後〉(What are the Bases For Evaluating a Literary Work — After Reading Comrade Qu Liuyi's Article).《文藝報》, 8 (1984).

Xie, Nie 謝聶. "Jiedu *Bi'an* de dianfuxing yinyu"〈解讀《彼岸》的顛覆性隱喻〉(Reading the Subversive Metaphors in *The Other Shore*).《星島日報》(Hong Kong), 21 April 1995.

Xing, Tiehua 邢鐵華. "Gao Xingjian paochude you yike 'caiqiu'"〈高行健拋出的又一顆「彩球」〉(Gao Xingjian Tosses Out Another Multi-Coloured Ball).《戲劇界》, 5 (1985).

Xing Zhi 行之. "Zhengfu guanzhong"〈征服觀眾〉(Conquering the Audience).《戲劇報》, 12 (1982).

Xu, Guorong 許國榮, ed. *Gao Xingjian xiju yanjiu*《高行健戲劇研究》(Studies on Gao Xingjian's Plays). Beijing: 中國戲劇出版社, 1985.

"*Yeren* — Tan Beijing renyi xinxide tupo"〈《野人》— 談北京人藝新戲的突破〉(*Wilderness Man* — On the Breakthrough of the New Production by Beijing People's Art Theatre).《香港文學》, 6 (1985).

"*Yeren* yiwu"〈《野人》咿唔〉(*Wilderness Man* and Mumbo-jumbo).《文藝報》, 13 July 1985.

Yin, Ning'an 尹寧安. "Yeren shi ge mi — huaju *Yeren* guanhou"〈野人是個謎 — 話劇《野人》觀後〉(The Wilderness Man is a Puzzle — After Seeing *Wilderness Man*).《中國青年報，星期日刊》, 19 May 1985.

Zhang, Fu 張玞. "Gao Xingjian yu Zhongguo dangdai xiju"〈高行健與中國當代戲劇〉(Gao Xngjian and Contemporary Chinese Drama). In Department of Chinese, University of Beijing, ed. *Zhuiyuji*《綴玉集》. Beijing: 北京大學出版社, 1990.

Zhang, Renli 張仁里. "Huaju wutai shang de yici xin tansuo"〈話劇舞台

上的一次新探索〉(A New Exploration on the Stage).《戲劇報》, 12 (1982).

Zeng, Zhennan 曾鎮南. "Shi *Yeren*"〈釋《野人》〉(Explaining *Wilderness Man*).《十月》, 6 (1985).

"Zhe yeshi lishi"〈這也是歷史〉(This Too is History).《讀書》, 7 (1983).

Zhong, Yibing 鍾藝兵. "Mantan *Yeren*"〈漫談《野人》〉(Random Talks on *Wilderness Man*).《戲劇報》, 7 (1985).

Zhou, Fanfu 周凡夫. "Sanchongxing guanzhong — kan Gao Xingjian de *Bi'an*"〈三重性觀眾 — 看高行健的《彼岸》〉(Tripartite Audience — Gao Xingjian's *The Other Shore*).《聯合報》(Hong Kong), 23 April 1995.

Zi Yong 子庸. "Yizhong xiandai xijuguan"〈一種現代戲劇觀〉(A Modern Theory of Drama).《文藝研究》, 1 (1985).

Japanese

Seto Hiroshi 瀬戸宏. *Chuugoku no Doujidaiengeki*《中國の同時代演劇》(Contemporary Chinese Drama). Japan: 好文出版, 1995.

Seto Hiroshi 瀬戸宏. "Gao Xingjian Toubou Daikai"〈高行健《逃亡》題解〉(On Gao Xingjian's *Exile*). In his *Chuugoku Gendai Gikyokushuu*《中國現代戲曲集》(Anthology of Modern Chinese Drama), Vol. 1. Japan: 晚成書房, 1994.

Western Languages

Alagic, Zoran. "Pa vandring med Gao Xingjian." *Värmlands Folkblad*. Sweden: 4 Nov. 1992.

Almansi, Guido. "Al Limite Estremo, di Gao Xingjian." *Panorma*. Roma: 2 June 1994.

Barmé, Geremie. "A Touch of the Absurd — Introducing Gao Xingjian and His Play *The Bus Stop*," *Renditions*, Nos. 19–20 (Spring & Autumn 1983).

Basting, Monica. "Tradition und Avantgarde in Gao Xingjians Theaterstück 'Die Wilden'." *Yeren*. Bochum, Deutsche: Studienvert Brockmeyer, 1988.

Broder, F. J. "Geschwätzig verquastes Kopftheater." *Frankischer Tag*. Deutsche: 28 Oct. 1992.

Broder, F. J. "Geschwätziges Kopftheater." *Nordbayerscher Kurier*. Deutsche: 29 Oct. 1992.

Carraz, Daniele. "Gao Xingjian: Une recherche zen de l'absurde." *Le Méridional*. Avignon: 18 July 1993.

Chen, Xiaomei. "A Wildman between Two Cultures: Some Paradigmatic Remarks on 'Influence Studies'." *Comparative Literature Studies*, Vol. 29, No. 4 (1992).

Clavel, André. "Lisez Gao Xingjian!" *L'Express*. 23 Nov. 1995.

Clavel, André. "Sur les cimes de l' âme." *Gazette de Lausanne*. Suisse: 3 Feb. 1996.

Contrucci, Jean. "Le Robinson du fleuve Jaune." *Le Provençal*. France: 24 Dec. 1995.

Decornoy, Jacques. "Sous la neige de la mémoire." *Le Monde diplômatique*. Paris: 30 Nov. 1995.

Douin, Jean Luc. "Le Grand bond en arrière." *Télérama*. Paris: 17 Jan. 1996.

Dutrait, Noël. "A Chen et Gao Xingjian, le retour du plaisir de conter." *Publication de l'Université de Provence*. France: 1998.

Ehnmark, Katarina. "Mångbottnat symboldrama." *Upsala Nya Tidning*. Sweden: 23 March 1992.

Florin, Magnus. "Jag vet att grodan är Gud." *Expressen*. Sweden: 11 Dec. 1992.

Franzén, Lars-Olof. "Vacklande under jord." *Gagens Nyheter*. Sweden: 21 March 1992.

Gao, Xingjian. "En kinesisk modernist, Lars Nygren." *Goteborgs-Posten*. Sweden: 29 Feb. 1988.

Hansell, Sven. "Kvinna, ditt namn ar kroppslighet." *Expressen*. Sweden: 21 March 1992.

Huss, Pia. "Ovanligt Kvinnoporträtt i tragikt samtidsdrama." *Svenska Dagbladet*. Sweden: 21 March 1992.

Kofler, Gerhard. "Warten, Flucht, Reise — Gao Xingjian und sein Stück 'Die Busstation' in Wien." *Der Standard*, Wien: 23 May 1990.

Kubin, Wolfgang. "Die Busstation." *Die Busstation*. Bochum, Deutsche: Studienvert Brockmeyer, 1988.

Lee, Mabel. "Walking out of Other People's Prisons: Liu Zaifu and Gao Xingjian on Chinese Literature in the 1990s." *Asian and African Studies*, No. 5. U.K.: 1996.

Lee, Mabel. "Personal Freedom in Twentieth-Century China: Reclaiming the Self in Yang Lian's *Yi* and Gao Xingjian's *Lingshan*." In Mabel Lee and Michael Wilding, ed. *History, Literature and Society: Essays in*

Honour of S.N. Mukherjee, Vol. 15. Sydney: Sydney Studies in Society and Culture, 1996.

Lee, Mabel. "Gao Xingjian's *Lingshan/Soul Mountain*, Modernism and Chinese Writer." *Heat*, No. 4. Sydney: 1997.

Lee, Mabel. "Gao Xingjian's Dialogue with Two Dead Poets from Shaoxing: Xu Wei and Lu Xun." *Essays in Honour of Marian Galik, Schweizerische Asiengesellschaft Band*, Vol. 30. 1998.

Leonardini, Jean-Pierre. "Une rencontre fructueuse Jean-Pierre Leonardini." *L'Humanité*. Paris: 21 July 1993.

Li, Jianyi. "Gao Xingjian's 'The Bus-Stop': Chinese Traditional Theatre and Western Avant-garde." Master's thesis, University of Alberta, 1991.

Lodén, Torbjörn. "World Literature with Chinese Characteristic: On a Novel by Gao Xingjian." *The Stockholm Journal of East Asian Studies*. Vol. 4. Stockholm University: 1993.

Ma Sen. "The Theatre of the Absurd in Mainland China: Gao Xingjian's *The Bus Stop*." *Issues and Studies: A Journal of China Studies and International Affairs*, Vol. 25, No. 8 (Aug. 1989).

Margerie, Diane de. "Fragments d'une Chine dévastée." *Le Figaro*. Paris: 11 Jan. 1996.

Martinez, Josefo. "Voyage dans la Chine profonde." *La Marseillaise*. Marseille: 26 Nov. 1995.

Meudal, Gérard. "La Longue marche du résident Gao." *Libération*. Paris: 21 Dec. 1995.

Nilsén, Rolf. "Gao kokar av berättarkraft." *Norrbottenskuriren*. Sweden: 2 Oct. 1992.

Nyberg, Daga. "Andlig odyssé i Kina." *Landstiningen*. Sweden: 11 Aug. 1992.

"Pa väg till Andarnas Berg Stig Hansén." *I Dag/GT Kvällsposten*. Sweden: 23 Sept. 1992.

Persson, Lasse. "Kinesen på Dramaten." *Expressen*. Sweden: 5 March 1988.

Peyraube, Alain. "Voyage au bout du la Chine." *Le Monde*. Paris: 16 Dec. 1995.

Pille, Bruno. "Gao Xingjian tire sa révérence." *La Nouvelle République du Centre-Ouest*. Joué-Lès-Tours, France: 30 Aug. 1994.

Pille, Bruno. "L'Eloge de la liberté assassinée." *La Nouvelle République du Centre-Ouest*. Joué-Lès-Tours, France: 9 Dec. 1994.

Pimpaneau, Jacques. "Gao Xingjian, auteur dramatique." *Le Rond Point janvier*. Paris: 1993.

Rind, Anita. "Les Amours de Petite Abeille et d'un jeune loubard." *Le Monde*. Paris: 4 Dec. 1982.

Robinson, Marc. "Passion Plays." *Voice*. New York: 26 June 1994.

Roubicek, Bruno. "*Wild Man*: A Contemporary Chinese Spoken Drama." *Asian Theatre Journal*, Vol. 7, No. 2 (Fall 1990).

Saag, Kristjan. "Spelet skymmer texten." *I Dag GT/Kvällsposten*. Sweden: 22 March 1992.

Senne, Thomas. "Der Mensch flieht letztlich vor sich selbst." *Main-Echo*. Deutsche: 5 Oct. 1992.

Tam, Kwok-kan. "Drama of Dilemma: Waiting as Form and Motif in *The Bus Stop* and *Waiting for Godot*." In Yun-Tong Luk, ed. *Studies in Chinese-Western Comparative Drama*. Hong Kong: The Chinese University Press, 1990.

Tay, William. "Avant-garde Theater in Post-Mao China: *The Bus Stop* by Gao Xingjian." In Howard Goldblatt, ed. *Worlds Apart: Recent Chinese Writing and Its Audiences*. Armonk, N.Y.: M. E. Sharpe, 1990.

Ulbricht, Dunja. "Im Angesicht des Todes." *Neue Presse*. Deutsche: 27 Oct. 1992.

Ulbricht, Dunja. "Verbotenes Stück aus China." *Heilbronner Stimme*. Deutsche: 30 Oct. 1992.

Wibling, Jörn. "Blivande nobel-pristagare i litteratur?" *Vastra Norrlands*. Sweden: 10 Nov. 1992.

Wischenbart, Rüdiger. "Zen im Theater des Absurden." *Der Standard*. Wien: 24 Sept. 1992.

Wunsch, Ulrich. "Auf der Flucht in guter Absicht." *Theater Heute*. Deutsche: No. 1, 1993.

Zimmermann, Gernot W. "Mauern, bitter und ironisch." *Der Standard*. Wien: 29 Sept. 1992.

Zou, Jiping. "Gao Xingjian and Chinese Experimental Theatre." Ph.D. dissertation, University of Illinois, 1994.

Appendix C

Major Productions of Gao Xingjian's Plays

1982 *Absolute Signal*《絕對信號》. Beijing People's Art Theatre, Beijing, China. Directed by Lin Zhaohua.

1983 *Bus Station*《車站》. Beijing People's Art Theatre, Beijing, China. Directed by Lin Zhaohua.

1984 *Bus Station*《車站》. Yugoslavia.

1985 *Wilderness Man*《野人》. Beijing People's Art Theatre, Beijing, China. Directed by Lin Zhaohua.

1987 *Hiding From the Rain*《躲雨》. Kungliga Dramatiska Teatern, Sweden. Directed by Peter Wahtqvist.

1987 *Bus Station*《車站》. Litz Drama Workshop, England.

1987 *Bus Station*《車站》. Horizonte Theatre, Hong Kong.

1988 *Wilderness Man*《野人》. Thalia Theatre, Hamburg, Germany. Directed by Lin Zhaohua.

1988 *Hades*《冥城》. Hong Kong Dance Company, Hong Kong. Directed by Chiang Ching.

1989 *Variations on a Slow Tune*《聲聲慢變奏》. Guggenheim Museum, New York, U.S.A. Directed by Chiang Ching.

1990 *The Other Shore*《彼岸》. National Arts College, Taipei, Taiwan. Directed by Chan Ling Ling.

1990 *Bus Station*《車站》. Wiener Unterhaltungs Theater, Vienna, Austria. Directed by Anselm Lipgens.

1990 *Wilderness Man*《野人》. Panther Theatre, Hong Kong. Directed by Luo Ka.

1992 *Exile*《逃亡》. Kungl Dramatiska Teatern, Sweden. Directed by Bjorn Granath.

1992 *Absolute Signal*《絕對信號》. Godot Theater, Taipei.

1992 *Exile*《逃亡》. Nürnberg Theater, Nürnberg, Germany. Directed by Johnanns Klett.

1992 *Dialogue and Rebuttal*《對話與反詰》. Theater des Augenblicks, Wien, Austria. Directed by Gao Xingjian.

1993 *Between Life and Death*《生死界》. Théâtre Renaud-Barrault Le Rond-Point, Paris, France. Directed by Alain Timárd.

1993 *Between Life and Death*《生死界》. Festival de Théâtre d'Avignon, France. Directed by Alain Timárd.

1993 *Between Life and Death*《生死界》. Centre for Performance, University of Sydney, Australia. Directed by Gao Xingjian.

1994 *Between Life and Death*《生死界》. Dionysia Festival mondial de Théâtre Contemporain, Veroli, Italie. Directed by Gao Xingjian.

1994 *Exile*《逃亡》. Poland National Theatre, Poznam, Poland. Directed by Edward Wojtaszek.

1994 *Exile*《逃亡》. RA Theatre Company, France. Directed by Madelaine Gautiche.

1995 *The Other Shore*《彼岸》. The Hong Kong Academy for Performing Arts, Hong Kong. Directed by Gao Xingjian.

1995 *Dialogue and Rebuttal*《對話與反詰》. Théâtre Molière, Paris, France. Directed by Gao Xingjian.

1996 *Between Life and Death*《生死界》. Teater Miejski Gdynia, Pologne.

1997 *Exile*《逃亡》. Ryunokai Gekidan 竜の会剧团, Osaka, Kobe, and Tokyo, Japan.

1997 *Between Life and Death*《生死界》. Theater for the New City, New York, U.S.A. Directed by Gao Xingjian.

1998 *Bus Station*《車站》. Theater of Cluj, Romania.

1998 *Exile*《逃亡》. Atelier Nomade, Benin, Ivory Coast.

1998 *Exile*《逃亡》. Haiyuza Gekidan 俳優座剧团, Tokyo, Japan.

1999 *Nocturnal Wanderer*《夜遊神》. Theatre des Halles, Avignon, France.

Radio Broadcasting

1984 *Bus Station*《車站》. National Broadcasting Station of Hungary.

1992 *Exile*《逃亡》. British Broadcasting Corporation, London, U.K.

1993 *Between Life and Death*《生死界》. Radio France Culture, Paris.

1997 *Exile*《逃亡》. Radio France Culture, Paris.

1997 *Between Life and Death* 《生死界》. Radio Free Asia, U.S.A.

1997 *Dialogue and Rebuttal* 《對話與反詰》. Radio France Culture, Paris.